McNALLY'S LUCK

Also by
Lawrence Sanders

McNally's Secret
The Seventh Commandment
Sullivan's Sting
Capital Crimes
Timothy's Game
The Timothy Files
The Eighth Commandment
The Fourth Deadly Sin
The Passion of Molly T.
The Seduction of Peter S.
The Case of Lucy Bending
The Third Deadly Sin
The Tenth Commandment
The Sixth Commandment
The Tangent Factor
The Second Deadly Sin
The Marlow Chronicles
The Tangent Objective
The Tomorrow File
The First Deadly Sin
Love Songs
The Pleasures of Helen
The Anderson Tapes

McNALLY'S LUCK

Lawrence Sanders

NEW ENGLISH LIBRARY

This is a work of fiction. The events described are imaginary,
and the settings and characters are fictitious and are not
intended to represent specific places or living persons.

1009775 02

British Library Cataloguing-in-Publication Data

Sanders, Lawrence
  McNally's luck.
  I. Title
  813.54 [F]

  ISBN 0-450-57407-5

First published by G. P. Putnam's Sons 1992
First published in Great Britain 1993

Published by New English Library,
a hardcover imprint of Hodder and Stoughton,
a division of Hodder and Stoughton Ltd,
Mill Road, Dunton Green, Sevenoaks, Kent TN13 2YA.
Editorial Office: 47 Bedford Square, London WC1B 3DP.

Photoset by E.P.L. BookSet, Norwood, London.

Printed in Great Britain by
St Edmundsbury Press Limited, Bury St Edmunds, Suffolk.

1

The cat's name was Peaches, and it was a fat Persian with a vile disposition. I knew that because the miserable animal once upchucked on my shoes. I was certain Peaches wasn't suffering from indigestion; it was an act of hostility. For some ridiculous reason the ill-tempered feline objected to my foot-wear, which happened to be a natty pair of lavender suede loafers. Ruined, of course.

So when my father told me that Peaches had been catnapped and was being held for ransom, I was delighted and began to believe in divine retribution. But unfortunately the cat's owner was a client of McNally & Son, Attorney-at-Law (father was the Attorney, I was the Son), and I was expected to recover the nasty brute unharmed. My premature joy evaporated.

"Why don't they report it to the police?" I asked.

"Because," the sire explained patiently, "the ransom note states plainly that if the police are brought in, the animal will be destroyed. See what you can do, Archy."

I am not an attorney, having been expelled from Yale Law, but I am the sole member of a department at McNally & Son assigned to discreet inquiries. You must understand that we represented some very wealthy residents of the Town of Palm Beach, and frequently the problems of our clients required private investigations

5

rather than assistance from the police. Most denizens of Palm Beach shun publicity, especially when it might reveal them to be as silly and sinful as lesser folk who don't even have a single trust fund.

Peaches' owners were Mr. and Mrs. Harry Willigan who had an estate on Ocean Boulevard about a half-mile south of the McNally manse. Willigan had made a fortune buying and developing land in Palm Beach and Martin counties, and specialized in building homes in the $50,000–$100,000 range. It was said he never took down the scaffolding until the wallpaper was up – but that may have been a canard spread by envious competitors.

With wealth had come the lush life: mansion, four cars, 52ft. Hatteras, and a staff of three servants. It had also brought him a second wife, forty years younger than he.

The McNallys had dined at his home occasionally – after all, he *was* a client – but I thought him a coarse man, enamoured of conspicuous consumption. He seemed to believe that serving beluga caviar on toast points proved his superiority to old-money neighbors, many of whom served Del Monte tomato herring on saltines. Laverne, his young wife, was not quite as crass. But she did flaunt chartreuse polish on her fingernails.

Willigan had children by his first wife, but he and Laverne were childless and likely to remain so if her frequent public pronouncements on the subject were to be believed. Instead of a tot, they had Peaches, and Harry lavished on that cranky quadruped all the devotion and indulgence usually bestowed on an only child. Laverne, to her credit, tolerated the cat but never to my knowledge called it Sweetums, as Harry frequently did.

And that's how the entire affair began, with the snatching of a misanthropic cat. It almost ended with the untimely demise of yrs. truly, Archibald McNally: bon vivant, dilettantish detective, and the only man in Palm

6

Beach to wear white tie and tails to dinner at a Pizza Hut.

I left father's office in the McNally Building and drove my fire-engine-red Miata eastward toward the ocean. I had a brief attack of the rankles because my unique talents were being used to rescue a treacherous beast whose loathing of me was exceeded only by mine of her. But I am a sunny bloke, inclined to accentuate the positive, and my distemper did not last. It happened to be June 21st, and when Aristotle remarked that one swallow does not make a summer, he obviously wasn't thinking of frozen daiquiries. That was my plasma of choice from the June solstice to the September equinox, and I was looking forward to the first of the season.

Also, my regenerated romance with Consuela Garcia was going splendidly. Connie had made no alarming references to wedlock – the cause of our previous estrangement – and we had vowed to allow each other complete freedom to consort with whomever we chose. But we were so content with each other's company that this declaration of an open relationship had never been tested. As of that morning.

Finally, my spirits were ballooned by an absolutely smashing day: hot sun, scrubbed sky, low humidity and a fresh sea breeze as welcome as a kiss. I thought God had done a terrific job and I thanked Him. As my mother is fond of saying, it never hurts to be polite.

The Willigans' mansion was a *faux* Spanish hacienda with red tile roof, exposed oak beams, and a numbing profusion of terra-cotta pots. The place was called *Casa Blanco* and when you tugged the brass knob on the front door, you expected a butler to appear wearing sombrero and serape.

Actually the butler who opened the door was wearing a black alpaca jacket over white duck trousers. He was an Australian named Leon Medallion, and when he came to

7

work for the Willigans he had to be restrained from addressing all guests as "Mate."

"Good morning, Leon," I said. "How are you this loverly day?"

"Great, Mr. McNally," he said enthusiastically. "Couldn't be better."

That was a shock. Leon usually took a dour view of existence in general and life on the Gold Coast in particular. More than once I had heard him mutter, "Florida sucks."

"And how are the allergies?" I asked.

He looked about cautiously, then stepped close to me. "Would you believe it," he said in a hoarse whisper, "but since that rotten cat's been gone, I haven't sneezed once."

"Glad to hear it," I said, "but I'm sorry to tell you that's why I'm here. I've been ordered to try to find Peaches."

He groaned. "Please, Mr. McNally," he said, "don't try too hard. I suppose you want to see the lady of the house."

"If she's in."

"She is, but I gotta go through all that etiquette shit and see if she's receiving."

He left me standing in the tiled foyer and shambled away. He returned in a few moments.

"She's at the pool and wants you to come out there," he reported. "She also says to ask if you'd like a drink."

I glanced at my watch: almost eleven-thirty. Close enough.

"Yes, thank you, Leon," I said. "Can you mix me a frozen daiquiri?"

"Sure," he said. "My favorite. Mother's milk."

I walked down the long entrance hall, the walls unaccountably decorated with swords, maces, and a few old muskets. The hallway led to a screened patio, and the rear door of that opened to a lawned area and the swimming pool.

Laverne Willigan was lounging at an umbrella table on the grass, her face shaded by a wide-brimmed planter's hat. It may not have been the world's smallest bikini she was wearing, but it wouldn't have provided a decent meal for a famished moth. Her tanned legs were crossed, and one bare foot was bobbing up and down in time to music coming from a portable radio on the table. A rock station, of course.

She had the decency to turn down the volume as I approached, for which I was grateful. I am not an aficionado of rock. I much prefer classical music, such as "I Wish I Could Shimmy Like My Sister Kate."

"Hiya, Archy," Laverne said breezily. "Pull up a chair. You order a drink?"

"I did indeed, thank you," I said, doffing my pink linen golf cap. I moved a canvas sling to face her. "You're looking positively splendid. Glorious tan."

"Thanks," she said. "I work at it. What else have I got to do?"

I hoped she wasn't expecting an answer, but I was saved from replying by the arrival of Leon bearing my daiquiri on a silver salver. It was in a brandy snifter large enough to accommodate a hyacinth bulb.

"Good heavens," I said, "that must be a triple."

"Nah," Leon said, "it's mostly ice."

"Well, if I start singing, send me home. Aren't you drinking, Laverne?"

"Sure I am," she said and picked up a glass as large as mine from the grass alongside her chair. "Bloody Mary made with fresh horseradish. I like hot stuff."

She frequently said things like that. Not suggestive things, exactly, and not double entendres, exactly, but comments that made you wonder what she intended. I had the impression that she was continually challenging men, and if an eager stud wanted to think she was coming on to him and responded, she wouldn't be offended. But I doubted if it ever went beyond high-intensity flirting. She had it made as mistress of *Casa Blanco*, and I hoped she was shrewd enough to know it.

We raised glasses to each other and sipped.

She said, "Through the lips and past the gums; look out, stomach, here it comes."

She actually said that; I am not making it up. I am merely the scribe.

Suddenly I became aware of activity in the Olympic-size swimming pool behind me and turned to look. A young woman in a sleek black maillot was doing laps, brown arms flashing overhead, long legs moving from the hips in a perfect flutter kick.

I watched, fascinated, as she swam the length of the pool, made a racing turn, and started back. There was very little splash and her speed was impressive.

"Who on earth is that?" I asked.

"My sister," Laverne said. "Margaret Trumble. You can call her Meg if you like, but don't call her Maggie or she's liable to break your arm. She's very strong."

"I can see that," I said. "What a porpoise!"

"And she jogs, lifts weights, skis, climbs mountains, and does t'ai chi. She's staying with us until she decides what to do."

I looked at her and blinked. "About what?"

"Right now she teaches aerobics in King of Prussia. That's in Pennsylvania."

"I know," I said. "I once met the queen of Prussia."

Laverne looked at me suspiciously, but continued. "Anyway, Meg is thinking of moving to Florida. She thinks there are enough richniks here so she could do well as a personal trainer. You know: go to people's homes, teach them how to exercise, put them on diets, plan individual workout programs for them. Meg says all the big movie and TV stars have private trainers, and so do business bigshots. She thinks she could get plenty of clients just in Palm Beach."

"She probably could," I said, watching Ms. Trumble zip back and forth through the greenish water. "She seems like a very disciplined, determined young lady."

"Not so young," Laverne said. "She's three years older than I am."

"It's still young to me," I said. "But I was born old. Anyway, it must be fun having your sister here for company."

"Yeah," she said and took a gulp of her drink.

Suddenly she whisked away her straw hat and tossed it onto the grass. She shook her head a few times so her long blonde hair swung free. It was not chemically brazen but softly tinted with reddish accents. I thought it quite attractive.

Her body, barely restrained by that minuscule bikini, was something else. It would be ungentlemanly to call it vulgar, but there was something fulsome about her flesh. There was just so *much* of it. It was undeniably sunned to an apricot tan, and certainly well-proportioned, but the very lavishness was daunting: whipped cream on chocolate mousse.

"Listen, Archy," she said, closing her eyes against the sun's glare. "Do you think you'll get Peaches back?"

"I'm certainly going to try. Could you show me the ransom note you received?"

"Harry's got it. He keeps it in the office safe. In the stock-room."

That was probably accurate since I happened to know she had worked for a year as receptionist in Harry Willigan's office. Then, discovering the boss's son was

11

happily married, had children, and lived in Denver, she had done the next best thing: she had married the boss.

"All right," I said, "I'll see him later. How much are the catnappers asking?"

She opened her eyes and stared, at me. "Fifty thousand," she said softly.

"Gol-*lee*! That's a lot of money for a cat."

"Harry will pay it if he has to," she said. "Sometimes I think he loves that stupid animal more than he does me."

"I doubt that," I said, but I wasn't certain. "When did Peaches disappear?"

"Last Wednesday. Harry was at work, I was at the beauty parlor and Ruby Jackson – she's our housekeeper and cook – had the day off. So only Leon and Julie Blessington were here. She's the maid.

"Where was your sister?"

"Gone to town to look for a place to live. She wants her own apartment. Anyway, it was around one o'clock in the afternoon when Leon and Julie realized Peaches was gone. They searched all over but couldn't find her."

"Maybe she just wandered off or went hunting mice and lizards."

Laverne shook her head. "Peaches is a house cat. We never let her out, because she's declawed and can't defend herself. Sometimes she went into the screened patio to get some fresh air or sleep on the tiles, but she never went outside. The back patio door is always kept closed."

"Locked?"

"No. But at night the door from the hallway to the patio is locked, bolted, and chained. So if anyone got into the patio at night, what could they steal – aluminium furniture?"

"But during the day, if Peaches was on the patio and no one was around, any wiseguy could nip in, stuff her in a burlap sack, and lug her away?"

12

"That's about it. Harry is fit to be tied. He screamed like a maniac at Leon and Julie, but it really wasn't their fault. They couldn't watch the damned cat every minute. Whoever thought she'd be kidnapped?"

"Catnapped," 1 said. "Leon and Julie are sure the outside door to the patio was closed?"

"They swear it was."

"No holes in the screening where Peaches might have slipped through?"

"Nope. Go look for yourself."

"I'll take your word for it. When did the ransom note arrive?"

"Thursday morning. Leon found it under the front door."

"I'll see it at Harry's office, but can you tell me what it said?"

She picked up her straw hat from the grass, clapped it on her head, tilted it far down in front to shade her eyes. She squirmed to find a more comfortable position in her canvas sling. I wished she hadn't done that. She took a deep breath and stretched, arching her back. I wished she hadn't done that.

"The note said they had taken Peaches and would return her in good health for fifty thousand dollars. If we went to the cops, they'd know about it and we'd never see Peaches alive again."

"Did they say how the payment was to be made?"

"No, they said we'd be hearing from them again."

"You keep using the plural. Did the note say *we* have the cat and you'd be hearing from *them?*"

"That's what it said."

"Uh-huh. Was the note in an envelope?"

"Yes. A plain white envelope."

"Was it typed or handwritten?"

"I thought it was typed, but Harry said it had been done

13

on a word processor."

"That's interesting. Is Peaches on a special diet?"

"She eats people-type food, like sautéed chicken livers and poached salmon. Things like that."

"Lucky Peaches," I said. "Well, I can't think of any more questions to ask."

"What will you do now, Archy?"

"Probably go to Harry's office and get a look at the ransom note. It may have – "

I stopped speaking and rose to my feet as I became aware that Margaret Trumble was approaching from the pool, drying her hair with a towel. There wasn't much to dry. Her hair was fairer than her sister's, almost silver, and cut quite short. In fact, she had a "Florida flattop", clipped almost to the scalp at the sides and back, with the top looking like a truncated whiskbroom.

I must admit she wore this bizarre hairdo with panache, as if other people's opinions were not worth a fig. But I found her coiffure charming, perhaps because her face was strong enough to carry it. Good cheekbones there, and a chin that was assertive without being aggressive.

Laverne introduced us, lauding me as "one of my dearest friends" – which was news to me. Meg Trumble's handclasp was firm but brief. She coolly nodded her acknowledgment of my presence – obviously an exquisite joy to her – and began toweling her bare arms and legs.

"How do you like South Florida, Miss Trumble?" I inquired politely.

She paused to look about at the azure sky, green lawn, palms, and a sumptuous royal poinciana.

"Right now it's beautiful," she said. Her voice was deep and resonant, totally unlike Laverne's girlish piping.

"Oh yes," I said. "'What is so rare as a day in June?'"

She looked directly at me for the first time. "Keats?" she asked.

14

"Lowell," I said, reflecting that though she might not know poetry, her pectorals were magnificent. "You're an excellent swimmer," I told her. "Do you compete?"

"No," she said shortly. "There's no money in it. Do you swim?"

"Wallow is more like it," I confessed.

She nodded again, as if wallowing was to be expected from a chap who wore a teal polo shirt and madras slacks.

"Laverne," she said, "I'd like to use the Porsche this afternoon. Can Leon drive me in?"

Her sister pouted. "I want Leon to get busy on the silver; it's getting so tarnished." She turned to me. "Archy, the Porsche is at the garage in West Palm for a tune-up. They phoned that it's ready. Could you drive Meg in to pick it up?"

"Of course," I said. "Delighted."

"That's a good boy," she said. "Meg, Archy will drive you to the garage and you can use the Porsche all afternoon. How does that sound?"

"Fine," the other woman said, expressing no gratitude to me. "I'll get dressed. I won't be long, Mr. McNally."

"Listen, you two," Laverne said. "Enough of that 'Miss Trumble' and 'Mr. McNally' crap. Be nice. Make it Meg and Archy. Okay?"

"Brilliant suggestion," I said.

The sister gave me a frosty smile and headed for the house.

"Don't mind her," Laverne advised me. "She's coming down off a heavy love affair that went sour."

"Oh? What happened?"

"It turned out the guy was married. Now she's in an 'All men should drop dead' mood. Treat her gently, Archy."

"That's the way I always treat women who lift weights," I said. "Thank you for the drink, Laverne.

15

Please call me at my office or home if you hear from the catnappers. And I'll let you know if I learn anything about Peaches."

"I don't much care," she said, "but when Harry is miserable he makes sure everyone is miserable, if you know what I mean. So find that lousy cat, will you."

I bid her adieu and was standing next to the Miata puffing my first English Oval of the day when Meg Trumble came striding from the house. She was wearing a tank dress of saffron linen, and I saw again how slender and muscled she was. Her bare arms and legs were lightly tanned, and she had the carriage of a duchess – a nubile duchess.

I gave her the 100-watt smile I call my Supercharmer. My Jumbocharmer hits 150, but I didn't want to unnerve her.

"You look absolutely lovely," I said.

"I would prefer you didn't smoke," she said.

I could have made a bitingly witty riposte and withered this haughty woman, but I did not lose the famed McNally cool. "Of course," I said, flicked my fag at a dwarf palm, and wondered why I had agreed to chauffeur Ms. Cactus.

We headed north on Ocean Boulevard, and when we passed the McNally home, I jerked my thumb. "My digs," I said.

She turned to stare. "Big," she said.

"I live with my parents," I explained, "with room enough for my sister and her brood when they come to visit. Laverne tells me you're thinking of moving down here."

"Possibly," she said.

And that was the extent of our conversation. Ordinarily I am a talkative chap, enjoying the give-and-take of lively repartee, especially with a companion of the female persuasion. But Meg Trumble seemed in an uncommuni-

16

cative mood. Perhaps she believed still waters run deep. Pshaw! Still waters run stupid.

Then we were in West Palm Beach, nearing our destination when, staring straight ahead, she suddenly spoke. "I'm sorry," she said.

What a shock that was! Not only was she making a two-word speech, but she was actually apologizing. The Ice Maiden had begun to melt.

"Sorry about what?" I asked.

"I'm in such a grumpy mood," she said. "But that's no reason to make you suffer. Please pardon me."

If I had accepted that with a nod of forgiveness and said no more, I would have saved a number of people (including your humble servant) a great deal of *tsores*. But her sudden thaw intrigued me, and I reacted like Adam being offered the apple: "Oh boy, a Golden Delicious!"

"Listen, Meg," I said, "after I leave you I planned to have a spot of lunch and then go back to my office. But why don't you have lunch with me first, and then I'll drive you to the garage."

She hesitated, but not for long. "All right," she said.

We went to the Pelican Club. This is mainly an eating and drinking establishment, although it is organized as a private social club. I am one of the founding members, and it is my favorite watering hole in South Florida. The drinks are formidable and the food, while not haute cuisine, is tasty and chockablock with calories and cholesterol.

The place was crowded, and I waved to several friends and acquaintances. All of them eyeballed Meg; the men her legs, the women her hairdo. Such is the way of the world.

I introduced her to Simon Pettibone, a gentleman of color who doubles as club manager and bartender. His wife, Jas (for Jasmine), was housekeeper and den mother;

17

his son, Leroy, was our chef, and daughter Priscilla worked as waitress. The Pelican could easily be called The Pettibone Club, for that talented family was the main reason for our success. We had a waiting list of singles and married couples eager to become full-fledged members, entitled to wear the club's blazer patch: a pelican rampant on a field of dead mullet.

Priscilla found us a corner table in the rear of the dining room. "Love your hair," she said.

"Thank you," I said.

"Not you, dummy," Priscilla said, laughing. "I'm talking to the lady. Maybe I'll get me a cut like that. You folks want hamburgers?"

"Meg?" I asked.

"Could I get something lighter? A salad perhaps?"

"Sure, honey," Priscilla said. "Shrimp or sardine?"

"Shrimp, please."

"Archy?"

"Hamburger with a slice of onion. French fries."

"Drinks?"

"Meg?"

"Do you have diet cola?"

"With your bod?" Priscilla said. "You should be drinking stout. Yeah, we got no-cal. Archy?"

"Frozen daiquiri, please."

"Uh-huh," she said "Now I know it's summer."

She left with our order. Meg looked around the dining room. "Funky place." she observed.

"It does have a certain decrepit appeal," I admitted. "How come no hamburger? Are you a vegetarian?"

"No, but I don't eat red meat."

"I know you don't smoke. What about alcohol?"

"No."

"Then you must have a secret vice," I said lightly. "Do you collect cookie jars or plastic handbags?"

18

Suddenly she began weeping. It was one of the most astonishing things I've ever seen. One moment she was sitting there quite composed, and the next moment tears were streaming down her cheeks, a perfect freshet. Then she hid her face in her palms.

I can't cope with crying women. I just don't know what to *do*. I sat there helplessly while she quietly sobbed. Priscilla brought our drinks, stared at Meg, then glared at me. I knew she thought I had been the cause of the flood: Priscilla believed breaking hearts was my hobby. Ridiculous, of course. I may be a philanderer, but if there is one thing I have inherited from my grandfather (a burlesque comic) it is this inflexible commandment: always leave 'em laughing when you say goodbye.

"Look, Meg," I said awkwardly, "did I say the wrong thing?"

She shook her head and blotted her face with a paper napkin. "Sorry about that," she said huskily. "A silly thing to do."

"What was it?" I asked. "A bad memory?"

She nodded and tried to smile. A nice try but it didn't work. "I thought I was all cried out," she said. "I guess I'm not."

"Want to talk about it?" I asked.

"It's so banal," she said. "You'll laugh."

"I won't laugh," I said. "I promise."

Priscilla brought our food, glanced at Meg, gave me a scowl, then left us again. While we ate our lunch, Meg told me the story of her demolished romance. She had been right: it *was* banal.

It had been a high-voltage affair with a handsome rogue. He had vowed undying love and proposed marriage, but continually postponed the date: he wanted to build up his bank account, his mother was ill, his business was being reorganized, etc. The excuses went on for

19

almost two years.

Then a girlfriend brought Meg a newspaper from her swain's town. He had won a hefty prize in the state lottery. The front-page photograph showed him grinning at the camera, his arm about the waist of a woman identified as his wife. That was that.

"I was a fool," Meg said mournfully. "I don't blame him as much as I blame myself – for being such an idiot. I think that's what hurts the most, that I could have been tricked so easily."

"Did you enjoy the relationship?" I asked.

She toyed with her salad a moment, head lowered. "Oh yes," she said finally, "I did. I really liked him, and we had some wonderful times together."

"So it's really a bruised ego that makes you weep."

She sighed. "I guess I always had a high opinion of my intelligence. I know better now."

"Nonsense," I said. "Intelligence had nothing to do with it. It's your emotions that were involved, and you were too trusting, and so you were vulnerable and got hurt: a constant risk for the hopeful. But would you rather be a crusty cynic who denies all possibility of hopes coming true?"

"No," she said, "I don't want to be like that."

"Of course you don't," I said. "Meg, when one is thrown from a horse, the accepted wisdom is to mount and ride again as soon as possible."

"I don't think I'm ready for that."

"You will be," I assured her. "You're too young, too attractive to be grounded."

Then we finished our lunch in silence. I was happy to note that despite her sorrow she had a good appetite: she emptied the really enormous salad bowl.

"Basil," she said.

"I beg your pardon," I said. "The name is Archy."

20

She laughed. "In the salad, silly. It was delicious. Archy, are you really one of Laverne's dearest friends?"

I tried to raise one eyebrow (my father's shtick) and failed miserably. "Not quite," I said. "Your sister has a penchant for hyperbole."

"You mean she lies?"

"Of course not. She just exaggerates occasionally to add a little spice to life. Nothing wrong with that. No, my relationship with your sister and brother-in-law is more professional that personal."

I handed over my business card and explained that I had been assigned by McNally & Son to locate the missing feline – the reason for my visit to *Casa Blanco*. I asked Meg when she had last seen Peaches, and she corroborated what Laverne had told me: she had been apartment hunting on the day the cat disappeared.

"Meg, do you think anyone of the staff might have had a hand in the catnapping?"

"I really don't know," she said. "None of them liked Peaches. And I didn't either."

"Glad to hear it," I said, and told her the story of how the beast had regurgitated on my lavender suede loafers.

She laughed again and leaned forward to put a hand lightly on my arm. "Thank you for making me laugh, Archy," she said. "I was afraid I had forgotten how."

"Laughter is a medicine," I pontificated. "Even better than chicken soup. You must promise to have at least one good giggle a day, preferably just before bedtime."

"I'll try, doctor," she vowed.

Coffee was another of her no-no's and neither of us wanted dessert, so I signed the tab and we went out to the Miata. I drove Meg to the garage and just before she got out of the car she thanked me for lunch.

"And for being such a sympathetic listener," she said. "I feel better. I hope I see you again."

21

"You shall indeed," I said, meaning that I would probably be nosing about *Casa Blanco* frequently in my search for Peaches.

But she looked intently into my eyes and repeated, "I do want to see you again," and then whisked away.

There was no misinterpreting that; it seemed evident Ms. Trumble was ready to ride a horse again, and I was the nag selected. I didn't know whether to be delighted or frightened. But I was certain I would not act wisely. Like most men, my life is often a contest between brains and glands. And you would do well to bet Gray Matter to place.

I returned to the McNally Building on Royal Palm Way, parked in our underground garage, and waved to Herb, the security guard. I took the elevator up to my tiny office and lo! on my desk was a telephone message: I was requested to call Consuela Garcia as soon as possible. I did.

"Hi, Connie," I said. "What's up?"

"Who was that baldy you had lunch with at the Pelican?" she demanded.

I believe it was Mr. Einstein who stated that nothing can move faster than the speed of light. It's obvious Albert had no knowledge of the Palm Beach grapevine.

2

I spent at least fifteen minutes trying to placate Connie. I explained that the luncheon had been professional business, part of an investigation into a catnapping. I said that Margaret Trumble, sister of Mrs. Laverne Willigan, had valuable testimony to offer, and I needed to question her away from the scene of the crime.

"Is she living with the Willigans?" Connie asked.

"Visiting."

"For how long?"

"I have no idea."

"Are you going to see her again?"

"If my investigation requires it," I said. "Connie, I am shocked – *shocked!* – by your suspicious tone. I only met Meg this morning and – "

"Oh-ho," she said bitterly, "it's *Meg*, is it?"

"Holy cow!" I burst out. "Laverne insisted I address her sister as Meg, and I complied as a matter of courtesy. Connie, your attitude is unworthy of you. What happened to our decision to have an open relationship: both of us free to date whomever we choose?"

"So you *are* going to see her again!"

"Only in the line of business."

"Just make sure it's not monkey business, buster," she said darkly. "Watch your step; my spies are everywhere."

And she hung up.

I did not take lightly her warning of "spies." Consuela Garcia was secretary to Lady Cynthia Horowitz, one of our wealthiest and most socially active matriarchs. Connie knew everyone in Palm Beach worth knowing, and many who weren't. I had no doubt that she was capable of keeping tabs on my to-and-froing. After all, Palm Beach is a small town, especially in the off-season.

It was a sticky situation but, I reflected, there was more than one way to skin a cat. And recalling that old saw brought me back to the search for the missing Peaches. I only hoped the catnappers were also aware of that ancient adage.

I phoned Harry Willigan's office, and a male receptionist answered. His employment, I reckoned, was Laverne's doing; after marrying the boss, she wanted her hubby's office cleared of further temptations. Smart lady. Harry had the reputation of being a willing victim of satyriasis.

I identified myself and asked for a personal meeting with Mr. Willigan as soon as possible. The receptionist was gone a few moments and then came back on the line to say that if I could come over immediately, I would be granted an audience to last no longer than a half-hour. I told him I was on my way.

Willigan's office was only a block from the McNally Building. Ten minutes later I was seated alongside the tycoon's littered desk, trying hard to conceal my distaste for a man who apparently thought a silk cowboy shirt with bolo tie and diamond clasp, silver identification bracelet, gold Piaget Polo, and a five-carat pinky ring were evidence of merit and distinction.

He was built like a mahogany stump and, to carry the arboreal analogy farther, his voice was a rough bark. I imagined he might have been a good-looking youth, but a lifetime of sour mash and prime ribs had taken their toll,

24

and now his face was a crumpled road map of burst capillaries. The nose had the hue and shape of a large plum tomato.

"What are you doing about Sweetums?" he screamed at me.

I quietly explained that I had barely started my investigation but had already visited his home to learn the details of the catnapping from his wife. I intended to return to question the servants and make a more detailed search of the premises.

"No cops!" he shouted. "Those bastards claim they'll kill Peaches if I go to the cops."

I assured him I would not inform the police, and asked to see the ransom note. He had taken it from the safe prior to my arrival and flung it at me across the desk. I questioned how many people had handled it. The answer: he, Laverne, his receptionist, Leon Medallion and perhaps the other servants at *Casa Blanco*. That just about eliminated the possibility of retrieving any usable fingerprints from the note.

It was neatly printed on a sheet of good paper, and appeared to have been written on a word processor, as Willigan had told his wife. What caught my eye was the even right-hand margin. The spacing between words had been adjusted so that all lines were the same width. Rather rare in a ransom note – wouldn't you say?

I asked if he had received any further communication from the catnappers, and Willigan said he hadn't. I then inquired if there was anyone he thought might have snatched the cat. Did he have any enemies?

He glowered at me. "I got more enemies than you got friends," he yelled. (A comparison I did not appreciate.) "Sure, I got enemies. You can't cut the mustard the way I done without making enemies. But they're all hard guys. They might shoot me in the back, but they wouldn't steal my Sweetums for a lousy fifty grand. That's penny-ante stuff to those bums."

I couldn't think of any additional questions to ask, so I thanked Willigan for his time and rose to leave. He walked me to the door, a meaty hand clamped on my shoulder.

"Listen, Archy," he said in his normal, raucous voice, "you get Peaches back okay and there's a nice buck in it for you."

"Thank you," I said stiffly, "but my father pays me a perfectly adequate salary."

"Oh sure," he said, trying to be jovial, "but a young stud like you can always use a little extra change. Am I right?"

Wretched man. How Laverne could endure his total lack of couth, I could not understand. But I suspected the Bloody Marys with fresh horseradish helped.

I walked back to the McNally Building, swung aboard the Miata, and headed for home. The old medulla oblongata had had enough of the misadventure of Peaches for one day. I gave all those bored neurons a treat by turning my thoughts to Meg Trumble and Laverne Willigan.

I found it amazing that the two were sisters. I could see a slight resemblance in their features, but their carcasses were totally dissimilar. If they stood side by side, Meg on the left, they'd look like the number 18.

And their personalities were so unlike. Laverne was a bouncy extrovert, Meg more introspective, a *serious* woman. I thought she was not as coarsely woven as Laverne, not as many slubs. As of that moment I was not smitten, but she intrigued me. There was a mystery to her that challenged. Laverne was about as mysterious as a baked potato.

I pulled into the driveway of the McNally castle, a tall

26

Tudorish pile with a mansard roof of copper that leaked. I parked on the graveled turnaround in front of our three-car garage, making sure I did not block the entrance to the left-hand bay where my father always sheltered his big Lexus. The middle space was occupied by an old, wood-bodied Ford station wagon, used mostly for shopping and to transport my mother's plants to flower shows.

I found her in the small greenhouse talking to her begonias, as usual. Her name was Madelaine, and she was a paid-up member of the Union of Ditsy Mommies. But she was an absolutely glorious woman, warm and loving. I had seen her wedding pictures, when she became Mrs. Prescott McNally, and she was radiant then. Now, pushing seventy, she was even more beautiful. I speak not as a dutiful son but as an eager student of pulchritude. (I carried in my wallet a small photo of Kay Kendall.)

Mother's specs had slipped down on her nose, and she didn't see me sneak up. I kissed her velvety cheek, and she closed her eyes.

"Ronald Colman?" she asked. "John Barrymore?"

"Tyrone Power," I told her.

"My favorite," she said, opening her eyes. "He was so wonderful in *The Postman Always Rings Twice*."

"Mother, that was John Garfield."

"I loved him, too," she said. "Where have they all gone, Archy?"

"To the great Loew's in the sky," I said. "But I'm still here."

"And I love you most," she said promptly, patting my cheek. "Ursi is baking scallops tonight. Isn't that nice?"

"Perfect," I said. "I'm in a scallopy mood. Ask father to open one of those bottles of muscadet he's been hoarding."

"Why don't you ask him, Archy?"

"Because he'll tell me that a jug chablis is good enough.

27

But if you ask, he'll break out the good stuff. He's putty in your hands."

"He is?" she said. "Since when?"

I kissed her again and went up to my suite to change. "Suite" is a grandiloquent word to describe a small sitting room, cramped bedroom, and claustrophobic bathroom on the third floor. But you couldn't beat the rent. Zip. And it was my private aerie. I had no complaints whatsoever.

I pulled on modest swimming trunks (shocking pink), a terry coverup, and sandals. Then I grabbed a towel and went down to the beach. The Atlantic was practically lapping at our doorstep; just cross Ocean Boulevard and there it was, shimmering in the late afternoon sunlight. The chop was not strong enough to give me second thoughts.

I try to swim two miles a day. Not out and back; that's for idiots. I swim parallel to the shore, about fifty feet out. I go a mile north or south and then return. I don't exactly wallow, as I told Meg Trumble, but I sort of plow along. However, since it is the only physical exercise I get – other than an occasional game of darts at the Pelican Club – it makes me feel virtuous and does wonders for the appetite. And thirst.

My father is very big on tradition. One of the ceremonies he insists on honoring is the cocktail hour, a preprandial get-together that usually lasts thirty minutes during which we imbibe martinis he mixes to the original formula of three parts gin to one of vermouth. Not dry enough for you? Complain to Prescott McNally, but be prepared to face a raised eyebrow – and a hairy one at that.

"Are you going out tonight, Archy?" my father asked that evening at the family gathering.

"No, sir," I said, "I hadn't planned to."

"Good," he said. "Roderick Gillsworth phoned this afternoon and wants to come over at nine o'clock. It concerns some matter he didn't wish to discuss at the office."

"And you want me to be present?" I asked, somewhat surprised.

The governor chomped on his olive which, in a small departure from his love of the hallowed, had been stuffed with a sliver of jalapeño. "Yes," he said, "Gillsworth particularly asked that you sit in."

"And how is Lydia?" mother asked, referring to the client's wife.

Father knitted his brows which, considering their hirsuteness, might have resulted in a sweater. "I asked," he said, "but the man didn't give me a direct answer. Very odd. Shall we go down to dinner?"

The scallops were super, the flavor enhanced by a muscadet the lord of the manor had consented to uncork. He's inclined to be a bit mingy with his vintage wines. It makes little difference to mother, who drinks only sauterne with dinner – a dreadful habit my father and I have never persuaded her to break. But I like a rare wine occasionally: something that doesn't come in a bottle with a handle and screw-top.

For desert, Ursi Olson, our cook-housekeeper, served big slices of a succulent honeydew with wedges of fresh lime. Surfeited, I climbed upstairs to my cave and did a spot of work before Roderick Gillsworth arrived.

During discreet inquiries in the past I had learned to keep a record of my investigations in a ledger. I have a tendency to forget things that may or may not turn out to be important.

So I scribbled short notes on the cases in which I was engaged. That evening I started a new chapter on the catnapping of the malevolent Peaches. I jotted down

29

everything I had learned during the day, which wasn't a great deal. When finished, I put my completed notes aside and glanced at my Mickey Mouse wristwatch (an original, not a reproduction). I saw that I had a quarter-hour before my presence was required in my father's study, to listen to what was troubling our client. I spent the time recalling what I knew of Roderick Gillsworth.

He was a poet, self-proclaimed. His first book, *The Joy of Flatulence*, was so obscure and prolix that critics were convinced he was a genius, and on the strength of their ecstatic reviews *TJOF* sold 527 copies. But Gillsworth's subsequent volumes didn't do as well, and he accepted employment as poet-in-residence at an exclusive liberal arts college for women in New Hampshire.

There he married one of his students, Lydia Barkham. She was heiress to a fortune in old money accumulated by a Rhode Island family that began by making string, graduated to rope, moved on to steel cables, and eventually sold out to a Japanese conglomerate at such a humongous price that one financial commentator termed it "Partial revenge for Pearl Harbor."

Lydia and Roderick Gillsworth moved to Palm Beach in the late 1970s and, despite their wealth, bought a relatively modest home on Via Del Lago, about a block from the beach. They lived quietly, entertained infrequently, and apparently had little interest in tennis, golf, or polo. This did not make them pariahs, of course, but they were considered somewhat odd. According to Palm Beach gossips (the entire population) the Gillsworths had what the French label a *marriage blanc*, and what your grandmother probably called a "marriage in name only." Naturally I cannot vouch for that.

Roderick continued to write poetry, but now his slim volumes were privately printed, handsomely bound in calf-skin, and given as Christmas gifts to personal friends.

30

The McNally family had eight of his books, the pages still uncut. The most recent collection of his poems was titled *The Cross-Eyed Atheist*.

When I entered my father's study on the ground floor, Gillsworth was already lounging in a leather wing chair. I went over to shake his hand and he didn't bother rising. I was an employee and about ten years younger than he, but I still felt it was bad manners. My father sat behind his big leather-topped desk, and I drew up a straight chair and positioned it so that I could observe both men without turning my head back and forth.

"Archy," the don said, "Mr. Gillsworth apparently has a personal problem he wishes to discuss. He is aware of your responsibility for discreet inquiries and the success you have achieved in several investigations with a minimum of publicity."

"No publicity," the poet said sharply. "I must insist on that: absolutely no publicity. Lydia would never forgive me if this got out."

Father stroked his mustache with a knuckle. That mustache was as bristly as his eyebrows, but considerably wider. It was the Guardsman's type and stretched the width of his face, a thicket that was a sight to behold when he was eating barbecued ribs. "Every effort will be made to keep the matter confidential, Mr. Gillsworth." he said. "What exactly *is* it?"

Our client drew a deep breath. "About three weeks ago," he began, "a letter arrived at our home addressed to my wife. Plain white envelope, no return address. At the time Lydia was up north visiting cousins in Pawtucket. Fortunately she had left instructions to open her mail and forward to Rhode Island whatever I thought important and might require her immediate attention. I say 'fortunately' because this particular letter was a vicious threat against Lydia's life. It spelled out the manner of her

31

murder in such gruesome and sickening detail that it was obviously the product of a deranged mind."

"Dreadful," my father said.

"Did the letter given any reason for the threat?" I asked.

"Only in vague terms," Gillsworth said. "It said she must die to pay for what she is doing. That was the phrase used: 'for what she is doing.' Complete insanity, of course. Lydia is the most innocent of women. Her conduct is beyond reproach."

"Do you have the letter with you, Mr. Gillsworth?" father asked.

The poet groaned, "I destroyed it," he said "And the envelope it came in. I hoped it might be a single incident, and I had no wish that Lydia would ever find and read that piece of filth. So I burned it."

Then we sat in silence. Gillsworth had his head averted, and I was able to study him a moment. He was a tall, extremely thin man with a bony face split by a nose that ranked halfway between Cyrano and Jimmy Durante.

He was wearing a short-sleeved leisure suit of black linen. With his mighty beak, scrawny arms, and flapping gestures he looked more bird than bard. I wondered what a young coed had seen in the poet that persuaded her to plight her troth. But it's hopeless to try and imagine what spouses find in each other. It's better to accept Ursi Olson's philosophy. She just shrugs and says, "There's a cover for every pot."

The silence stretched, and when the seigneur didn't ask the question that had to be asked, I did.

"But you've received another letter?" I prompted Gillsworth.

He nodded, and the stare he gave me seemed dazed, as if he could not quite comprehend the inexplicable misfortune that had befallen him and his wife. "Yes," he said in

32

a voice that lacked firmness. "Two days ago. Lydia is home now, and she opened the letter, read it, showed it to me. I thought it even more disgusting and frightening than the first. Again it said that she must die for what she was doing, and it described her murder in horrendous and obscene detail. Obviously the work of a homicidal maniac."

"How did your wife react to the letter?" my father asked gently.

Gillsworth shifted uncomfortably in his wing chair. "First," he said, "I must give you a little background. My wife has always been interested in the occult and in psychic phenomena. She believes in supernatural forces, the existence of spirits, ESP, and that sort of thing." He paused.

I was curious and asked, "Do you also believe in those things, sir?"

He made one of his floppy gestures. "I don't believe and I don't disbelieve. Quite frankly, the supernatural is of minor interest to me. My work is concerned with the conflict between the finite expression of the human psyche and the Ur-reality concealed within. I call it the Divine Dichotomy."

My father and I nodded thoughtfully. What else could we do?

"To answer your question, Mr. McNally," Gillsworth continued, addressing mein papa, "my wife reacted to the letter with complete serenity. You may find it remarkable – I certainly do – but she has absolutely no fear of death, no matter how painful or horrid its coming. She believes death is but another form of existence, that we pass from one state to another with no loss, no diminution of our powers, but rather with increased wisdom and added strength. This belief – which she holds quite sincerely, I assure you – enables her to face her own death with

33

equanimity. And so that letter failed to frighten her – if that was its purpose. But it frightens *me*, I can tell you that. I suggested to Lydia that it might be wise if she returned to Rhode Island for an extended visit until this whole matter can be cleared up."

"Yes," father said, "I think that would be prudent."

"She refused." Gillsworth said. "I then suggested both of us take a trip, perhaps go abroad for a long tour. Again she refused. She will not allow the ravings of a lunatic to alter her life. And she is quite insistent that the matter not be referred to the police. She accepts the entire situation with a sangfroid that amazes me. I cannot take it so lightly. I finally won her permission to seek your counsel with the understanding that you will make no unauthorized disclosure of this nasty business to the police or anyone else."

"You may depend on it," my father said gravely.

"Good," the poet said. "Would you care to see the second letter?"

"By all means."

Gillsworth rose and took a white envelope from his outside jacket pocket. He strode across the room and handed it to my father.

"Just a moment, please," I said. "Mr. Gillsworth, I presume only you and your wife have touched the letter since it was received."

"That's correct."

"Father," I said, "I suggest you handle it carefully, perhaps by the corners. The time may come when we might wish to have it dusted for fingerprints."

He nodded and lifted the flap of the opened envelope with the tip of a steel letter opener taken from his desk. He used the same implement to tease out the letter and unfold it on his desktop. He adjusted the green glass shade of his brass student lamp and began to read. I

34

moved behind his shoulder and peered but, without my reading glasses, saw nothing but a blur.

Father finished his perusal and looked up at the man standing before his desk. "You did not exaggerate, Mr. Gillsworth," he said, his voice tight.

"Would you read it aloud, sir?" I asked him "I'm afraid I left my glasses upstairs."

He read it in unemotional tones that did nothing to lessen the shock of those words. I shall not repeat the letter lest I offend your sensibilities. Suffice to say it was as odious as Gillsworth had said: a naked threat of vicious murder. The letter was triple-distilled hatred.

Father concluded his reading. The client and I returned to our chairs. The three of us, shaken by hearing those despicable words spoken aloud, sat in silence. The pater looked at me, and I knew what he was thinking. But he'd never say it, never dent my ego in the presence of a third person. That's why I loved him, the old badger. So I said it for him.

"Mr. Gillsworth," I said as earnestly as I could, "I must tell you in all honesty that although I appreciate your confidence in me, I am beyond my depth on this. It requires an investigation by the local police, post office inspectors, and possibly the FBI. Sending a threat of physical harm through the mail is a federal offense. The letter should be analyzed by experts: the typewriter used, the paper, psychological profile of the writer, and so forth. It's possible that similar letters have been received by other Palm Beach residents, and yours may provide a vital lead to the person responsible. I urge you to take this to the proper authorities as soon as you can."

My father looked at me approvingly. "I fully concur with Archy's opinion," he said to Gillsworth. "This is a matter for the police."

"No," the poet said stonily. "Impossible. Lydia has

expressly forbidden it, and I cannot flout her wishes."

Now my father's glance at me was despairing. I knew he was close to rejecting Gillsworth's appeal for help, even if it meant losing a client.

"Mr. Gillsworth," I said, leaning toward him, "would you be willing to do this: allow me to meet and talk with your wife. Let me try to convince her how seriously my father and I take this threat. Perhaps I can persuade her that it really would be best to ask the authorities for help."

He stared at me an excessively long time. "Very well," he said finally. "I don't think it will do a damned bit of good, but it's worth a try."

"Archy can by very persuasive," my father said dryly. "May we keep the letter, Mr. Gillsworth?"

The poet nodded and rose to leave. Handshakes all around. My father carefully slid the opened letter into a clean manila file folder and handed it to me. Then he walked Roderick Gillsworth out to his car. I carried the folder up to my cave and flipped on the desk lamp.

I put on my glasses and read the letter. It was just *awful* stuff. But that wasn't what stunned me. I saw it was on good quality paper, had been written with a word processor, and had an even right-hand margin.

How does that grab you?

3

I went to sleep that evening convinced that the Peaches letter and the Gillsworth letter had been written on the same machine, if not by the same miscreant. But what the snatching of a cranky cat had to do with a murderous threat against a poet's wife, the deponent kneweth not.

I awoke the next morning full of p. and v., eager to devote a day to detecting and sorry I lacked a meerschaum pipe and deerstalker cap. Unfortunately I also awoke an hour late, and by the time I traipsed downstairs my father had left for the office in his Lexus and mother and Ursi had taken the Ford to go provisioning. Jamie Olson was seated in the kitchen, slurping from a mug of black coffee.

We exchanged matutinal greetings, and Jamie – our houseman and Ursi's husband – asked if I wanted a "solid" breakfast. Jamie is a septuagenarian with a teenager's appetite. His idea of a "solid" breakfast is four eggs over with home fries, pork sausages, a deck of rye toast, and a quart of black coffee – with maybe a dram of aquavit added for flavor. I settled for a glass of OJ, a buttered bagel, and a cup of his coffee – strong enough to numb one's tonsils.

"Jamie," I said, sitting across the table from him, "do you know Leon Medallion, the Willigan's butler?"

"Uh-huh," he said.

Our Swedish-born houseman was so laconic he made Gary Cooper sound like a chatterbox. But Jamie had an encyclopedic knowledge of local scandals – past, present, and those likely to occur. Most of his information came from the corps of Palm Beach servants, who enjoyed trading tidbits of gossip about their employers. It was partial recompense for tedious hours spent shining the master's polo boots or polishing milady's gems.

"You ever hear anything freaky about Leon?" I asked. "Like he might be inclined to pinch a few pennies from Mrs. Willigan's purse or perhaps take a kickback from their butcher?"

"Nope."

"How about the cook and the maid? Also straight?"

Jamie nodded.

"I know Harry Willigan strays from the hearth," I said. "Everyone knows that. What about his missus? Does she ever kick over the traces?"

The houseman slowly packed and lighted his pipe, an old discolored briar, the stem wound with adhesive tape. "Mebbe," he said. "I heard some hints."

"Well, if you learn anything definite, pass it along to me, please. Their cat's been swiped."

"I know."

"Have you heard anything about the Gillsworths, the poet and his wife?"

"She's got the money," Jamie said.

"That I know."

"And she's tight. He's on an allowance."

"What about their personal lives? Either or both seeking recreation elsewhere?"

"Haven't heard."

"Ask around, will you?" I urged. "Just in a casual way."

38

"Uh-huh," Jamie said. "The Miata could use a good wash. Get the salt off. You going to be around this morning?"

"No," I said, "I have to hit the road. But I should be back late this afternoon. I'd appreciate it if you could get to it then."

"Sure," he said and accepted with a nod the tenner I slipped him. I wasn't supposed to do that, and my father would be outraged if he knew. But Jamie and I understood the *pourboire* was for the information he provided, not a domestic chore. The Olsons were amply paid for managing the McNally household.

I drove southward to the Willigans' hacienda. That ominous message sent to Lydia Gillsworth had given new urgency to my search for Peaches' abductors. It didn't seem incredible to me that the two cases might be connected; I had learned to accept the bizarreness of life.

Leon Medallion opened the door to my ring, and if it wasn't so early in the morning I would have sworn the fellow was smashed. His pale blue eyes were bleary and his greeting was slurred, as if he had breakfasted on a beaker of the old nasty.

He must have seen my astonishment because he said, "I ain't hammered, Mr. McNally. I got my allergies back again. I been sneezing up a storm and now I'm stuffed with antihistamines."

"So it wasn't the cat after all?"

"I guess not," he said mournfully. "But this place has enough molds and pollens to keep my peepers leaking for the rest of my life. You find Peaches?"

"Not yet, Leon. That's why I stopped by – to talk to you and the rest of the staff. Is Mrs. Willigan home?"

"Nah, she took off about a half-hour ago."

"And Miss Trumble?"

"In the pool doing her laps. The woman's a bloomin'

39

fish. You want to talk to all us peons together?"

"Might as well," I said, "No use repeating the same questions three times."

We assembled in the big kitchen: Leon; Ruby Jackson, the cook-housekeeper; the maid, Julie Blessington; and me. Ruby was a tiny, oldish woman who looked too frail to hammer a scallopine of veal. Julie was younger, larger, and exceedingly plain. Trust Laverne not to employ a skivvy who might light her husband's fuse.

I questioned the three of them for about twenty minutes and got precisely nowhere. Only Julie and Leon had been in the house the afternoon Peaches disappeared. They swore the back door of the screened patio had been securely closed. There were no holes in the screening through which the cat might have vamoosed.

None of the three had seen strangers hanging about recently. No one lurking in the shrubbery; nothing like that. And none could even hazard a guess as to who might have shanghaied Peaches. They all testified to Harry Willigan's mad infatuation for his pet and hinted they'd all be happy to endure the permanent loss of that irascible feline. I could understand that.

I hadn't expected to learn anything new and I didn't. I thanked them for their cooperation and wandered out to the back lawn. Meg Trumble was still slicing back and forth in the pool, wearing the shiny black maillot that looked like a body painting. She saw me approach, paused to wave, then continued her disciplined swim. I moved a sling chair into the shade and waited.

She finished her workout in about five minutes. I loved the way she got out of the pool. No ladder for her. She simply placed her hands flat on the tiled coping and in one rhythmic surge heaved up and out, a bent leg raised for a foothold. It was a joy to see, and I never could have done it in a million years.

She came padding to me across the lawn, dripping and using her palms to scrape water from hair, face, arms. "Good morning, Archy," she said, smiling. "Isn't it a lovely day?"

"Scrumptious," I said, staring at her admiringly. She really was an artfully constructed young lady. "Would you care to have dinner with me tonight?"

"What?" she said, startled.

"Dinner. Tonight. You. Me."

"I don't – " she said, confused. "I shouldn't – I better – Perhaps if – "

I waited patiently.

"May I pay my own way?" she asked finally.

"Keep talking that way," I said, "and you'll be asked to resign from the female sex. No, you may not pay your own way. I'm inviting you to have dinner with me. Ergo, you will be my guest."

"All right," she said faintly. "What shall I wear?"

I was able to repress the reply that came immediately to mind.

"Something informal," I said instead. "A flannel muu-muu in a Black Watch tartan might be nice."

"Are you insane?" she said.

"Totally," I assured her. "Pick you up around seven."

I left hastily before she had second thoughts. I walked through the house, down that long corridor lined with antique weapons. They made me wonder if someone might, at that very moment, be taking a scimitar to Peaches. I do believe the plight of that offensive beast was beginning to concern me.

I exited and closed the front door behind me. Took two strides toward the Miata and stopped. Turned around and rang the bell again. Eventually the butler reappeared.

"Sorry to bother you, Leon," I said, "But a question occurred to me that I neglected to ask before. Was

41

Peaches ever taken to the vet?"

"Oh sure," he said. "Once a year for her shots, but more often than that for a bath and to have her teeth and ears cleaned. And once when she got a tapeworm."

"How was she taken? Do you have a carrier – one of those suitcase things with air holes and maybe a wire mesh at one end?"

"Yeah, we got a carrier."

"Could I take a look at it please?"

"I'll dig it out," he said and departed, leaving me standing in the foyer.

I waited. And waited. And waited. It must have been at least ten minutes before he returned. He looked flummoxed.

"Can't find the damned thing," he reported. "It's always been kept in the utility room, but it's not there now. It's probably around here somewhere."

"Sure it is," I said, knowing it wasn't. "Give me a call when you find it, will you."

I drove officeward, not pondering so much on the significance of the missing cat carrier as wondering what inspired me to ask about it in the first place. Frequently, during the course of an investigation, I get these utterly meshuga ideas. Most of them turn out to be Looney Tunes, but occasionally they lead to something important. I had a creepy feeling this particular brainstorm would prove a winner.

My office in the McNally Building had the spaciousness and ambience of a split-level coffin. I suspected my father had condemned me to that closet to prove to the other employees there was no nepotism in his establishment. But allowing me one miserable window would hardly be evidence of filial favoritism, would it? All I had was an air-conditioning vent.

So it was understandable that I rarely occupied my

42

cubby, using it mainly as a message drop. On those rare occasions when I was forced to write a business letter, my father's private secretary, Mrs. Trelawney, typed it for me and provided a stamp. She also informed me when my salary check was available, the dear lady.

On that morning a telephone message placed precisely in the middle of my pristine desk blotter requested that I call Mrs. Lydia Gillsworth. I lighted and smoked my first cigarette of the day while planning what I might say to a woman who had received a dreadful prediction of her doom.

Actually, when I phoned, she could not have been more gracious and lighthearted. She inquired as to my health and that of my parents. She expressed regret that she did not see the McNallys more often. She said she had brought a small Eyelash begonia back from Rhode Island especially for my mother, and as soon as it recovered from jet lag, she would send it over. I thanked her.

"Now then, Archy," she said, "Roderick says you'd like to talk to me about that silly letter I received."

"If I may, please," I said. "I really don't think it should be taken lightly."

"Much ado about nothing," she said firmly. "People who mail letters like that exhaust all their hostility by writing. They never *do* anything."

"I would like to believe you're correct, Mrs. Gillsworth," I said. "But surely it will do no harm if I look into it a bit."

"Rod said you thought the police should be consulted. I will not allow that. I don't wish this matter to become public knowledge and perhaps find its way into the tabloids."

She spoke so decisively that I knew it would be hopeless to plead with her, but I reckoned her command could be finessed. I have sometimes been called "devious"; I much

43

prefer "adroit." It calls up the image of a skilled fencer and a murmured "Touché."

"No police," I agreed. "Just a private, low-key investigation."

"Very well then," she said. "Can you come over at two o'clock this afternoon?"

"With pleasure," I said. "Thank you."

"And I'll take another look at the Eyelash begonia," she added. "If it seems fit to travel, perhaps you can carry it back to your mother."

"Delighted," I said bravely.

After she hung up, I took the box of English Ovals from my jacket, stared at it a moment, then returned it unopened to my pocket. I was attempting to renounce the things and was at the point where denying myself a cigarette yielded almost as much satisfaction as smoking one. Almost – but not quite.

I phoned Sgt. Al Rogoff at the Palm Beach Police Department. Al was a compadre of many years, and we had worked together on several cases, usually to our mutual benefit.

"Sergeant Rogoff," he answered.

"Archy McNally," I said. "How was the vacation?"

"Great," he said. "I spent a week bonefishing off the Keys."

"Liar," I said. "You spent a week in Manhattan and went to the ballet every night."

"Shhh," he said, "not so loud. If that got around, you know what a ribbing I'd take from the Joe Six-packs?"

"Your secret is safe with me." I said. "How about lunch in an hour?"

"Nope," he said promptly. "I could make it but I'm not going to."

"Al!" I said, shocked. "Since when do you turn down a decent lunch? I'll pay the bill."

"You'll pay the bill for the food," he said, "but every time I have lunch with you I end up paying a lot more – like more work, more stress, more headaches. No, thanks. You solve your own problems."

"I have no problems," I protested. "I'm not working a case. I merely wanted to have a pleasant social get-together."

"Oh sure," he said. "When shrimp fly. I appreciate the invitation, but I'll pass."

"Well, will you at least answer one little question for me?"

"Trot it out and I'll let you know."

"Has the Department had any complaints lately from people receiving poison-pen letters? Vicious stuff. Threats of murder."

"I knew it!" Rogoff said, almost shouting. "I knew you'd never feed me without getting me involved in one of your cockamamy investigations. Who got the letter?"

"I can't tell you that, " I said. "Client confidentiality. And I'm not trying to get you involved. I just want to know if it's part of a local pattern."

"Not to my knowledge," he said. "I'll ask around but I haven't heard of any similar squeals."

"Al," I said, "the crazies who mail filth like that – do they ever do what they threaten?"

"Sometimes they do," he said, "And sometimes they don't."

"Thank you very much." I said. "That's a big help."

"We're here to serve." He said. Then, gruffly, "Keep me up to speed on this, Archy. I don't like the sound of it."

"I don't either," said I, and we hung up.

I drove home for lunch reflecting that Sgt. Rogoff was right; sooner or later I'd have to get him involved. I needed professional help on the Willigan and Gillsworth letters: analysis of the paper and the printing machine used, perhaps a psychological profile of the writer. I laughed aloud at what Al's reaction would be when he learned I wanted his assistance to recover an abducted pussycat.

It was not, after all, a major criminal act. In fact, considering Peaches' personality, I didn't think it was a crime at all. I remembered *The Ransom of Red Chief*, and wondered if the case might end with the catnappers paying Harry Willigan to take back his disagreeable pet.

My mother had departed for the monthly meeting of her garden club so I lunched in the kitchen with Ursi and Jamie Olson. We had a big platter of cold cuts, a bowl of German potato salad, and the marvelous sour rye Ursi bakes once a week. We all made sandwiches, of course, with a hairy mustard and cold bottles of St. Pauli Girl to cool the fire.

It was all so satisfying that I went up to my digs for a short nap. I had a demented dream that involved Peaches wearing pajamas in convict stripes. The pj's then turned into a sleek black maillot. Can you help me, Dr. Freud?

I awoke in time to freshen up, smoke a cigarette (No. 2), and vault into the freshly washed Miata for my trip to the Gillsworth home. I was looking forward to my conversation with Lydia, a lovely woman.

She was younger than her husband by about ten years, which would put her in my age bracket. But I always thought of her as a married woman and that made her seem older. I can't explain it. Why do married people strike one as older than singles of the same age? I must puzzle that out one of these days.

Physiognomically Lydia Gillsworth was unique – at least in my experience. She had an overbite so extreme that I once heard it cruelly remarked that she was the only woman in Palm Beach who could eat corn on the

46

cob through a picket fence. But to compensate for this anomaly she had the county's most wonderful eyes. They used to be called bedroom eyes: large, deep-set, luminous. It was almost impossible to turn one's gaze away from those seductive orbs.

And charm? A plentitude! She had the rare faculty of making you believe she thought you the most fascinating creature on God's green earth. She listened intently, she asked pertinent questions, she expressed sympathy when needed. All with integrity and dignity. Can a woman be a *mensch* – or is that a term reserved for honorable men? If it is, then Lydia was a *menschess*.

I knew the Gillsworths had no staff of live-in servants but employed a Haitian housekeeper who worked thrice a week. So I wasn't surprised when the mistress herself opened the door in answer to my knock. She drew me inside in a half-embrace and kissed my cheek.

"Archy!" she cried. "This *is* nice! Guess what I have for you."

"An autographed photo of Thelma Todd?"

"No," she said, laughing, "a pitcher of pink lemonade. Let's go out on the patio. It's a super day."

She led the way through the Gillsworth home. It was decorated in the French Country style: everything light, airy, in muted colors. Fresh flowers were abundant, and the high-ceilinged rooms seemed to float in the afternoon sunlight. Overhead fans billowed gossamer curtains, and the uncarpeted floor, random-planked and waxed to a high gloss, reflected the antique bestiary prints framed on the whitewashed walls.

The patio was small but trig. It faced west but a striped awning shielded it from the glare of the setting sun. We sat at a glass-topped table and drank iced pink lemonade from pilsners engraved with a vine design.

She wasted no time with small talk. "Archy," she said,

47

"I do wish Roderick hadn't consulted your father and you about that letter." She was as close to petulance as I had ever seen her. "It's so embarrassing."

"Embarrassing? Mrs. Gillsworth, through no fault of yours, you have received a very venomous message. I could understand your being concerned, but why should you be embarrassed?"

"Because I seem to be causing such a foofaraw. Isn't that a lovely word? I've wanted to use it for ages. The letter doesn't bother me; it's such a stupid thing. But I am upset by the disturbance it's causing. Poor Rod hasn't been able to write a line since it arrived, and now you've been dragooned into trying to find the writer when I'm sure there are a dozen other things you'd rather be doing. That's why I'm embarrassed – because I'm causing so much trouble."

"One," I said, "I wasn't dragooned; I volunteered. Two, there is nothing I'd rather be doing than getting to the bottom of this thing. Three, your welfare is important to your husband and to McNally & Son. None of us take the matter lightly. Speaking for my father and myself, we would be derelict in our duty if we did not make every effort possible to identify the sender. And only you can help."

"I don't see how I can, Archy," she said, pouring us more lemonade. "I haven't the faintest idea who might want to murder me."

"Have you ever been threatened in person?"

"No."

"Have you had any recent arguments with anyone?"

"No."

"What about some event in your past? Can you think of anyone who might have harbored a grudge, even for years and years?"

"No."

"Have you, however unintentionally, given anyone cause to believe he or she has been injured by you, insulted, offended, or even slighted?"

"No.

I sighed. "Mrs. Gillsworth, the writer of that piece of filth is obviously not playing with a full deck. Please think hard. Is there anyone amongst your friends and acquaintances you have felt, occasionally or often, might be emotionally or mentally off the wall?"

She was silent a moment, and I hoped she was obeying my adjuration to "think hard."

"No," she said finally, "I know of no one like that."

"What about a chance meeting with someone unknown to you? A clerk in a store, for example. A parking attendant. A waiter. Have you had any problems at all with people who serve the public? Any disagreements, no matter how trivial? Complaints you've made?"

"No, I can't recall anything like that."

I could not believe this woman was deliberately lying, but I found it hard to believe her denial of any altercation whatsoever with clerk, waiter, or bureaucrat. The world being what it is, we all have occasional disputes with those being paid to serve us.

I finished my lemonade. It was a bit sweetish for my taste. Lydia attempted to fill my glass again, but I shook my head, held a palm over the glass.

"Delicious," I told her, "but I'm fighting a losing war against calories. Mrs. Gillsworth, do you know of anyone who envies you?"

She was startled, then looked at me with a wry smile. "What an odd question to ask."

"Not so odd," I said. "You are an attractive, charming lady. Everyone in Palm Beach knows you are well-to-do, if not wealthy. You are happily married to an intelligent, creative man. Your life seems to be serene and trouble-

49

free. You have a lovely home and you dress beautifully. It appears to me that there are many reasons why you might be envied."

That discomposed her and she showed her perturbation by standing suddenly to lower the patio awning farther so that we sat in warm shade.

"You know, Archy," she said, frowning, "it has never occurred to me that I might be envied. But when you list my blessings in that fashion, I can understand why I might be. But I assure you I have never heard anyone express anything that could be construed as envy. Oh, I've had compliments on my gowns or on the house, but those were just conventional social remarks. Nothing that suggested the speaker was jealous."

Then we sat in silence a moment. I was depressed by all her negative reactions to my questions. She had given me nothing, not a hint of a lead that might give direction to my discreet inquiries. She caught my mood, because she leaned forward and placed a hand lightly on my arm.

"I'm sorry, Archy," she said softly. "I really think you should drop it."

"No, ma'am," I said stubbornly, "I won't do that. The letter you received frightens me."

She gave me a smile that surprised me. It was an amused smile, as if she appreciated my concern but thought my determination excessive.

"Let me try to explain how I feel," she said. "And give you the reason why that letter doesn't terrify me. I don't know whether or not my husband spoke to you about my faith, but I believe deeply that life is but one form of existence and what we call death is another. I believe that when we die, we pass into another world as viable as this one but much more wonderful because it is inhabited by all those who have gone before. The soul never dies. Never! So corporeal existence is just a temporary state.

50

When we give it up, voluntarily or not, we pass to a higher spiritual plane, just as a butterfly emerges from a cocoon. I am not trying to convert you, Archy; really I'm not! I'm just trying to explain why death holds no terrors for me."

I abstained from reminding her that the death promised by the poison-pen letter involved torture and agony; it would not be a peaceful passing to her higher spiritual plane. But I was curious. "Tell me, Mrs. Gillsworth, are there many people, do you think, who share your beliefs?"

She laughed. "Many more than you think, I assure you. I call them 'kindred souls.' That's a nice, old-fashioned phrase, isn't it? Oh yes, there are many who feel as I do. Right here in Palm Beach, as a matter of fact. A number of us meet frequently to discuss out-of-body experiences and attempt to communicate with those who have already passed over."

I hoped she didn't notice, but I came to attention like a gun dog on point.

"Oh?" I said, as casually as I could. "These gatherings – something like a club, are they? You meet at members' homes?"

"Not exactly," she said, seemingly gratified by my interest. "They're orchestrated by our psychic adviser and held in her home. Mrs. Gloriana. A wonderful woman. So sensitive."

"That *is* fascinating," I said, and it *was* because I now had a name. "Is she a medium? A seer?"

"*Not* a seer," Lydia said definitely. "Hertha doesn't attempt to predict the future or tell your fortune or any claptrap like that. But I suppose you might call her a medium. We prefer to think of her as a channel, our means of communication to the great beyond."

She spoke so simply and sincerely that I had no

inclination to snicker. I am something of an infidel myself but I never scorn belief. If you are convinced the earth is flat, that's okay with me as long as it gives you comfort.

"And this is Mrs. Gloriana's profession?" I asked. "I mean, she does this for a living?"

"Oh yes. But don't get the idea that it's some kind of a con game. Hertha is licensed and bonded."

"But she does charge for her services?" I said gently.

"Of course she does," Mrs. Gillsworth said. "And why shouldn't she, since her talents are so special. But her fees are quite reasonable and she takes credit cards."

"Uh-huh," I said. "And these meetings – sort of like séances, are they?"

"Well . . . " she said hesitantly, "somewhat. But there are no blobs of protoplasm floating in space or weird noises. We meet in a well-lighted room, sit in a circle around a table, and hold hands. To increase our psychic power, you see. Then Mrs. Gloriana tries to communicate with the other world. Her contact is a Mayan shaman who passed over hundreds of years ago. His name is Xatyl. Through him, Hertha attempts to reach people her clients wish to question. Sometimes they are famous people but usually they are relatives. I've spoken to my great-grand-mother many times."

"And communication with the, ah, deceased is made through Xatyl via Mrs. Gloriana?"

"Not always," Lydia said sharply. "The contact fails as often as it succeeds. Sometimes the departed person re-quested is not available, or the line of communication is too faint to produce results because our combined psychic power that particular night is simply not strong enough to allow Mrs. Gloriana to get through to Xatyl."

"Incredible," I said, shaking my head, "and positively entrancing. Does Mrs. Gloriana provide private, uh, con-sultations?"

"Of course she does. But she'll warn you that the chances of a successful contact are less for an individual than for a group. Because the psychic power is usually not sufficient, you see. A gathering of believers with linked hands generates much more energy than one person."

That seemed reasonable to me. If you accepted the original premise, it even sounded *logical*.

"Tell me something else," I said, "and this is just idle curiosity on my part, but has your husband ever attended the meetings with Mrs. Gloriana?"

"Oh, Rod came to three or four," she said lightly, "but then he just drifted away. He never scoffed, but he never accepted the concept wholeheartedly. Rod's interests are more intellectual than spiritual. And he's uncomfortable in groups. He needs solitude to create."

"I can appreciate that," I said. "He has his work to do, and very important work it is, too." I stood up. "Mrs. Gillsworth, I thank you for your time and hospitality."

"You intend to continue your investigation?"

I nodded. "I can't promise success, but I must try."

"I haven't been much help, have I?"

"I'm sure you've provided all the information you possibly can."

"And you promise not to take this ridiculous matter to the police? It's really of no consequence."

I made no reply. She conducted me back through the house, then suddenly stopped and put a hand on my arm.

"Wait just a moment, Archy," she said. "I must show you something I brought back from Rhode Island for Rod's collection. I found it at a country shop near Woonsocket."

Roderick Gillsworth collected antique canes and walking sticks.

In fact, collecting was an absolute frenzy in Palm Beach, and the more outré the collectables, the stronger

53

the passion. I myself had succumbed to the madness and was buying up every crystal shotglass I could find. The star of my collection was an etched Lalique jigger.

I had seen Gillsworth's collection before, and he had some beauts, including several sword canes, one that concealed a dagger, a walking stick that held a half-pint of whiskey, and a formal evening stick which, when one peered through a small hole in the handle, revealed a tiny photo of a billowy maiden wearing nothing but long black stockings and a coy smile.

The cane Lydia had brought her husband from Rhode Island was a polished, tapered cone of ash topped with a heavy head of sterling silver in the shape of a unicorn. It really was an impressive piece, probably about two hundred years old, and I longed to know what it cost – but didn't ask, of course.

I complimented Mrs. Gillsworth on her purchase and thanked her again for the pink lemonade. But I was not to escape so easily.

She brought me that Eyelash begonia intended for my mother. I thought it should have been called a Godzilla begonia but thanked Lydia once again and lugged it out to the Miata. I drove home slowly, mulling over everything I had just learned. I am an amateur muller. I get that from my father, who is a world-class muller and has been known to ponder for two minutes trying to decide whether or not to salt a radish.

Mother was still absent when I arrived home so I left the monstrous plant on her workbench in the potting shed. I had plenty of time for my ocean swim before the family cocktail hour. It was while plowing through the murky sea that I had an idea which was absolutely bonkers. What if Mrs. Lydia Gillsworth had written the poison-pen letter herself and mailed it to herself?

I could think of several possible motives. (1) She

54

wished to elicit sympathy from friends. (2) She wanted attention from her husband, who apparently spent most of his time cuddling with his muse. (3) She yearned for a little drama in a life that had become hopelessly humdrum. (4) She herself was around the bend and was now subject to irrational impulses.

A case could be made for suspecting Lydia as the culprit, but it fell apart when I remembered the similarly printed ransom note delivered to the Willigans. I doubted if Mrs. Gillsworth even *knew* the Willigans, and it was absurd to believe her guilty of swiping their cat.

I showered and dressed carefully for my date with Meg Trumble. I was in a Bulldog Drummond mood and wore total black: raw silk jacket, jeans, turtleneck, socks, and loafers. My father took one look, elevated an eyebrow, and commented, "You look like a shadow." But of course his taste in male attire is stultified. He thinks my tasseled loafers were twee. I think of him as the Prince of Wingtips.

We sipped our martinis, and mother told us how delighted she was with Lydia Gillsworth's gift. The pater asked offhandedly if I had made any progress with the "Gillsworth matter," and I said I had not.

"And the Willigan's missing cat?" he added.

"Negative," I said, and was tempted to tell him I was convinced the two cases were connected. But I didn't, fearing he might have me certified.

We finished our drinks, and my parents went downstairs to dine. I went out to the Miata and sat long enough to smoke my third English Oval of the day, knowing that in Meg Trumble's company I would have to forgo nicotine.

Then I drove down to the Willigans' home, ruminating on where I could take Meg for dinner. It had to be someplace so distant that my presence with another

55

woman might escape the notice of Consuela Garcia's corps of informants. I finally decided to make the journey to Fort Lauderdale.

I was familiar with W. Scott's warning about tangled webs. But I wasn't really practicing to deceive Connie.

Was I?

4

'I had suggested to Meg that she dress informally and so she did: Bermuda shorts of blue silk, a tank top the color of sea foam, and a jacket in a muted shepherd's plaid that she wore over her shoulders cape-fashion. All undoubtedly informal, but so elegantly slender was her figure and so erect her carriage that she made even casual duds look as formal as a Givenchy ball gown.

"Smashing," I told her. "Have you ever modeled?"

"I tried once," she said, "but I don't photograph well. I come out all edges and sharp corners. The photographer said I looked like a stack of slates."

"Stupid photographer," I grumbled. "He probably prefers cheeseburgers to veal piccata."

Meg laughed. "Is that the way you think of me? As veal piccata?"

"It's a splendid classic dish," I said.

I turned southward and she asked where we were going. I told her I knew a fine restaurant in Fort Lauderdale, and would she mind traveling for about an hour?

"Couldn't care less," she said. "I'm so happy to get out of that house."

"Oh?" I said. "Problems?"

"My brother-in-law," she said. "I can't stand the way he treats Laverne. The man is really a mouthy lout. I don't know how my sister puts up with him."

"Maybe she loves him," I said mildly.

Meg hooted. "Laverne loves the perks of being Mrs. Harry Willigan. But she's paying her dues. I'd never do it. If a man screamed at me the way Harry does, I'd clean his clock."

"I'll remember that."

"See that you do," she said, so solemnly that I couldn't decide if she was serious or putting me on.

I had hoped it would be a pure night, the air crystal, the sky glittering like a Cartier ad in *Town & Country*. But it was not to be. That murky ocean should have warned me; there was a squall brewing offshore, and the cloud cover was thickening.

"I think it's going to rain," Meg said.

"It wouldn't dare," I said. "I planned a romantic evening, and it's hard to be romantic when you're sopping wet."

"Oh, I don't know," she said thoughtfully, which convinced me this woman had *depths*.

Her prediction was accurate; rain began to spatter when we hit Deerfield Beach, south of Boca Raton. I didn't think it would last long – summer squalls rarely did – but it could be a brief vertical tsunami.

"We can stop and put up the top," I told Meg, "and then continue on to Lauderdale. Or we can take potluck and stop at the first restaurant we see that offers shelter for the car. Which shall it be?"

"You call it," she said.

So we continued on, the Miata hatless and the rain becoming more determined. Then, at Lighthouse Point, I spotted a Tex-Mex joint that had a portico out front. We pulled under just in time to avoid a Niagara that would have left us bobbing in a filled bathtub.

"Good choice," Meg said. "I love chili."

Marvelous woman! Not the slightest complaint that her jacket was semi-sodden and her short hair wetly plastered to her skull. We scampered inside the restaurant, laughing, and at that moment I really didn't care if the Miata floated away in our absence.

It was not the Oak Room at the Plaza. More of a Formica Room with paper roses stuck in empty olive jars on every table. It was crowded, which I took as a good omen. We grabbed the only empty booth available and slid in. Paper napkins were jammed in a steel dispenser, and the cutlery looked like Army surplus. But the glassware was clean, and there was a bowl of pickled tomatoes, mushrooms, and jalapeños, with tortilla chips, for noshing until we ordered.

The menu, taped to the wall, was a dream come true. We studied the offerings with little moans of delight. Dishes ranged from piquant to incendiary, and I reckoned that we might have been wise to wear sweats.

The stumpy waiter who came bustling to take our order had a long white apron cinched under his armpits. He also had a mustache that Pancho Villa might have envied.

"Tonight's spassel," he announced proudly, "is pork loin basted with red *mole* sauce and served with black bean relish in a tortilla with roast tomato chili sauce. Ver' nice."

"Mild?" I asked him.

"You crazy?" he said.

But we skipped the spassel. Meg relaxed her stricture against red meat to order an appetizer of Kick-Ass Venison Chili. (I am not making it up; that's what it was called.) Her entrée was Cajun Seafood Jambalaya (including crawdads) in a hot creole sauce with garlicky sausage rice.

I went for an appetizer of Swamp Wings (fried frog legs with pepper sauce) and, for a main course, Sirloin Fajita. It was described on the menu as a grilled marinated steak basted with Jack Daniel's and served with sautéed peppers and onions and a lot of other swell stuff, all inflammatory. Meg asked for a diet cola and I ordered a bottle of Corona beer.

"And a stomach pump for two," I was tempted to add, but didn't.

I shall not attempt to describe the actual consumption of that combustible meal. Suffice to say that it was accompanied by gasps, brow-mopping, and frequent gulps of cold diet cola and Mexican beer. Our tonsils did not actually shriek in protest, but my stomach began to glow with an incandescent heat, presaging an insomniac night.

Of more importance to this narrative was our conversation that evening, for it included tidbits of information that would have aided my investigation – if I had had the wit to recognize clues in Meg's casual remarks. But I was too busy gnawing fried frog legs and swilling Corona to pay close attention. Do you suppose S. Holmes ever neglected a case because Mrs. Hudson brought him a plump mutton chop?

"Good news," Meg said, working on her chili. "I found an apartment. I already have the keys. I'm moving in tomorrow."

"Wonderful!" I said. "Where?"

"Riviera Beach. It's just a small place and I only have it till October. But the off-season rent is reasonable. I'm going to fly back to Pennsylvania, pack up more clothes and things, and then drive my Toyota back. Now I'll be able to stop freeloading on my sister."

"And get away from Harry," I added.

"That's the best part," she said. "I'll still see Laverne, of course, but not in that house."

We discussed her hope of becoming a personal trainer to Palm Beach residents seeking eternal youth through diet and exercise. I offered to supply a list of friends and acquaintances who might be potential clients.

"That would be a big help, Archy," she said gratefully. "Laverne has already given me some names, but I need more prospects. How about you?"

I laughed. "I'm really not the disciplined grunt-and-groan type. I try to do a daily swim, as I told you, and I play tennis and golf occasionally. I admit I'm hardly in fighting trim, but regular workouts are not my cup of sake. Too lazy, I suspect. I'm surprised you're willing to accept men as clients. I thought you'd limit your efforts to reducing female flab."

"Oh no," she said. "I'll be happy to train men. As a matter of fact, Harry Willigan has already volunteered to be my first client. But he's not interested in improving his health and fitness."

"No?" I said. "What is he interested in?"

I knew the answer to that, and it was just what I expected.

"Me," Meg Trumble said.

Our entrées arrived and we plunged in.

"I hope your sister isn't aware of her husband's interest," I said.

"Of course she's aware. She trusts me, but secretly she'll probably be relieved to have me out of the house."

That amused me. "If there was anything going on between you and Harry, your moving out wouldn't end it. Facilitate it more likely."

60

"Well, there's nothing going on," she said crossly, "and never will be. I told you what I think of that man."

"I share your opinion," I assured her. "He can be grim. It's amazing that Laverne puts up with his nonsense."

"Oh, she ignores him as much as she can. And she has other interests. She's taking tennis lessons, and she's very active in local clubs. She's at meetings two or three nights a week. But enough about Laverne and Harry. How are you making out on finding Peaches?"

"Not very well," I said. "No progress at all, except for one oddity that needs looking into."

I thought it would do no harm to tell her about the missing cat carrier. I thought it would surprise her, and that she'd immediately guess what I had already assumed: someone in the Willigan household had stuffed Peaches in the carrier and hauled her away.

But Meg kept her head lowered, picked through the jambalaya for shrimp, and said only: "Oh, I'm sure it will turn up somewhere around the house."

We finished our dinner with scoops of lemon sherbet, which helped diminish the conflagration – but not enough.

"Everything hokay?" the mustachioed waiter asked.

"Fine," I said. "If you don't mind a charred epiglottis."

I paid the tab with plastic and we went out to the Miata. I took along a handful of paper napkins and wiped the seats reasonably dry. The squall had passed, the night air was freshening, and there were even a few stars peeking out from behind drifting clouds.

"Yummy dinner," Meg said. "Thank you. I really enjoyed it."

"We must dine there again," I said. "Perhaps after the turn of the century."

The drive home was a delight. We sang "It Ain't Gonna Rain No Mo'," and several other songs of a more recent vintage. Meg had a throaty alto, and I thought we harmonized beautifully. Then, like an idiot, I suggested we do "Always," and she started weeping again. Not heaving sobs; just a quiet cry.

"Sorry," I said.

"Not your fault," she said sniffling. "It's memories. I'll get over it."

"Of course you will," I said, not all that sure.

But she shook off the brief attack of the megrims and, spirits restored, began describing her new apartment. Suddenly she stopped.

"Hey, Archy," she said. "Would you like to see it? It's not too late, is it?"

"Not late at all," I said, "and I'd like to see it."

It took a good hour to get back to Riviera Beach, but the weather improved as we drove. It became mellow with a salty breeze, palm fronds rustling, the sea providing a fine background of whispering surf. It turned out to be the pure night I had hoped for. I wish I could say the same for my thoughts.

Meg now had her own private pad; that was provocative. Even more stimulating was the fact that it was in Riviera Beach, as distant from Connie Garcia's espionage network as I could reasonably hope. The McNally luck seemed to be holding, and I resolved not to waste it. Luck is such a precious commodity, is it not? Especially on a voluptuous night in the company of a young woman whose clavicles drove me mad with longing.

I lied gamely and told Meg how attractive her apartment was. In truth, I found it utterly without charm. It had obviously been furnished as a rental property; everything was utilitarian and designed to withstand rough usage. Nondescript pictures were bolted to the walls and the dinnerware on the open kitchen shelves was white plastic and looked as if it might bounce if dropped.

62

"Of course it's a little bleak right now," Meg admitted. "It needs some personal things scattered about. But the air conditioner works fine and there's even a dishwasher. I can stand it till October. By that time I hope to have something better lined up."

"I'm sure you will," I said. "Is the phone connected?"

"Not yet. I'll have that done when I return. After I get settled in and fill up the fridge, I hope you'll come over for dinner."

"Love to," I said. "We'll have a housewarming."

She looked at me speculatively. "We could have one right now," she said. "It's a king-sized bed."

"I like to be treated royally," I said.

I feared she might be a white-bread lover. You know: spongy and bland. Men and women who devote all their energies to body-building and no-smoke, no-drink discipline are sometimes incapable of the kinder, gentler arts, like love-making.

I needn't have worried about Meg Trumble. Rather than white bread, she was pumpernickel, robust and zesty. She never used her strength to dominate, but I was always aware that her complaisance was voluntary, and so vigorous was her response to my efforts that I reckoned she could, if she wished, twist me into a pretzel.

It is generally thought that highly spiced foods act as aphrodisiacs. But I do not believe our behavior that night on coarse, motel-type sheets can be credited to Kick-Ass Venison Chili and Swamp Wings. I think Meg's fervor was partly inspired by her determination to banish aching memories, and my excitement fed on her passion.

Depleted (temporarily), we stared at each other with pleased recognition: two strangers who had discovered they spoke the same language.

"And you said you weren't in fighting trim," Meg scoffed. "You didn't mention loving trim."

"It was your doing," I told her. "Your beauty and *joie de vivre*. I rose to the occasion and, with your assistance, shall do so again."

"By all means," she said, moving closer.

It was a bit after midnight when we departed from Riviera Beach and headed homeward. We had tarried in her new apartment long enough to bathe together in a delightfully cramped shower stall, using a sliver of soap as thin as a potato chip. The towels had all the absorbency of Alençon, but by that time nothing could lessen our beaming felicity.

I pulled into the driveway of the Willigan estate, crawled out of the car, and went around to open Meg's door. I held out a hand to assist her.

"Thank you for a lovely evening, Miss Trumble," I said, completely po-faced. "The pleasure of your company at dinner was exceeded only by the kindness of your hospitality."

"Thank you, Mr. McNally," she said, just as deadpan. "I trust our paths may cross again."

"A consummation devoutly to be wished," I said, and then we both dissolved and kissed. Lingeringly.

Science defines a kiss as the close juxtaposition of two or more orbicular muscles in a state of contraction. Science has a lot to learn.

I drove home in an ecstatic mood, knowing there would be no insomnia and no nightmares that night. And there weren't. I slept the sleep of the just.

Just exhausted and just content.

I awoke the next morning infected with a galloping case of *joie de vivre* I had obviously contracted from my companion of the night before. At breakfast, mother commented on my good humor and sought the cause.

"Did you have a pleasant dinner engagement, Archy?" she asked.

"Very."

"Connie?"

"No," I said. "Margaret Trumble, sister of Laverne Willigan. I think I may be in love."

My father uttered a single syllable that sounded suspiciously like "Humph."

I told him I would not be driving to the office with him that morning, as I sometimes did, but would be busy with discreet inquiries.

"Oh?" he said. "The cat?"

"No, sir," I said. "The Gillsworth letter."

He nodded. "The more important of the two. Do you have a lead?"

"Anorexic," I said. "But it's all I have."

He left for the office, mother went out to the greenhouse to bid good morning to her begonias, and I went upstairs to my den. I brought my journal up to date, which didn't take long, and then made a phone call.

"Lady Cynthia Horowitz's residence," she recited. "Consuela Garcia speaking."

"Hi, Connie," I said. "Archy. How about lunch today?"

"Love to," she said, "but can't. I'm working on the madam's Fourth of July bash, and I'm having lunch with the fireworks people."

Her friendly tone was gratifying. Obviously she had not been informed of my dinner date the previous night. And since we had agreed on an open relationship, I saw absolutely no reason to feel guilty. So why did I feel guilty?

"Another time then," I said breezily.

"When?" she asked.

Meg Trumble had said she planned to fly back to King of Prussia, so that romance would be on hold until her return. It seemed an ideal time to reassure Connie that our attachment remained intact.

"Dinner tonight?" I suggested.

"You're on," she said. "How about Tex-Mex food?" For a brief instant my world tottered, but then she went on: "There's a new place in Lantana that's supposed to have great chili. Want to try it?"

"Sounds good to me," I said bravely. "Pick you up around seven?"

"I'll be ready."

"Oh, Connie, one more thing: did you ever hear of a woman named Mrs. Hertha Gloriana?"

"The séance lady? Of course I've heard of her. A lot of people swear she's a whiz."

"You don't happen to have her address and phone number, do you?"

"No, but I think she's listed in the Yellow Pages."

"The Yellow Pages!"

"Sure. Under Psychic Advisers. Why are you laughing?"

"I don't know," I said. "It just seems odd to have Psychic Advisers listed in the Yellow Pages. I mean, if you had a tumor, would you look in the Yellow Pages for Brain Surgeons?"

"You know, Archy," she said, "you have a freaky sense of humor."

"I guess," I said, sighing. "Thanks, Connie. See you tonight."

I went downstairs to my father's study. All his telephone directories had leather slipcovers. Stodgy? I agree. But you must understand that, to my knowledge, he was the only man in South Florida who wore rubbers when it rained.

There she was in the Yellow Pages, listed under Psychic Advisers: a two-column display ad that stated Mrs. Hertha Gloriana was licensed, bonded, provided "advice and direction," and accepted all major credit cards. It didn't say if she was a Freudian, Jungian, or W. C. Fields-ian.

I decided a personal encounter was preferable to a phone call, so I boarded the Miata and headed for West Palm Beach. That city has seven times the population of the Town of Palm Beach and, as this is written, is in the process of shedding its image as a poor country cousin and enjoying a long overdue rejuvenation.

Mrs. Hertha Gloriana's address was on Clematis Street in an area that was now awash with new office buildings, pricey boutiques, and quaint shoppes for all kinds. It would never be Worth Avenue, of course, but what will?

I had imagined the haunt of a medium would resemble one of those Dracula castles in the cartoons of Charles Addams. But Mrs. Gloriana had a fourth-floor suite in one of the new glass and stainless steel buildings.

Her office was impressive, the large, airy waiting room decorated in mauve and aqua. There was a man seated behind the receptionist's desk. He was idly leafing through a copy of *Vanity Fair* and didn't look up when I entered. He was about my age, a handsome devil in a dark, saturnine kind of way. And he was dressed beauti-fully. As you may have gathered, I fancy myself some-thing of a Beau Brummell, but this dude made me look like Bozo the Clown.

He was wearing a suit of dove gray flannel that didn't come off a plain pipe rack. His shirt had white French cuffs and a collar wide enough to accommodate a knitted black silk cravat tied in a Windsor knot. The body of the shirt was striped horizontally with lavender bands. What a dandy he was!

He finally looked up. "May I help you, sir?" he in-quired pleasantly enough.

"May I speak to Mrs. Gloriana, please."

He smiled. "Do you have an appointment?"

67

"Afraid not."

"Mrs. Gloriana prefers appointments. Would you care to set a date?"

"No possibility of seeing her now?"

He pursed his lips and appeared to be giving my request serious consideration. "Mrs. Gloriana is busy with a client at the moment. May I ask how you learned of us?"

I didn't believe mentioning the Yellow Pages would cut much ice. A personal recommendation might prove more efficacious.

"Mrs. Lydia Gillsworth suggested I consult Mrs. Gloriana."

He brightened immediately. "Mrs. Gillsworth. Of course. A charming lady."

He stood and came from behind the desk. He was a tall one and lean as a fencer. He was wearing, I noted, a heavy ring of Navaho silver set with a large turquoise in the expensive sky-blue shade.

"I'm Frank Gloriana," he said. "Hertha's husband."

We shook hands. He had a hard, bony grip.

"Archibald McNally," I said. "Happy to meet you."

He stared at me a moment. "McNally?" he repeated. "The law firm across the lake?"

"That's correct," I said. "McNally & Son. I'm the son."

His smile was cool. "I've heard excellent things about your outfit. As a matter of fact, I may need some legal advice shortly, and McNally & Son heads a short list of possibles I have drawn up."

"Glad to hear it," I said. "We have a number of specialized divisions, and I'm sure we can provide the services you require."

"I'm sure you can. Your visit here today – it concerns some legal business of your firm?"

"Oh no," I said hastily, "nothing like that. It's a personal thing, and I'm afraid you'll find it rather silly."

"Try me," he said.

"A close friend has lost his cat," I said earnestly. "Lost, strayed, or stolen. He really loves the animal and has been worried sick since it's been gone. He's advertised but with no results. It occurred to me that Mrs. Gloriana might possibly be able to give me some hints or suggestions as to where his pet can be found."

"It's possible," he said immediately. "Hertha has had remarkable success in visualizing where missing objects or people might be located. I don't believe she's ever worked on an animal before, but I see no reason why she couldn't. She once enabled a builder in Atlanta to find his missing bulldozer."

"Wonderful," I said. "Where was it?"

"In his foreman's garage." Gloriana said with a slightly sardonic smile. "Listen, why don't you make yourself comfortable out here, and I'll go in and see how much longer Hertha will be. Perhaps she'll have time to fit you in before her next appointment."

"I'd appreciate that," I said.

He departed through an inner door, closing it carefully behind him. I flopped into a mauve-and-aqua armchair alongside a glass cocktail table. It held a selection of thin books and magazines, most of them dealing with astrology, channeling, crystals, mysticism, and occult philosophies of the Far East.

There was also a stack of fliers, advertising circulars that looked as if they had been designed for mailing. A small sign read TAKE ONE – so I did. It stated that Mrs. Gloriana, a licensed and bonded adviser, would prepare a "psychic profile" for anyone providing her with the exact time, date, and place of birth, names of parents and grandparents, and a snapshot or personal possession of the sender.

The cost of the psychic profile was a hundred dollars in

US funds, payable in advance.

I was stuffing a copy of this intriguing offer into my jacket pocket when Frank Gloriana returned. He saw at once what I was doing.

"Our new project," he said. "What do you think?"

"It makes no promises," I observed.

"Oh no," he said quickly, "no promises. The profile merely analyzes and suggests directions the subject might wish to take that could possibly enrich their lives. It is a serious attempt to provide psychic counseling. I assure you it is not a bunko scheme."

"I never thought for a moment it was."

"We've just started," he said "but the response to newspaper and magazine ads has encouraged me to plan a direct mail campaign. I think it could turn out to be a very successful enterprise, and that's the reason why I may need legal advice on setting up a separate business venture." He paused and laughed: a thin, toneless ha-ha. "But you didn't come to listen to my business problems. Hertha is available now. Follow me, please."

He led the way through that inner portal, down a short hallway to an interior room. The door stood open, and I could see the chamber was furnished more as a residential sitting room than a commercial office. A young woman – younger than Frank Gloriana by at least five years, I guessed – rose from a high-backed mauve-and-aqua wing chair as we entered.

"Dear," he said "this gentleman is Archibald McNally. Mr. McNally, my wife, Hertha. I'll leave you two alone."

And he left us, closing the hall door softly behind him.

She floated to me and offered a hand so soft and tender I feared I might crush it in my sinewy paw.

"Mrs. Gloriana," I said, "this *is* a pleasure."

I had always imagined a medium as an old woman, heavy through the bosom and hips, with dyed and frizzled

70

hair, caked makeup, a frowsy appearance, and perhaps the overwhelming scent of patchouli. In this case, all wrong. Hertha Gloriana was, if you will pardon the wordplay, a very rare medium indeed.

She was definitely a Pre-Raphaelite type, with a nimbus of chestnut hair, skin as white and smooth as wax, and features so classic they might have graced a coin. There was something ethereal in her beauty, I thought, and something delicate and unworldly in her manner. She moved slowly with a languid ease, and if she had suddenly levitated to the ceiling, I wouldn't have been a bit surprised. She was so insubstantial, you see.

"Mr. McNally," she murmured, voice low and breathy, "Frank has told me why you are here. Perhaps I can help. *Perhaps*. But I cannot promise. You do understand that, don't you?"

"Of course," I said, trying to determine the exact shade of her eyes. Periwinkle blue, I finally decided. "I would appreciate your trying."

"What is the cat's name?"

"Peaches."

"Female?"

"Yes."

"What breed?"

"Persian, I believe."

"Describe her, please."

"Plump. Silver-gray with tabby markings."

"How old?"

"I don't really know," I confessed. "Perhaps five years."

"Affectionate?"

"Not really. Not with strangers."

She nodded. "Please leave your address and phone number with my husband. If I'm able to do anything, he will contact you."

71

Apparently our consultation was at an end, but she continued to stare at me. Our eyes were locked, and her gaze was so intent and unblinking that I wanted to look away but could not.

She came close. She was wearing a light floral scent. She put a hand gently on my arm. "You are troubled," she said.

"About the cat? Well, yes. This close friend of mine is very – "

"No," she interrupted, "not the cat. You, personally, are troubled."

"Not really," I said, my short laugh sounding nervous to me. "Nothing I can't handle."

She continued to stare. "Two women, two loves," she said. "That is troubling you."

I wasn't impressed: it smacked too much of a fortune teller on a carnival midway. Many men – at least many I know – are frequently involved with more than one wo-man. It's hardly a unique situation, is it? Mrs. Gloriana was not demonstrating any special clairvoyant talent.

She stepped back and smiled: a tremulous smile, very vulnerable. "Do not worry," she told me. "The problem will eventually be solved."

"Glad to hear it," I said.

"But not by you," she added. "It was nice meeting you, Mr. McNally. I'll do my best to get a message about Peaches."

"Thank you," I said and turned away. I was at the door when I looked back. I hadn't heard her move but she was seated again in the high-backed wing chair, regarding me gravely. I made up my mind.

"Mrs. Gloriana," I said, "Lydia Gillsworth has told me of the meetings she attends during which you are some-times able to contact those who are – who are – "

"Dead," she said.

"Yes," I said. "I was wondering if I might possibly sit in at one of your gatherings. I find the whole concept fascinating."

Her stare never wavered. "Very well," she said softly. "Ask Lydia to bring you to our next session. She knows the time and place."

"Thank you," I said again and left her sitting there, distant and complete.

There was a middle-aged couple in the waiting room, holding hands. And Frank Gloriana was seated behind the desk, impassive and doing nothing.

"Your wife said she'd let me know if she is able to help," I told him and handed over my card.

He glanced at it. "You wish to be billed at your office, Mr. McNally?"

All business, this lad.

"Please," I said. "Thank you for your assistance."

I went out into the corridor. I had a lot of impressions I needed to sort out, but there was something I wanted to do first.

When I had entered the office, Frank Gloriana had stalled me by saying the medium was busy with a client. Then, after a period of time, he reported she was now available. But I had seen no client leave the office.

That was understandable if there was another exit from the Gloriana suite. Psychiatrists frequently have such an arrangement to protect the privacy of their analysands. I mean, it would be a bit off-putting, would it not, to enter a shrink's office and bump into your spouse, lover, or boss coming out.

So, before I pushed the elevator button, I roamed the fourth-floor corridor looking for another doorway to the Gloriana offices. There was none. Which probably meant that Hertha had not been busy with another client when I arrived.

73

There were several innocent explanations. Frank Gloriana's prevarication might mean nothing.

Or it might mean something.

5

On my way back to the McNally Building I stopped at Harry Willigan's office. He was in his usual vile mood, and I wondered if he got his disposition from Peaches or if the cat had learned how to be nasty from her master.

He demanded to know what progress I was making in the search for his beloved pet. Very little, I told him, but my investigation would be aided if he'd let me have a photocopy of the ransom note.

"What the hell for?" he screamed at me.

I explained as patiently as I could that I wanted the letter analyzed by an expert. The vocabulary and grammar might enable the specialist to make some shrewd guesses as to the education, occupation, nationality, and social status of the writer. That wasn't total kaka, of course; there are analysts who can glean such information from the language of a document.

Finally, Willigan had his receptionist make a photocopy for me. I folded it carefully and tucked it into my jacket pocket along with the Gloriana flier. Then I left as quickly as I could, with Willigan shouting obscene threats of the mayhem he'd wreak if he ever got his hands on those effing catnappers. I believed him.

Back in my office, I found a message on my desk asking me to call Connie Garcia as soon as possible.

"Archy," she wailed, "about tonight – Lady Horowitz wants me to come back here after dinner and go over the budget for the Fourth of July shindig with her."

"Aw," I said, "that's too bad. Want to postpone our date?"

"No," she said definitely. "I haven't seen you in ages. Instead of driving to Lantana for chili, we'll grab a bite at the Pelican Club and you can get me back here by eight-thirty or so. Okay?"

"Sure," I said, much relieved that I wouldn't have to incinerate my uvula two nights in a row. "But I guess that means no fun and games later. I'm disappointed."

"Me, too," she confessed. "It's been so long that every time I sneeze, dust comes out my ears."

"We'll have to do something about that," I said.

Long pause. Then, suspiciously:

"You haven't been making nice-nice with that Meg Trumble, have you, Archy?"

"Who?"

She sighed. "Now it's coming out *your* ears, and it's not dust. If I discover you've been cheating, you know what'll happen to you, don't you?"

"I'll be singing soprano?"

"You've got it, son," she said. "See you tonight."

She hung up, and I sat there a few minutes remembering that her Latin temper was not to be trifled with. Once, during our initial liaison, she had caught me dining with another young lady and had dumped a bowl of linguine Bolognese on my head. Took me a week of shampoos to get rid of all those damned chicken livers.

It was a dangerous game I was playing, I reflected mournfully, and wondered if a vow of celibacy might be

75

the answer. But than I recalled Hertha Gloriana's prediction: my problem would eventually be solved, and not by me. A welcome thought. I had enough bad habits without adding chastity.

I took the Gloriana flier from my pocket and reread it. Mommy didn't raise her boy to be an idiot, and my first reaction was that the offer of individualized psychic profiles was a scoundrelly con game. I figured the Glorianas had printed up a standard profile they mailed back to all the suckers, similar to those canned horoscopes you can buy at news-stands.

But, despite my cynicism, I found it hard to believe Hertha Gloriana was an out-and-out swindler. Husband Frank – the business manager – could be a flimflam artist capable of cutting a shady deal. But not Hertha, not that soft, vulnerable waif. Her eyes were too blue. How's that for logical deduction?

But there was a way I could test Hertha's bona fides, and I resolved to launch my mini-plot that evening. I was certain Connie Garcia would cooperate. She'd think it was a hoot.

Musing about the Glorianas and the apparently thriving business they owned, I realized how little I knew about parapsychology. I decided it was time I learned more about what I was investigating. I phoned Lydia Gillsworth. It was then almost noon.

"Oh, Archy," she said after an exchange of cordial greetings, "I do hope this isn't about that stupid letter I received."

"Not at all," I said, lying valiantly. "This call includes a confession and a request. I was so interested in what you told me about Hertha Gloriana the other day that I went to see her this morning. I used your name shamelessly. I hope you don't object."

"Of course not. Isn't she a remarkable woman?"

"She is that," I said. "And lovely."

"Careful, Archy." Mrs. Gillsworth said, laughing. "Hertha is happily married, and Frank carries a gun."

That shook me. "Why on earth would he do that?"

"He says it's just a precaution. Sometimes they have to deal with irrational or deeply disturbed people."

"I can imagine," I said. "The lunatic fringe."

"Exactly," she said. "If you don't mind my asking, why did you consult Hertha?"

I told her my loopy story about the close friend whose beloved cat was missing and how I had asked Mrs. Gloriana to visualize the pet's present whereabouts. Lydia didn't think my request unusual at all.

"I'm sure Hertha will be able to help," she said. "She's very good at locating lost things. She told Laverne Willigan where to find her pearl earrings."

I suspect that if I had been wearing dentures they might have popped out at that moment. I know my jaw flopped open and I stared about wildly to make certain the world was still there.

"And where were the earrings?" I asked hoarsely.

"Behind her dresser drawer. They had caught on the inside molding."

"I know Mrs. Willigan," I said as casually as I could. "Her husband is a client of ours. Does Laverne attend those séances Mrs. Gloriana holds?"

"Oh yes, she never misses a session."

I didn't want to push it any farther.

"That's another part of my confession, Mrs. Gillsworth," I said. "I asked Hertha if I might sit in on one of your meetings. She said I could, and have you bring me to the next gathering."

"Of course," she said. "As a matter of fact, there's one tonight at seven o'clock."

"Ah, what a shame," I said. "I have a dinner date I

77

dare not break. Well, I'll make certain I'm at the next one, with your kind assistance. And now the request: I'd like to learn more about spiritualism, and I wondered if you had any books on the subject you'd be willing to lend me. Return guaranteed. I'm especially intrigued about the possibility of contacting those who have, uh, departed this life for existence on another plane."

"Oh, Archy, I have a whole library of books on the subject. You'll find them fascinating, I'm sure. Suppose I select three or four that will give you the basic information on our beliefs."

"I'd certainly appreciate that. When may I pick them up?"

"Let me see . . . I have a little shopping to do, but I should be back around two o'clock. Can you stop by then?"

"Love to. Thank you so much for all your help, Mrs. Gillsworth."

I drove home for lunch and found I had the McNally manse to myself. Mother and the Olsons had departed on a shopping safari to replenish our larder, but a note left on the kitchen table informed me that a Caesar salad, heavy on the garlic, had been prepared for my pleasure and was chilling in the fridge.

I had a glass of California chablis with the salad and popped a few fresh strawberries for dessert. Then I trudged upstairs to my digs, donned my reading specs, and placed the photocopy of Peaches' ransom note next to the poison-pen letter sent to Lydia Gillsworth. I compared them carefully, and to my inexpert eye they definitely appeared to have been composed on the same machine.

Even more telling, both documents included the word "horrendous." That is not an adjective commonly used in written communications. What could I think but that both letters had quite likely been written by the same person? It was not hard evidence, I admit, but I was more convinced than ever that the catnapping and the threats against Mrs. Gillsworth were somehow connected.

I started to scrawl notes in my journal about the morning encounter with Hertha and Frank Gloriana, but I tossed my gold Mont Blanc aside, unable to concentrate.

What was confounding me was Laverne Willigan's apparent interest in spiritualism. She always seemed to me such a *physical* woman, whose main enthusiasms were chocolate eclairs, tanning her hide, and amassing expensive baubles. It came as a shock to hear she attended séances.

It was obvious I had misjudged Laverne; she was more than a featherbrain with a *zoftig* bod. It made me wonder if my opinions of other actors in this drama were similarly in error. Perhaps Harry Willigan, beneath his bluster, was a devotee of macramé, and Frank Gloriana a keen student of the bass lute. Anything, I concluded glumly, was possible.

But my sour mood dissipated as I drove southward to my meeting with Lydia Gillsworth. Now there was a woman who harbored no hidden passions or guilts; I was ready to swear to that. She was complete and without artifice.

She was waiting for me in a sitting room that was an aquarium of light. She had just purchased several twig baskets of dried flowers, and their presence made the room seem like a country garden. She took such an innocent joy in the hydrangea, pepperberries, and love-in-a-mist that her pleasure was infectious. I requested and received a pink strawflower to place in the buttonhole of my Technicolor jacket.

She had three books ready for me, neatly stacked in a small Saks shopping bag.

"Now, Archy," she said, "you must promise to read these slowly and completely."

"I promise," I vowed.

"Your first reaction," she went on, "will be laughter. You'll say to yourself, 'What nonsense this is!' But if you open your mind and heart to these ideas you'll find yourself wondering if the whole concept might not be true. Do try to wonder, Archy."

"I shall."

"You must not think about spiritualism in a logical manner," she said severely. "It is not a philosophy; it is a faith. So don't try to analyze. Just let the belief enter into you and see if it doesn't answer a lot of questions you've always asked."

She was so sincere and earnest that I was more impressed by her than by her words. Mr. Webster defines "nice" as, among other things, "well-bred, virtuous, respectable." Lydia Gillsworth was all of that, I thought, and observing her eager efforts to set me on the right path, I felt great affection for her.

Among the zillion problems I've never been able to solve is whether there can be a true friendship between a man and a woman if sexual attraction is totally lacking. I'm just not sure. But at that moment, in Mrs. Gillsworth's sunlit country garden, listening to her quiet voice and gazing into her limpid eyes, I did feel a kinship that I believed came near to love.

I thanked her for the books and rose to leave. She came close and held me by the shoulders. She gave me a smile of surpassing warmth.

"Be prepared, Archy," she said, almost mischievously. "These books may change your life."

"Any change would be an improvement," I said, and she laughed and leaned forward to kiss my cheek.

I returned home thinking what a *sweet* woman she was.

80

I felt empathy for the terror those dreadful letters aroused in Roderick Gillsworth. It may sound odd to you, but I now considered threats against Lydia's life an act of blasphemy; that's how convinced I was of her goodness.

Back in my cave, I did little more than glance at the books she had loaned me. I read the introductions and scanned the chapter headings, then tossed the volumes aside. Oh, I planned to read them in their entirety eventually, but I knew it would be heavy going.

I went for my ocean swim, dutifully attended the family cocktail hour, and at seven o'clock that evening I was waiting in the driveway of the Lady Cynthia Horowitz estate, having announced my arrival to the housekeeper. Ten minutes later Consuela Garcia came scampering out, slid into the Miata, and away we went.

I don't care how exacting your standards may be, I assure you, male or female, that if you ever saw Connie you'd think me a dolt for casting a libidinous eye at any other woman. She is not beautiful in a conventional way, but she is certainly attractive and so sparkling that she could persuade a golem to dance a gavotte.

She is rather shortish and plumpish, but she sports a year-round tan and usually lets her long, glossy black hair float free. I think I mentioned previously that I once saw her in a string bikini. More impressive than Mount Rushmore, I assure you.

That evening she was wearing a white silk shirt with white denim jeans. Atop her head was a jaunty straw boater with a cerise silk band. It had once been my hat, and it still rankled that it looked better on her than it had on me. All in all, she looked so fetching that once again I lamented my philandering. I suspect it may be due to a defective gene.

I was happy to see the Pelican Club was not too mobbed when we arrived. Priscilla was able to seat us at a

81

corner table in the dining area.

"Just right for lovebirds," she said, and looked at me. "Or should I say one lovebird and one cuckoo."

"What sass!" I said. Then to Connie: "It's so hard to get good help these days."

"Watch yourself, Simon Legree," Priscilla said, "or I'll tell pop to slip a Mickey in your margarita."

"In that case I'll have a vodka gimlet," I said. "Connie?"

"Ditto," she said. "Pris, what's Leroy pushing tonight?"

"Yellowtail with saffron rice and an endive salad."

That's what we both ordered, and after our drinks were brought, I wasted no time in broaching my nefarious plot. I handed Connie the Glorianas' flier advertising individualized psychic profiles. She read it swiftly and then looked up at me.

"A swindle?" she asked.

"I think so," I said. "I'd like to prove it, and you can help. Have you ever met Hertha or Frank Gloriana?"

"Nope."

"Do you think they've ever heard of you?"

"I doubt it."

"Good," I said. "Now here's what I'd like you to do: answer the ad in your own name from your home address. But make up a completely phony woman. Fake the date and place of birth. Fake the names of parents and grandparents. Buy some cheap gimcrack and send it along as this non-existent woman's personal possession. I want to see what kind of a psychic profile you'll get for an imaginary person."

Connie laughed. "You're a tricky boyo, you know that? You really think the Glorianas will provide an analysis of a make-believe woman?"

"For a hundred bucks they will," I said. "I'll bet on it.

Send a personal check along with your letter, and I'll make sure you get reimbursed. Will you do it?"

"Of course," she said. "It'll be fun. but why are you going to so much trouble, Archy?"

I had a con ready.

"An elderly gent is addicted to the mumbo-jumbo the Glorianas are peddling. He's spending a fortune on private séances, fake demonstrations of telepathy and psychokinesis, and similar stuff. His grown children, our clients, are furious, figuring the old man is wasting their inheritance. They think the Glorianas are frauds. My father told me to investigate."

Connie bought it.

"Okay," she said, "I'll order a psychic profile for a woman who doesn't exist. Ah, here's our food. Now shut up and let me eat."

"Yes, ma'am," I said.

We finished dinner in record time, stopped at the bar for ponies of Frangelico, and then I drove Connie back to the Horowitz mansion.

"Sorry you have to work late," I said. "Next time we'll make a night of it."

"We better," she said. "Archy, tell the truth. Have you been faithful to me?"

I avoided a direct lie, as is my wont. Subterfuge is the name of the game.

"Connie," I said somberly, "I must be honest. Last week I flipped through a *Playboy* in the barbershop, and I confess I had lust in my heart."

She tried not to laugh but failed. "Just make sure it stays in your heart," she said, "and doesn't migrate southward. Thanks for the dinner, luv."

She gave me a very nice kiss, slid out of the Miata, and stalked back to her office. I waited until she was safely inside, and then I drove home singing "If You Knew Susie

83

– Like I Know Susie." Actually, I've never met a woman named Susie, but one never knows, do one?

When I pulled into our driveway I saw Roderick Gillsworth's gray Bentley parked on the turnaround. The windows of my father's study were lighted, and he came out into the hallway when I entered.

"Archy," he said, "Gillsworth just arrived with bad news. Join us, please."

The poet was slumped in a leather club chair, biting at a thumbnail. The governor went behind his massive desk and I pulled up a straight chair.

"Another letter arrived today," my father said grimly and gestured toward a foolscap lying on the desk blotter. "Even more despicable than the others. And more frightening."

I hardly heard his final comments. I was thinking of "Another letter arrived today" and wondering why Lydia Gillsworth hadn't mentioned it. But perhaps she had. I recalled that during our telephone conversation, she had said, "I hope this isn't about that stupid letter I received." I had assumed she was speaking about the previous letter, not referring to a new one.

"Well, Archy?" father demanded impatiently, and I realized he had asked me something that simply hadn't registered.

"I beg your pardon, sir," I said. "Would you repeat the question?"

He stared at me, obviously saddened by the imbecile he had sired. "I asked if you had made any progress at all in identifying the writer of this filth."

"No, sir," I said, and let it go at that.

Gillsworth groaned. "What are we going to *do*?" he said, his last word rising to a falsetto.

I had never seen the man more distraught. In addition to the nail biting, he was blinking furiously and seemed

84

unable to control a curious tremor of his jaw; it looked as if he was chewing rapidly.

"Mr. Gillsworth," I said, "I really think the police should be brought in. Or if your wife continues to forbid it, then private security guards should be hired. Round-the-clock. It will be costly, but I feel it's necessary until the perpetrator can be found."

The seigneur fell into one of those semi-trances that signified he was giving my proposal heavy thought, examining the pros and cons, and considering all the options in-between.

"Yes," he said finally, "I think that would be wise. Mr. Gillsworth, we have dealt several times in the past with a security service that provides personal guards. We have always found their personnel trustworthy and reliable. May I have permission to employ guards for your wife, twenty-four hours a day?"

"Oh God, yes!" Gillsworth cried, his skinny arms flapping. "Just the thing! Why didn't I think of it?"

"Where is Mrs. Gillsworth at the moment?" I asked.

"She went to a séance this evening," he said. "She should be home by now. May I use your phone?"

"Of course," father said.

Gillsworth stood, walked rather shakily to the desk phone, and dialed his number. He held the receiver clamped tightly to his head. While we all waited, I noted how he was perspiring. His face was sheened with sweat, and there was even a drop trembling at the tip of his avian honker. Poor devil, I thought; I knew exactly how he felt.

Finally he hung up. "She's not home," he said hollowly.

"No cause for alarm," my father said. "She may have stayed a few extra moments at the séance. She drove her own car?"

"Yes," the poet said. "A Caprice. I don't understand

85

why she isn't home. She's rarely late."

"She may be delayed by traffic. Try again in five or ten minutes. Meanwhile, I suggest we all have a brandy. Archy, will you do the honors?"

I welcomed the assignment. In truth, I had caught Gillsworth's fear and needed a bit of Dutch courage. I went to the marble-topped sideboard and poured generous tots into three snifters. I served the poet and father.

Gillsworth finished half of his drink in one gulp and gasped. "Yes," he said, "that helps. Thank you."

"Father," I said, "when you talk to the security people about personal guards, I think it might be smart to ask that female operatives be assigned. I believe Mrs. Gillsworth might be more inclined to accept the constant presence of women rather than men."

"Yes, yes!" Gillsworth said, animated by the cognac and flapping his arms again. "You're quite right. A capital idea!"

The senior McNally nodded. "Good thinking, Archy," he said, and I felt I had been pardoned for my earlier inattention. "Mr. Gillsworth, would you have any objection if the female guard or guards moved into your home? Temporarily, of course."

"None at all," the poet said. "We have extra bedrooms. I'd welcome the presence of someone who'll watch over Lydia every minute I'm not with her. May I use the phone again?"

"Naturally," father said.

He called, and a moment later I saw his entire body relax and he actually grinned.

"You're home, Lydia," he said heartily. "All safe and sound? Good. Doors and windows locked? Glad to hear it. I'm at the McNallys', dear, and I should be home in fifteen minutes or so. See you soon."

He hung up and rubbed his palms together briskly.

"All's well," he reported. "I'll stay with her until your security people arrive. When do you think that will be?"

"Probably early in the morning," father told him. "I'll call the night supervisor, and he can get things started. I'll request a female guard be sent to your home early tomorrow. Will that be satisfactory?"

"Eminently," Gillsworth said, and finished his brandy. "I feel a lot better now. I'm going to tell Lydia I insist the guards remain until this whole horrible mess is cleared up. Thank you for your help, Mr. McNally – and you too, Archy. I better go now."

"I'll see you to your car," my father said. "Please wait here for me, Archy."

He went out with the client, and I sneaked another quick cognac. Just a small one.

My father returned and regained his throne. "Personal guards are an excellent idea," he said. "I only hope Mrs. Gillsworth doesn't refuse them."

"I don't believe she will, sir," I said. "Especially if it's explained that their assignment will not be made public. But I still think the police should be informed of the letters. Granted they cannot provide round-the-clock surveillance, but they might be able to trace the source of the paper used and identify the make of the printing machine that was used."

Father looked at me steadily. "Then you were telling the truth? You've made no progress at all?"

"That's not completely accurate," I admitted, "but what I have is so slight that I didn't want to mention it in Gillsworth's presence."

Then I told him of Hertha and Frank Gloriana, who might or might not be frauds, and how Lydia attended their séances. I said nothing about Laverne Willigan's connection with the Glorianas, nor did I mention that I believed the poison-pen letters and Peaches' ransom note

87

had been composed on the same word processor by the same author.

Why didn't I tell my father these things? Because they were very thin gruel indeed, vague hypotheses that would probably make no sense to anyone but me. Also, I must admit, I didn't want to tell the pater everything I knew because he was so learned, so wise, so far my intellectual superior. What I was implying by my reticence was "I know something you don't know!" Childish? You bet.

He looked at me, somewhat bewildered. "You think the Glorianas are responsible for the threatening letters?"

"I just don't know, sir. But Mrs. Gillsworth gave me no other names. Apparently she's convinced that no one in her social circle – relatives, friends, acquaintances – could possibly be capable of anything like that. So Hertha Gloriana is the only lead I have."

"It's not much," he said.

"No," I agreed, "it's not. But they do say the medium is the message."

He gave me a sour smile. "Well, stay on it," he commanded, "and keep me informed. Now I must call the security – "

But just then the phone rang.

He broke off speaking and stared at it a moment.

"Now who on earth can that be?" he said and picked it up.

"Prescott McNally," he said crisply. Then:

"What? *What?* Oh my God. Yes. Yes, of course. We'll be there immediately."

He hung up slowly and turned a bleak face to me.

"Lydia Gillsworth is dead," he said. "Murdered."

I don't often weep but I did that night.

6

We later learned that Roderick Gillsworth had called 911 before phoning my father. By the time we arrived at the poet's home, the police were there and we were not allowed inside. I was glad to see Sgt. Al Rogoff was the senior officer present and apparently in charge of the investigation.

Father and I sat in the Lexus and waited as patiently as we could. I don't believe we exchanged a dozen words; we were both stunned by the tragedy. His face was closed, and I stared unseeing at the starry sky and hoped Lydia Gillsworth had passed to a higher plane.

Finally, close to midnight, Rogoff came out of the house and lumbered over to the Lexus. Al played the good ol' boy because he thought it would further his career. But I happened to know he was a closet intellectual and a ballet maven. Other Florida cops might enjoy discussing the methods of Fred Bundy; the sergeant preferred talking about the technique of Rudolf Nureyev.

"Mr. McNally," he said, addressing my father, "we're about to tape a voluntary statement by Roderick Gillsworth. He'd like you to be present. So would I, just to make sure everything is kosher."

"Of course," father said, climbing out of the car. "Thank you for suggesting it."

"Al – " I started.

"You stay out here, Archy," he commanded in his official voice. "We've already got a mob scene in there."

"I have something important to tell you," I said desperately.

"Later," he said, and he and my father marched into the Gillsworth home.

So I sat alone for another hour, watching police officers and technicians from a fire-rescue truck search the grounds with flashlights and big lanterns. Finally Rogoff came out of the house alone and stood by my open window peeling the cellophane wrapper from one of his big cigars.

"Your father is going to stay the night," he reported. "With Gillsworth. He says to tell you to drive home. He'll phone when he wants to be picked up."

I was shocked. "You mean Gillsworth wants to sleep in this house tonight? We could put him up or he could go to a hotel."

"Your father suggested it, but Gillsworth wants to stay here. It's okay; I'll leave a couple of men on the premises."

Then we were silent, watching as a wheeled stretcher was brought out of the house. The body was covered with a black rubber sheet. The stretcher was slid into the back of a police ambulance, the door slammed. The vehicle pulled slowly away, the siren beginning to moan.

"Al," I said as steadily as I could, "how was she killed?"

"Hit on the head repeatedly with a walking stick. It had a heavy silver spike for a handle. Pierced her skull."

"Don't tell me it was in the shape of a unicorn."

He stared at me. "How did you know?"

"She showed it to me. She brought it back from up north as a gift for her husband. He collected

90

antique canes."

"Yeah, I saw his collection. Is that what you wanted to tell me?"

"No. Something else. Remember me asking you about poison-pen letters? Lydia Gillsworth was the person getting them."

"Son of a bitch," the sergeant said bitterly. "Why didn't you tell me?"

"Because she refused to let us take it to the police. And if we had, would you have provided twenty-four-hour protection?"

"Probably not," he conceded. "Where are the letters now?"

"At home."

"How's about you drive me there and hand them over. Then drive me back here. Okay? You weren't planning to get to bed early, were you?"

"Not tonight," I said. "Let's go."

I drove, and Al sat beside me juicing up his cigar.

"Tell me what happened," I asked him.

"Not a lot to tell," he said. "Gillsworth was at your place, talked to his wife on the phone, told her he'd see her soon. He says he drove directly home. Says he found the front door open although she had told him all doors and windows were locked. She was facedown in the sitting room. Signs of a violent struggle. Spatters of blood everywhere. Baskets of flowers knocked to the floor. A grandfather clock tipped over. It had stopped about ten minutes before Gillsworth arrived."

"My God," I said, "he almost walked in on a killing."

"Uh-huh."

"Did he see anyone when he drove up?"

"Says not."

"Anything stolen?"

"Doesn't look like it. He can't spot anything missing."

91

"How's he taking it?"

"Hard. He's trying to do the stiff-upper-lip bit, but it's not working."

"She was a lovely woman, Al."

"She's not now," he said in the flat tones he used when he wanted to conceal his emotions.

When we entered the house, mother was waiting in the hallway. She wore a nightgown under a tatty flannel robe, and her feet were thrust into fluffy pink mules. She glanced at Sgt. Rogoff in his uniform, then put a hand against the wall to steady herself.

"Archy," she said, "what's wrong? Where is father? Has he been hurt?"

"He's all right," I said. "He's at the Gillsworth home. Mother, I'm sorry to tell you that Lydia has been killed."

She closed her eyes and swayed. I stepped close and gripped her arm.

"A car accident?" she asked weakly.

I didn't answer that. One shock at a time.

"Father will be staying with Gillsworth tonight," I said. "I came back with the sergeant to pick up some papers."

She didn't respond. Her eyes remained closed and I could feel her trembling under my hand.

"Mother," I said, "it's been a bad night, and the sergeant and I could use a cup of black coffee. Would you make it for us?"

I hoped that giving her a task would help, and it did. She opened her eyes and straightened.

"Of course," she said. "I'll put the kettle on right away. Would you like a sandwich, sergeant?"

"Thank you, no, ma'am." he said gently. "The coffee will do me fine."

Mother bustled into the kitchen, and I led Rogoff into my father's study. The letter was still lying on the desk blotter.

92

"There it is," I told Al. "Both the Gillsworths handled it but not my father and not me. Maybe you'll be able to bring up some usable prints."

"Fat chance," he growled, sat down behind the desk, and leaned forward to read.

"That was the third letter received," I said. "The first was destroyed by Gillsworth. The second is upstairs in my rooms. I'll get it for you."

A few moments later I returned with the second letter in the manila folder. I did not bring along the photocopy of Peaches' ransom note. Willigan had told us, "No cops!" And he was paying the hourly rate.

Rogoff had his cigar burning and was leaning back in my father's chair. He read the second letter and tossed the folder onto the desk.

"Ugly stuff," he said.

"A psycho?" I suggested.

"Maybe," he said. "Maybe someone trying to make us think they were written by a psycho."

"What will you do with the letters?"

"Send them to the FBI lab. Try to find out the make of machine used, the paper, the ink, and so forth. See if they've got any similar letters in their files."

"Even right-hand margins," I pointed out.

"Oh, you noticed that, did you? Got to be a word processor or electronic typewriter. We'll see. How about that coffee?"

When we entered the kitchen, mother was filling our cups. And she had put out a plate of Ursi Olson's chocolate-chip cookies, bless her.

"The coffee is instant," she said anxiously to Rogoff. "Is that all right?"

"The only kind I drink," he said, smiling at her. "Thank you for your trouble, Mrs. McNally."

"No trouble at all," she assured him. "I'll leave you

93

men alone now."

We sat opposite each other at the kitchen table, hunching over our coffee and nibbling cookies.

"You suspect the husband, don't you?" I said.

The sergeant shrugged. "I've got to, Archy. Seventy-five percent of homicides are committed by the spouse, a relative, a friend, or acquaintance. These cookies are great."

"She was alive when he left here, Al," I reminded him. "He talked to her on the phone. You think he drove home and killed her?"

"Doesn't seem likely, does it?" he added slowly. "But what really helps him is that there were no bloodstains on his clothes. I told you that place looked like a slaughterhouse. Blood everywhere. The killer had to get splashed. What was Gillsworth wearing when he left here?"

I thought a moment. "White linen sports jacket, pale blue polo shirt, light gray flannel slacks."

Rogoff nodded. "That's what he was wearing when we got there. And he looked fresh as a daisy. His clothes, I mean. Absolutely unstained. And he sure didn't have enough time to change into identical duds. Also, we searched the house. No bloodstained clothes anywhere."

We sipped our coffee, ate more cookies. The sergeant re-lighted his cold cigar.

"So Gillsworth is off the hook?" I asked.

"I didn't say that. He's probably clean, but I've got to check out the timing. A lot depends on that. How long did it take him to drive from here to his place? Also, what time did the victim leave the séance? How long would it take her to drive home? What time did she arrive? Was someone waiting for her? There's a lot I don't know. After I find out, maybe Gillsworth will be off the hook. Right now he's all I've got."

I stared at him. "Al, is there something you're

94

not telling me?"

"Would I do that?"

"Sure you would," I said. "Look, I know this is your case. You wear the badge; you're the law. You can order me to butt out. You're entitled to do that. But I'm telling you now I'm not going to do it. That woman meant a lot to me. So no matter what you say, I'm going to keep digging."

He looked at me strangely. "That's okay," he said. "You stay on it. Just keep me up to speed – all right?"

We finished our coffee, went to the study where Rogoff collected the letters. When we came out into the hallway mother was waiting with a small overnight bag.

"I packed father's pajamas, robe, and slippers," she said "And his shaving gear and a fresh shirt for tomorrow morning."

I'll never cease to be amazed at how *practical* women can be, even under stress. I imagine that when the flood came and Noah was herding everyone aboard the ark, Mrs. Noah plucked at his sleeve and asked, "Did you remember to empty the pan under the icebox?"

Rogoff took the little valise and promised to deliver it to father. This time I drove the open Miata; after inhaling Al's cigar, I wanted fresh air – lots of it.

We didn't speak on the trip back to the Gillsworth home. But when we arrived and the sergeant climbed out, he paused a moment.

"Archy, I know Roderick Gillsworth was your father's client. Was Mrs. Gillsworth?"

"Yes, she was."

"I hear she had plenty of money. Did your father draw her will?"

"I don't know, Al. Probably."

"Who inherits?"

"I don't know that either. Ask my father."

Then I drove back to the McNally fiefdom for the final time that night. I feared I'd have trouble getting to sleep but I didn't. First I recited a brief prayer for a noble lady. I consider myself an agnostic – but just in case . . .

The weekend had started badly and didn't improve. The weather was no help; Saturday morning was dull and logy – just the way I felt when I awoke. I had an OJ, cinnamon bun and coffee with Jamie Olson in the kitchen. He was wrapping a fresh Band-Aid around the cracked stem of his ancient briar. I had given him a gold-banded Dupont for Christmas, but he saved it for Sunday smoking.

"Heard about Mrs. Gillsworth," he said in a low voice. "Too bad."

"Yes," I said. "It was in the papers?"

"Uh-huh. And on the TV."

"Jamie, if you hear anything about enemies she may have had, or maybe an argument with someone, I wish you'd let me know."

"Sure," he said. "You asked about that Mrs. Willigan."

"So I did. What about her?"

"She's got a guy."

"Oh?" I said and took a gulp of my coffee. "Where did you hear that?"

"Around."

"Know who it is?"

"Nope. No one knows."

"Then how do they know she's got a guy?"

He looked up at me. "The women know," he said, and added sagely, "They always know."

"I guess," I said and sighed.

I went back upstairs to work on my journal. It was a slow, gloomy morning, and I couldn't seem to get the McNally noodle into gear. I was stuck in neutral and all I could think about was pink lemonade and strawflowers in twig baskets. It wasn't the first time a friend had died, but never so suddenly and so violently. It made me want to telephone every friend I had and say, "I love you." I knew that was goofy but that's the way I felt.

My phone rang about ten-thirty, and I thought it would be my father asking me to come fetch him. But it was Leon Medallion, the Willigans' houseman.

"Hiya, Mr. McNally," he said breezily, "Soupy weather – right?"

"Right," I said. "What's up, Leon?"

"Remember asking me about the cat carrier? Well, I found it. It was in the utility room, where it's supposed to be. I guess I missed it the first time I looked."

"That's probably what happened," I said. "Thanks for calling, Leon."

I hung up and the old cerebrum slipped into gear. Not for a moment did I think Medallion had missed spotting Peaches' carrier on his first search of the utility room. Then it was gone. Now it had been returned. Puzzling. And even more intriguing was the fact that I had mentioned the carrier's disappearance to Meg Trumble.

I was still diddling with that nonplus when my phone rang again. This time it was my father, announcing he was ready to return. He specifically requested that I drive the Lexus. He didn't have to say that; I knew very well he thought riding in my red two-seater dented his dignity.

He was waiting outside when I arrived at the Gillsworth home. He placed his overnight bag in the back and motioned for me to slide over to the passenger side so he could get behind the wheel. He thinks I drive too fast. But then he thinks motorized wheelchairs go too fast.

"I'm going to drop you at home, Archy," he said, "and then go the office. Gillsworth wants me to inform his wife's relatives."

97

"Shouldn't he be doing that, sir?"

"He should but he's still considerably shaken and asked me to handle it. Not a task I welcome. Also, I want to review Lydia's will."

"Did Sergeant Rogoff question you about that?"

"He did, and Gillsworth had no objection to full disclosure. To the best of my recollection, she left several specific bequests to nieces, nephews, an aunt, and her alma mater. But the bulk of her estate goes to her husband."

"Hefty?" I asked.

"Quite," he said. "I told the sergeant all that, and he asked for the names and addresses of the beneficiaries. He is a very thorough man."

"Yes, sir," I agreed, "he is that. He wants me to continue my investigation of the poison-pen letters."

"So he said. I also want you to, Archy. Lydia was a fine lady, and I would not care to see this crime go unsolved or her murderer unpunished."

"Nor would I, father. Do you know where Rogoff is now?"

"He came to the Gillsworth home early this morning. He was driving his pickup, and with Roderick's permission he loaded the grandfather clock into the truck and drove off with it."

"The clock that was tipped over during the assault?"

"Yes."

"What on earth does Al want with that?"

"He didn't say. Here we are. Please take my overnight bag inside and tell mother I'll be at the office. I'll phone her later."

I followed his instructions and then went into his study and used his phone to call the Glorianas' office. I wasn't certain mediums worked on Saturdays, but Frank Gloriana answered, and I identified myself.

98

"Ah, yes, Mr. McNally," he said. "About the missing cat . . . I intended to contact you on Monday."

"Then you have news for me?"

"My wife has news," he corrected me. "When might you be able to stop by?"

"Now." I said. "If that's all right."

"Just let me check the appointment book," he said so smoothly that I was convinced he was scamming me again. "Well, I see we have a very busy afternoon ahead of us, but if you can arrive within the hour I'm sure we can fit you in."

"Thank you so much," I said, playing Uriah Heep. "I'll be there."

Mother wanted me to stay for lunch, but I had no appetite at all. And besides, I had recently noted that the waistbands of my slacks were shrinking alarmingly. So I went upstairs and pulled on a silver-gray Ultrasuede sport jacket over my violet polo shirt. Then I went outside and jumped into the Miata for the trip to West Palm Beach.

As I've mentioned before, basically I'm a cheery sort of chap, and that black cloud that had been hovering over my head since I heard of Lydia Gillsworth's death began to lift as I drove westward. That doesn't mean I ceased to mourn, of course, or that I was any less determined to avenge her. But the world continues to spin, and one must continue to spin along with it or step off. And I wasn't ready to do that.

Actually, I hadn't called the Glorianas to inquire about Peaches. The fate of that miserable feline was small spuds compared to finding the killer of Lydia Gillsworth. But I reckoned the cat's disappearance would serve as a good excuse for seeing the medium again. Not only did I want to learn more about her relationship to Lydia, but the woman herself fascinated me.

When I entered the Glorianas' suite there was no crush

99

of clients Frank had forecast during our phone conversation. In fact, he was alone in that mauve and aqua office, listlessly turning the pages of a magazine and looking bored out of his skull. He glanced up as I came in, put the magazine aside, and rose to greet me.

He was wearing an Armani double-breasted in taupe gabardine and sporting a regimental tie. It happened to be the stripe of the Royal Glasgow Yeomanry, a regiment of which I doubted he had ever been a member. We shook hands, and he reached to stroke the sleeve of my Ultrasuede jacket.

"Nice," he said. "Would you mind telling me what it cost?"

I knew then he was no gentleman. "I don't know," I said. "It was a gift." I think he guessed I was lying, but I didn't care.

He nodded and turned back to his desk. "I'll tell Hertha you're here," he said, then paused with his hand on the phone. "We heard about Lydia Gillsworth," he said. "Dreadful thing."

"Yes," I said, "wasn't it."

He pushed a button, spoke softly into the phone, and hung up. "She's ready for you," he reported. "This way, please."

He again conducted me down the hallway to his wife's chamber. There were two other closed doors in that corridor but they were unmarked, and I had no idea what lay behind them. Gloriana ushered me into the medium's sanctum, then withdrew.

She was standing alongside her high-backed chair, and when the door closed she came floating forward to place her hands on my shoulders. I marveled at how petite she was: a very small wraith indeed, and seemingly fragile.

"Lydia has gone over," she said in that muted voice, "and you are desolated."

100

"It was a shock," I agreed. "I still find it hard to accept."

She nodded, led me to her wing chair, and insisted I sit there. She remained standing before me. I thought it an awkward position for a conversation, but it didn't seem to trouble her.

"Did Lydia tell you how she felt about physical death?" she asked.

"Yes, she did."

"Then you must believe the spirit we both knew still exists. This is not the only world, you know."

She said that with such conviction that I could not doubt her sincerity. But I thought her a world-class fruitcake. Strangely, her feyness made her more attractive to me. I'm a foursquare hedonist myself, but I've always been intrigued by otherworldly types. They live as 'if they're collecting Frequent Flier points for a one-way trip to the hereafter.

"Mrs. Gloriana," I started, but she held up a soft palm.

"Please," she said, "call me Hertha. I feel a great kinship with you. May I call you Archy?"

"Of course," I said, pleased. "Hertha, Lydia promised to bring me to one of your séances. In fact, she suggested the meeting last evening, but I was unable to make it. Perhaps if I had, things might have turned out differently."

"No," she said, staring at me, "nothing would have changed. Do not blame yourself."

I hadn't, but it was sweet of her to comfort me.

"I would still like to attend one of your gatherings. Would that be possible?"

She was silent for a long moment, and I wondered if I was to be rejected.

"There will be no more sessions until October, Archy," she said finally. "So many people have gone

101

north for the summer."

The off-season seemed a curious reason to halt spirit communication, but I supposed the medium charged per communicant, so there was a good commercial justification for it.

"Do you ever hold private séances?" I asked. "Could that be arranged?"

She turned and began to move back and forth, hugging her elbows. She was wearing a flowered dress of some gossamer stuff, and it wafted as she paced.

"Perhaps," she said. "But the chances of success would be lessened. The psychic power of a circle of believers is naturally much stronger than that of an individual. I could ask Frank and his mother to join us. Would that be acceptable?"

"Of course."

"And do you have a friend or two you could bring along? Individuals who are sympathetic to spiritualism even if they are not yet firm believers?"

"Yes, I think I could provide at least one person like that.

"Very well," she said. "I'll plan a session and let you know when arrangements have been finalized."

Her language surprised me. She spoke as if she was scheduling a corporate teleconference.

"Fine," I said "I'm looking forward to it. And now about Peaches . . . Have you received any messages on the cat's whereabouts?"

She stopped moving and turned to face me. But instead of the intent gaze I expected, her eyes slowly closed.

"Faint and indistinct," she said, and now her wispy voice took on what I can only call a singsong quality. "The cat is alive and healthy. I see it in a very plain room. It's just a single room with bed, dresser, small desk, armchair." Her eyes opened. "I am sorry, Archy, but that is

102

all I have. I cannot see where this room is located. But if you wish, I will keep trying."

"Please do," I urged. "I think you've done wonders so far."

She didn't reply, and I had nothing more to ask about Peaches. I rose, moved toward the door, then paused.

"Hertha," I said, "when we have our séance, do you think we could contact Lydia Gillsworth?"

She looked at me gravely. "It might be possible."

"Could we ask her the name of her murderer?"

"Yes," she said, "we will ask."

"Thank you," I said. "Please let me know when the session will be held."

She nodded and then moved close to me. Very close. She lifted up on her toes and kissed me full on the mouth. It was not a kiss of commiseration between two fellow mourners. It was a physical kiss, sensual and stirring. Her lips were soft and warm. So much for my vision of her as a wraith. Ghosts don't kiss, do they?

She pulled away and must have seen my shock, for she smiled, opened the door and gently pushed me out.

There was no one in the reception room. The place seemed deserted.

I drove home in a State of Utter: utterly startled, utterly confused, utterly flummoxed. I confess it wasn't the catnapping or murder that inspired my mental muddle; it was that carnal kiss bestowed by Mrs. Gloriana. What did she *mean* by it? Kisses usually have meaning, do they not? They can signal a promise, serve as a lure, demonstrate a passion – any number of swell things.

Hertha's kiss was an enigma I could not solve. It *had* to be significant, but where the import lay I could not decide. As you may have guessed, my ego is not fragile, but I could not believe the lady had suddenly been over-whelmed by my beauty and brio. I am no Godzilla, but I

103

am no young Tyrone Power either. I mean women are not repelled by my appearance, but neither do they swoon in my presence or feel an irresistible desire to nibble my lips.

I was still trying to puzzle out the mystery of that inexplicable kiss when I arrived home just as my father was garaging his Lexus. We paced back and forth together on the graveled turnaround before going inside.

"Have you heard from Sergeant Rogoff?" he asked.

"No, father. I expect he's busy."

"Have you made any progress?"

I was tempted to reply, "Yes, sir. I was smooched by a medium." But I said, "No, sir. Nothing of importance. Was Lydia's will as you remembered it?"

He nodded. "Roderick is the main beneficiary – which causes a problem. We also drew his will: a simple document since his estate is hardly extensive. He leaves what little cash he has and his personal effects to his wife. He bequeaths the original manuscripts of his poems to the Library of Congress."

"They'll be delighted," I said.

"Don't be nasty, Archy," he said sharply. "You and I may feel they are nonsense; others may see considerable literary merit."

I said nothing.

"The problem," my father continued, "is that Roderick is now a wealthy man. It is imperative that he revise his will as soon as possible. As things stand, the bulk of Lydia's estate is in a kind of legal limbo. If Gillsworth should die before dictating a new will, the estate might be tied up for years. I'd like to suggest to him that a new testament is necessary, but the man is so emotionally disturbed at the moment that I hesitate to broach the subject. I invited him to dine with us tonight, but he begged off. Too upset, he said. That's understandable."

"Yes, sir," I said. "I don't suppose he's quite realized

the enormity of what's happened. Do you think he is aware of his wife's will?"

"I know he is. He was present when I discussed the terms with Lydia. Let's go in now. Considering recent events, I think we might schedule the family cocktail hour a bit earlier today."

"Second the motion," I said.

But despite the preprandial drinks and a fine dinner (duckling with cherry sauce), it was a lugubrious evening. Conversation faltered; the death of our neighbor seemed to make a mockery of good food and excellent wine. I think we all felt guilty, as if we should be fasting to show respect. Ridiculous, of course. An Irish wake makes much more sense.

After dinner I retired to my nest and worked on my journal awhile. Then I tried to read those books on spiritualism Mrs. Gillsworth had lent me. Heavy going. But I began to understand the basic appeal of the faith. It does promise a kind of immortality, does it not? But then so does every other religious belief, offering heaven, paradise, nirvana – whatever one wishes to call it.

It was all awfully serious stuff, and as I've stated on more than one occasion, I am not a serious johnny. In fact, my vision of the final beatitude is of a place resembling the Pelican Club where all drinks are on the house.

So I tossed the books aside and went back to wondering about the motive for Hertha Gloriana's kiss. I came to no conclusion except to resolve that if there was an encore I would respond in a more manful and determined fashion.

Only to further the investigation, of course.

7

The most noteworthy happening of the following Sunday was that I accompanied my parents to church. I am not an avid churchgoer. As a matter of fact, I had not attended services since a buxom contralto in the choir with whom I had been consorting married a naval aviator and moved to Pensacola. After that, my faith dwindled.

But that morning I sat in the McNally pew, sang hymns, and stayed awake throughout the sermon, which was based on the dictum that it is more blessed to give than to receive. I supposed that included a stiff bop on the snoot. But the final prayer was devoted to Lydia Gillsworth, a former member of the congregation. The short eulogy was touching, and I was glad I was there to hear it.

We returned home to find a police car parked outside our back door. Sgt. Al Rogoff, in civvies, was in the kitchen drinking coffee with the Olsons. He stood up when we entered and apologized for his presence on a Sunday.

"But there are some things to talk about," he said to my father. "Including funeral arrangements. The Medical examiner will release the . . . " He glanced at mother, and his voice trailed off.

"Of course, sergeant." Père McNally said. "Suppose you come into the study. I'll phone Gillsworth and find out what his wishes are."

"Fine," Al said, then looked at me before he followed my father. "You going to be around awhile?" he asked.

"I can be," I said.

"Do try, Archy," Rogoff said with that heavy sarcasm he sometimes affects. "I want to talk to you."

"I'm on the third floor," I told him. "Come up when you and father have finished."

I trudged upstairs, took off my Sunday-go-to-meeting costume, and pulled on flannel bags and a fuchsia Lacoste. I was wondering if I had time to nip downstairs for a tub of ice cubes when there was a knock on the door.

It was the first time the sergeant had been in my rooms, and he looked about with interest.

"Not bad," he said.

"The best thing about it is the rent."

He laughed. "Zilch?" he asked.

"You got it," I said. "Al, would you like a wee bit of the old nasty?"

"What's available?"

"Marc."

"What the hell is that?"

"Brandy made from wine sludge."

"I'm game. But just a small one."

I poured two tots, and Al sampled his. He gasped and squinched his eyes.

"That'll take the tartar off my teeth," he said.

I had few accommodations for visitors, so the sergeant sat in the swivel chair behind my desk while I pulled up a rather tatty leather ottoman.

"How did you and father make out with Gillsworth?"

"Okay. He is going to take the casket up north. Apparently there's a family plot in a Rhode Island cemetery. She'll be buried there."

We sipped our minuscule drinks slowly. There is no

107

other way to imbibe marc and survive.

"Al," I said, "I understand you hauled away the grandfather clock from the murder scene."

"That's right. It's a nice antique. Bleached pine case."

"What was the reason for taking it?"

"I wanted to find out if it was in working order before it was toppled."

"And was it?"

"Yep, according to the expert who examined it. When it was knocked over, one of the gears jolted loose and the clock stopped."

"So the time it showed was the time of the murder?"

"Seems like it, doesn't it."

I sighed. "You're not giving anything away, are you? Have you finally decided Gillsworth is clean?"

"He appears to be," Rogoff said grudgingly. "The time it takes to drive from here to his place at a legal speed checks out. Ordinarily his wife would have been home earlier from the séance, but she stayed awhile to talk with one of the women."

"Who told you that?"

"The woman."

"This is like pulling teeth," I said. "Would you mind telling me the woman's name, sergeant?"

"Mrs. Irma Gloriana, the mother-in-law of the medium. You know her?"

"Mrs. Irma Gloriana?" I said carefully. "No, I've never met the lady. What's she like?"

"A tough broad," Al said, then paused and cast his eyes heavenward. "Forgive me, Susan B. Anthony," he said. "I meant to say that she's a strong-willed individual of the female gender."

"That's better," I said approvingly. "Otherwise I might have to charge you with PI – Political Incorrectness. Did you meet the medium?"

"Nope. She and her husband weren't home. I'll catch up with them tomorrow, along with all the others who were at the séance. I have their names."

"Where was the séance held?"

"At the Glorianas' condo. It's in a high-rise near Currie Park."

"A luxury high-rise?"

"Not very," Rogoff said. "In fact, I thought it was a ratty place. I guess communing with the dear departed doesn't pay as well as selling pizzas."

"Guess not," I said. "How did you get on to this Mrs. Irma Gloriana?"

"Gillsworth gave me her name. He had been to three or four séances with his wife and knew where they were held. But after a while he stopped going. Says the whole idea of spiritualism just doesn't grab him."

"Uh-huh. Did you time how long it would take Lydia to drive home from the séance?"

"That was the whole point, wasn't it? Of course I timed it. If Lydia left when the mother-in-law says she did, then she would have arrived home about when her husband talked to her from your father's study."

"So everything fits and Gillsworth is cleared?"

"I guess so," Rogoff said dolefully. "Could I have another shot of that battery acid? A tiny one. Just enough to dampen the glass."

I poured and said, "Al, what's bothering you? You don't seem to be convinced."

He drew a heavy breath and blew it out. "As you said, 'Everything fits.' Whenever that happens, I get antsy and start wondering if I've missed something. What's chewing me is that I've only got the statement of one witness as to the time the victim went home. I'd prefer to have several. But all the others who attended the séance had already left, and the medium and her husband had gone out to dinner. So only Mrs. Irma Gloriana can say when Lydia started home."

"You think she's lying?"

He stirred restlessly in the swivel chair. "Why the hell should she? What could possibly be her motive for lying? No, she's probably telling the truth. Now what about you? What have you been up to?"

"Not a great deal," I said, all innocence. I had been pondering how much to tell him. Not everything, of course, because I was certain he wasn't telling me everything. In the past we had cooperated on several investigations to our mutual benefit, but I always reckoned – and I think Rogoff did, too – that part of our success was due to the fact that we were as much competitors as partners. I believe we both enjoyed it. Nothing like rivalry to put a little Dijon on the sandwich. Adds zest, *n'est-ce pas?*

It was at that precise moment that the McNally talent for improv showed its mettle.

"Al," I said earnestly, "I just had an idea I think you'll like."

"Try me."

"Until you get the FBI report on those poison-pen letters, the séance and everyone connected with it represents our best lead – right?"

"Not necessarily," he argued. "Archy, we're just starting on this thing. We'll have to identify and question all the victim's neighbors, friends, and acquaintances, and establish their whereabouts at the time of the homicide."

"Agreed," I said. "A lot of legwork. But while you're doing that, why don't I zero in on the Glorianas? What I had in mind was going to them, passing myself off as a half-assed spiritualist, and setting up a séance with the medium. I'm not suggesting you ignore them entirely, but let me go at them from the angle of an eager client."

110

He stared at me thoughtfully. "Why do I have the feeling I'm being euchred?"

"You're *not* being euchred," I said heatedly. "The more I think of it, the better it sounds. I can be Mr. Inside and you can be Mr. Outside. The Glorianas will never know we're working together. They won't even realize we know each other. But between us, we should be able to get a complete picture of their operation."

He was silent a long time, and I feared I had lost him. But finally he sighed, finished his drink, and stood up.

"All right," he said. "I can't see where it will do any harm. You set up a séance and try to get close to the medium."

"I'll try," I said.

"And you'll keep me informed of anything you turn up?"

"Absolutely," I said. "And you'll keep me informed on your progress?"

"Positively," he said, and we smiled at each other.

After he left, I sat in the swivel chair, finished my marc, and licked the rim of the snifter. I was satisfied with the plot I had hatched. I wasn't deceiving Al, exactly, but now I had an official imprimatur for doing something I had already done. It's called finagling.

I jotted a few notes in my journal, trying to recall everything the sergeant had told me. One contradiction immediately apparent was his description of the Glorianas' condo as "ratty" while their glittering offices in a new building indicated a profitable enterprise. But their mauve and aqua suite, I decided, could be a flash front. During my two visits I certainly hadn't seen hordes of clients clamoring for psychic counsel. And despite Frank's elegant duds, I thought him something of a sleaze.

The weather was still blah, but being the sternly disciplined bloke I am, I went for my ocean swim nonetheless.

111

Surprisingly, the sea was calm as the proverbial millpond, so as I plowed along I was able to think about the coming séance and plan a course of action.

When Hertha Gloriana suggested I provide a friend who might join the circles of believers and augment its psychic powers, I had intended to ask Consuela Garcia to accompany me. Connie was a go-for-broke kiddo and she'd think the whole thing an adventure she could gossip about for weeks.

But then I remembered I had asked Connie to answer the Glorianas' ad for a "personalized psychic profile." The risk was too great that they would recognize her name, and that might eliminate whatever chance I had of proving their mail order project a fraud. I decided that instead of Connie, I'd ask Meg Trumble to attend the séance with me.

What a fateful decision that turned out to be!

I returned from my swim in time to dress for the family cocktail hour – my third change of apparel that day. It was while dispensing our first martini that my father delivered unexpected news.

"Roderick Gillsworth would like to see you, Archy," he said.

I blinked. "What on earth for?"

"He didn't say. He suggested you come over this evening after dinner. I think perhaps you better phone first."

"All right," I said doubtfully. "Rather odd, wouldn't you say sir?"

"I would. But I'd like you to take advantage of your meeting, if you feel the time is opportune, to mention the necessity of his drafting a new will. Just refer to it casually, of course. It may serve to start him thinking of his financial responsibilities."

"I'll do what I can," I said. "But I really can't imagine why he should want to talk with me."

112

Mother looked up. "Perhaps he's lonely," she said quietly.

Sunday dinner was a more relaxed occasion than that of the previous night. I think my parents and I were determined not to let our sorrow at Lydia Gillsworth's death affect the serenity of our household. What a cliché it is to say that life goes on, so I shall say it: "Life goes on." And Ursi Olson's mixed grill (lamb chops, tournedos, médaillons of veal) was a splendid reminder.

We finished our key lime mousse and coffee a little after eight-thirty. I phoned Gillsworth, and he asked if I could arrive around nine. He sounded steady enough. I said I'd be there and inquired if there was anything he needed that I might bring along. First he thanked me and said there was not. But then, after a pause, he asked timidly if the McNallys could spare a bottle of vodka. His supply was kaput and he would repay as soon as he could get to a liquor store.

I saw nothing unusual in this request, but I feared it might trouble my father. (Tabloid headline: "Grieving Hubby Drinks Himself into Insensibility on Attorney's Booze") So I sneaked a liter of Sterling from our reserve in the utility room and hustled it out to the Miata without being caught.

Crime scene tape was still in place around the Gillsworth home, but there were no police cars in sight. Roderick himself answered my knock and greeted me with a wan smile. He said he was alone, finally, and thanked me for bringing the plasma.

"Have the reporters been a nuisance?" I asked as he led me to his study. (I was happy he hadn't selected the sitting room where the body was found.)

"Not too bad," he said. "Your father handled most of them, and I refused to grant television interviews. Make yourself comfortable while I fetch some ice cubes. Would

113

you like a mix?"

"Water will be fine," I said, and when he left, I settled into a threadbare armchair and looked about with interest.

I had never before been in a poet's den, and it was something of a disappointment: just a small book-lined room with worn desk, battered file cabinet, an unpainted worktable laden with reference books and a typewriter. It was an ancient Remington, not electronic and definitely not a word processor. I don't know what I expected to find in this poet's sanctum sanctorum – perhaps a framed photograph of Longfellow or a Styrofoam bust of Joyce Kilmer. But there were no decorative touches. That drab room could easily be the office of any homeowner: a nook too cramped and depressing to be used for anything but answering threats from the IRS.

He returned with a bucket of ice cubes, a flask of water, and two highball glasses. He placed them on the table alongside my bottle of Sterling.

"I'm a miserable bartender," he confessed. "Would you mix your own?"

"Certainly, sir." I said.

"That's another thing," he added. "Your 'sir' and 'Mr. Gillsworth,' while appreciated, really aren't necessary. I've always addressed you as Archy. If you called me Rod, my ego would not be irretrievably damaged."

"Force of habit," I said. "Or rather force of training. I may be the last son in America who addresses his father as 'sir'."

"Your father's different."

"Yes," I said, sighing, "he is that."

I built my own drink: a little vodka, a lot of water. He mixed his own: a lot of vodka, a little water. I took the armchair again, and he lowered himself into a creaky swivel chair behind his desk.

"Rod," I said, beginning to recite a short speech I had rehearsed, "I haven't had a chance to express my condolences on the death of your wife. It was a terrible tragedy that saddened my parents and me. We shall always remember Lydia as a good neighbor and a gracious lady."

"Yes," he said, "she was. Thank you."

I sipped, but he gulped, and I wondered if he swilled in that fashion to make certain he'd sleep that night.

"It makes my poems seem so meaningless," he mused, staring into his glass. "So futile."

"It shouldn't have that effect," I said, "Surely your wife's tragic death could provide inspiration for poetry in an elegiac mood."

"Perhaps," he said. "In time. At the moment my mind is empty of everything but sorrow. I hope you're right. I hope that eventually I'll be able to express my bereavement and by writing about it exorcise my pain and regain some semblance of emotional tranquility."

I thought that rather much. In fact it sounded like a speech *he* had rehearsed. But perhaps poets talked that way. Or at least this poet.

He took another heavy swallow of his drink and slumped in his chair. His eyes were reddened, as if from weeping, and his entire face seemed droopy. I fancied that even his long nose had sagged since I last saw him. He was now a very gloomy bird indeed.

"Archy," he said, "I understand that you will continue investigating the poison-pen letters."

"That's correct."

"You'll be working with Sergeant Rogoff?"

I nodded.

"What do you think of him? Is he competent?"

"More than competent," I said. "Al is a very expert and talented police officer."

Gillsworth made a small sound I think he intended as a

laugh. "I believe he suspects me."

"That's his job, Rod," I explained. "The investigation is just beginning. The sergeant must suspect everyone connected with Mrs. Gillsworth until their whereabouts at the time the crime was committed can definitely be established."

"Well, my whereabouts have definitely been established. I was with you and your father."

"Rogoff understands that," I said as soothingly as I could. "But he can take nothing for granted. Every alibi must be verified."

He finished his drink and poured himself another, as massive as the first.

"What angers me the most," he said, "is that he won't give me any information. I ask him what is being done to find the maniac who killed my wife, and he just mutters, 'We're working on it.' I don't consider that adequate."

"At this stage I doubt if there is anything to tell you. And even when progress is made, the police are very cautious about revealing it. They don't want to risk raising false hopes, and they are wary about identifying any person as being under suspicion until his or her guilt can be proved."

Gillsworth shook his head. "It's maddening. Now I've got to accompany Lydia's casket up north for the funeral. Her family is sure to ask what is being done to find the killer, and all I'll be able to tell them is that the police are working on it."

"I know it's frustrating," I said sympathetically. "It's difficult to be patient, but you must remember the police have had the case for only forty-eight hours."

"How long do you think it will take to solve it?"

"Rod, there is absolutely no way to predict that. It could be days, weeks, months, years."

He groaned.

116

"But there is no statute of limitations on homicide," I said. "The police will keep at it as long as it takes – and so will I."

"Thank you for that," he said. "I see you need a refill. Please help yourself." While I was doing exactly that, he said, "Archy, will you be exchanging information with Rogoff?"

"I hope so."

"While I'm up north for Lydia's funeral, may I phone you to ask if any progress has been made? I don't want to call Rogoff, he'll tell me nothing."

"Of course you can phone me," I said. I was about to add that naturally I'd be unable to reveal anything without Rogoff's permission. But Gillsworth's animus toward the sergeant seemed evident, and not wanting to exacerbate it, I said no more.

"I'll really appreciate it if you can keep me informed."

"How long will you be gone, Rod?"

"Two or three days. I'd like to give you a set of house keys before you leave tonight. Would you be kind enough to look in once or twice while I'm gone."

"I'd be glad to."

"Thank you. Our cleaning lady, Marita, has been given two weeks off, so she won't be around. And I have handed over a set of keys to the police. I don't know why they wanted them, but that sergeant grunted something about security. Oh God, what a mess this whole thing is."

"Rod, I hate to add to your burdens, but my father asked me to mention something to you. It is imperative that you make out a new will. Unfortunately, circumstances have changed, and your present will is simply inadequate."

His head snapped up as if I had slapped him.

"I hope I haven't offended you by referring to it," I said hastily.

117

"No, no," he said. "That's all right. I was just shocked that it hadn't even occurred to me. Your father is correct, as usual. As you probably know, Lydia inherited a great deal of money, and now I suppose it comes to me. What a filthy way to get rich."

"It was her wish," I reminded him.

"I know, but still . . . Very well, you can tell your father that I'll certainly give it a lot of thought, and when I return from the funeral I'll get together with him."

"Good," I said. "A will isn't something that should be delayed."

He looked at me with a twisted smile. "A legal acknowledgement of one's mortality," he said. "Isn't that what a will is?"

"I suppose so," I said. "But for a man in your position it's a necessity."

He poured himself another drink with a hand that trembled slightly. I wondered how many more of those bombs he'd be able to gulp without falling on his face. I wanted to caution him but it wasn't my place.

He must have guessed what I was thinking because he grinned foolishly and said, "I'll sleep tonight."

"That you will."

"You know, these are the first drinks I've had since Lydia died. I wanted a drink desperately while waiting for the police to arrive, but it seemed shameful to need alcohol to give me courage to see it through. But now I don't care. I need peace even if it comes from a bottle and even it it's only temporary. Can you understand that?"

"Of course," I said. "As long as you have no intention of leaving the house tonight."

"No intention," he mumbled, his voice beginning to slur. "Positively no intention."

"That's wise," I said, finished my drink, and stood up. I had no desire to witness this stricken man's collapse.

"Then if you'll give me your house keys, I'll be on my way."

He rooted in the top drawer on his desk and finally handed me three keys strung on an oversized paperclip. "Front door, back door, and garage," he said.

"I'll look in while you're gone," I promised. "And may I tell father you'll consult him about a new will when you return?"

"Yes," he said. "New will. I'll think about it."

He didn't stagger when he accompanied me to the front door, but he moved very, very slowly and once he placed a palm against the wall for support. He turned to face me at the entrance. I couldn't read his expression.

"Archy," he said, "do you like me? Do you?"

"Of course I like you," I said.

He grabbed my hand and clasped it tightly between both of his. "Good man," he said thickly. "Good man."

I gently drew my hand away. "Rod, be sure to lock up and put the chain on."

Outside, the door closed, I listened until I heard the sounds of the lock being turned and the chain fumbled into place. Then I took a deep breath of the cool night air and drove home.

I garaged the Miata and saw lights in my father's study. His door was open, which I took as an invitation to enter. He was seated in the leather club chair, a glass of port at his elbow. He was reading one of the volumes from his leather-bound set of Dickens. The book was hefty, and I guessed it to be *Dombey and Son*. He was stolidly reading his way through the entire Dickens oeuvre, and I admired his perseverance. Even more amazing, he remembered all the plots. I don't think even Dickens could do that.

He looked up as I entered. "Archy," he said, "you're home. You saw Gillsworth?"

"Yes, sir. He gave me a set of his house keys and asked

119

that I look in once or twice while he's up north at the funeral."

I was waiting for him to ask me to sit down and have a glass of something, but he didn't.

"You brought up the subject of the will?"

"I did. He said he'd give it some thought and consult you when he returned."

"I suppose that's the best that can be hoped for. What condition is he in?"

"When I left him, he was half in the bag and still drinking."

One of father's eyebrows ascended. "That's not like Gillsworth. I've never known him to overindulge."

"Emotional strain," I suggested.

"No excuse," the lord of the manor pronounced and went back to his Dickens.

I climbed the stairs to my perch, thinking of what an uncompromising man my father was. And as I well knew, his bite was worse than his bark.

I undressed, showered, and scrubbed my choppers. Then I pulled on a silk robe I had recently purchased at a fancy-schmancy men's boutique on Worth Avenue. It bore a design of multicolored parrots carousing in a jungle setting. One of those crazy birds had a startling resemblance to Roderick Gillsworth.

I treated myself to a dram of marc and lighted an English Oval – my first cigarette of the day! I slouched in the padded swivel chair, put my bare feet up on the desk, and ruminated on why the poet had asked if I liked him. His question was as perplexing as Hertha Gloriana's kiss.

I didn't think it was the vodka talking; Gillsworth was seeking reassurance. But of what – and why from me? I could only conclude that his wife's death had left him so bereft that he had reached out to make contact with another human being. I happened to be handy.

But that explanation was not completely satisfying. Sgt. Rogoff had often accused me of having a taste for complexity, of searching for hidden motives and unconscious desires when I'd do better to accept the obvious. Al could be right, and mother was correct in suggesting that Gillsworth was simply lonely. But I was not totally convinced.

Take as a case in point the recent behavior of yrs. truly. When the poet had asked, "Do you like me?" I had automatically replied, "Of course I like you." That was the polite and proper response to an intimate query from a man who was apparently suffering and needed, for whatever reason, a boost to his morale. And I had duly provided it.

But if the truth be known, I didn't like him. I didn't *dis*like him; I just felt nothing for him at all. That was my secret, and hardly something I'd reveal to him. I mention it now merely as an illustration of how the obvious frequently masks reality.

I was still musing gloomily on the strangeness of human nature when my phone rang. It was then almost midnight, and a call at that hour was not calculated to lift the McNally spirits. My first thought was: now who's died?

"H'lo?" I said warily.

"Archy?" A woman's voice I could not immediately identify.

"Yes. To whom am I speaking?"

"Such elegant grammar! Meg Trumble."

Relief was better than a schooner of marc.

"Meg!" I practically shouted. "How *are* you?"

"Very well, thank you. I didn't wake you up, did I?"

"Of course not. It's the shank of the evening."

"Well, I did call earlier, but I guess you were out. Behaving yourself, I hope."

"Unfortunately. You're calling from King of Prussia?"

"Yes, but I'm leaving early tomorrow morning, and I

121

do mean early. I should be in Florida by Tuesday."

"Can't wait," I said. "Listen, if you arrive in time, give me a call and we'll have dinner. You'll be ready to unwind after all that driving."

"I was hoping you'd say that," she said. "I'm not even telling Laverne when I expect to arrive, but I'll phone you as soon as I get in. See you Tuesday night."

"Good-o," I said. She hung up, and I sat there grinning like an idiot at the dead phone.

It was incredible what a goose that phone call gave to my dismal mood. I was immediately convinced I would rescue Peaches, find the killer of Lydia Gillsworth, the sun would shine full force on the morrow, and I would lose at least five pounds.

When A. Pope wrote about hope springing eternal, he obviously had A. McNally in mind.

8

I don't believe I've ever mentioned my peculiar infatuation with hats. I love hats. When I was attending Yale Law (briefly), I wore suede and tweed caps, fedoras, bowlers, and once, in a moment of madness, a fez. But all that headgear was a mite heavy for South Florida, so when I returned to Palm Beach I opted for mesh caps, panamas, and a marvelous planter's sombrero with a five-inch brim.

122

Recently I had written to a custom hat maker in Danbury, Conn., and had ordered three linen berets in white, puce, and emerald green. They arrived on Monday morning, and I was highly pleased. They were soft enough to roll up and tuck in a hip pocket, yet when they were donned and the fullness pulled rakishly over to one side, I felt they gave me a certain devil-may-care look.

I went down to a late breakfast wearing my new puce beret. Fortunately my father had already departed for the office so I didn't have to endure his incredulous stare. Mother took one look, laughed delightedly, and clapped her hands.

"Archy," she said, "that beret is *you!*"

I was so gratified by her reaction that I wore the cap while breakfasting on fresh grapefruit juice, three slices of Ursi Olson's marvelous French toast with honey-apricot preserve, and a pot of black coffee. I was finishing my second cup when mater remarked casually, "Oh, by the way, Archy, Harry Willigan phoned just before you came down. He'd like you to call him as soon as possible. He sounded in a dreadful temper."

Dear mother! She made certain I had a nourishing breakfast before breaking the bad news. I went into father's study and called the Willigan home. Julie Blessington, the maid, answered the phone. I identified myself and asked to speak to the master. In a moment our splenetic client came on the line and began screaming at me.

He was spluttering and shouting so loudly that it was difficult to grasp the reason for his rancorous outburst. I finally determined that a second ransom note had been found that morning, slid under the Willigan's front door.

"When was it found?" I asked.

"I told you already – this morning."

"How early this morning?"

123

"Very early. When Ruby Jackson came down to make breakfast."

"You think it was delivered last night?"

"Who the hell knows? You're the detective, aincha?"

"Plain white envelope?"

"Yeah, same as before."

"Who in your house has handled it?"

"Ruby handled the envelope. I handled the envelope and the letter inside."

"Don't let anyone else touch it, Mr. Willigan. What does the letter say?"

"Peaches is crying a lot. Poor Sweetums. She misses me."

"Uh-huh," I said. "What else?"

"They want me to put together a bundle of fifty thousand dollars. Used bills, unmarked, no numbers in sequence, nothing over a hundred."

"Any instructions for delivery?"

"Nah. I should just have the cash ready. They'll tell me when and how to get it to them."

"I better come over and pick up the letter," I said. "Will you be there, sir?"

"No, I won't be here," he said aggrievedly. "I got a meeting I'm late for already. I'll leave the letter with Laverne. You get it from her."

"Please tell her not to handle it."

"All right, all right," he said angrily, "I'll tell her. Listen, Archy, you've got to work harder on this thing. As far as I can see, you're spinning your wheels."

"Not exactly," I said. "I have a very important lead I can't discuss on the phone."

"Yeah?" he said. "Well, it better pan out or I'm hiring me a *professional* private eye. And I might even pull my business from McNally & Son unless I get some results."

And with that naked threat he slammed down the

124

phone before I had a chance to reply. The response I had already would have shocked my father. He believes a soft answer turneth away wrath. Sometimes it does. And sometimes a knuckle sandwich is required.

I went upstairs to exchange my puce beret for the white one because I feared the puce would clash with a flag-red Miata. (Genius is in the details.) Then I drove toward the Willigans' estate. My spasm of fury at our client's insulting treatment ebbed as I noted the sun was shining brightly and the sky looked as if it had just come from the tumble-dry cycle. A splendid day!

The door of the Willigan hacienda was opened by Leon Medallion, glum of countenance, eyes bleared by whatever allergy was affecting him that morning.

"Another ransom note, Leon," I said.

He nodded gloomily. "The old man was in a ferocious temper. When he starts shouting up a storm like that, I disappear. He can be mean."

"I'm supposed to pick up the letter from Mrs. Willigan. Is she here?"

"Out by the pool toasting her buns. You can find your way, can't you? I'm still polishing the effing silver, trying to get the tarnish off. This climate is murder on silverware, brass, and copper."

"Maybe we should all switch to plastic," I suggested.

He brightened. "Fair dinkum, mate," he said.

It hadn't been an exaggeration to say Laverne was toasting her buns. She was lying prone on a padded chaise pulled into the sunlight. She was wearing a thong bikini, and I was immediately reminded of a Parker House roll. She raised her head as I approached. It was wise of her not to rise farther since she had unhooked her bra strap.

"Hi, Archy," she said breezily. "Love your tam."

"Beret," I corrected, "and I thank you. I hope you're using a sunscreen."

125

"Baby oil," she said.

"You won't roast," I told her, "You'll fry. May I pull up a chair?"

"Sure," she said. "And if you're a good boy I'll let you oil my back."

She was at it again, and I decided she was a lady who enjoyed playing the tease. There is a coarse epithet for women like that – but I shall not offend by repeating it.

I placed a canvas director's chair close to her chaise, but not within oiling distance, and sat where I could see her face.

"Another letter from the catnappers," I said.

"That's right. Harry said to give it to you. It's on the taboret in the hallway. They want him to get the cash ready."

"So I understand. I imagine the next letter will give instruction for delivery."

"Archy, do you have any notion of who might have swiped Peaches?"

"A few frail leads," I said, "but nothing really definite. Laverne, I have a fantastic idea I'd like to try out on you. Do you know what a psychic is?"

Her face was half-buried in the padding, and I couldn't observe her reaction.

"Sure," she said, voice muffled. "People who are supposed to have second sight. They claim that they can predict the future and things like that."

"Things like locating missing persons and objects," I said. "My idea is to contact some local psychic and see if he or she can get a vision of where Peaches is now."

Laverne raised her head to stare at me with an expression I could not decipher. "That's the nuttiest idea I've ever heard," she said. "You don't believe that voodoo stuff, do you?"

"I don't believe and I don't disbelieve. But it's worth

trying, wouldn't you say?"

"No, I would not say," she said with what seemed to me an excess of vehemence. "It's crazy. Don't do it, Archy. If Harry finds out you've gone to someone who reads tea leaves or whatever it is they do, he'll fire both you and your father."

"Yes," I said regretfully, "I guess you're right. As I said it was just a wild idea. I better forget it."

"That's smart," she said settling down again. "By the way, I heard from Meg. She'll be back sometime this week. She's got her own apartment now in Riviera Beach. Will you be glad to see her again, Archy?"

"Of course. She's a very attractive lady."

Her head came up again, and this time she grinned at me. "I think you ought to make a move there," she said. "I think Meg is ready."

I was happy to learn that Meg didn't tell Laverne *everything*.

"Laverne!" I said as if shocked. "She's your sister!"

"That's why I want her to have fun. Give her a break, darling. It doesn't have to be heavy. Just for laughs."

"I don't know," I said doubtfully. "I'm not sure she has eyes for me."

"Try it," Laverne urged. "It would do her a world of good. I realize she's a skinny one, but remember: the nearer the bone, the sweeter the meat."

Yes, she *did* say that. Was there a more vulgar woman in Palm Beach? If there was, I hadn't met her and had no desire to.

"I'll take it under advisement," I said and stood up. "I better pick up that letter and see if it's any help in finding the catnappers."

"And you'll forget all about going to a psychic?"

The first two rules of successful deception are keep it short and never repeat. Ask me; I know. Laverne was obviously an amateur at deceit.

"I've already forgotten," I assured her. "Don't get too much sun or you might start peeling."

Her reply is unprintable in an account that may possibly be read by impressionable youngsters and innocent oldsters.

I found the second ransom note on the taboret in the hallway. I handled it carefully by the corners and slipped it into my jacket pocket. No one was about so I let myself out and drove home, still smiling at Laverne's final comment and wondering why she felt it necessary to conceal her acquaintance with the Glorianas.

At home, I went immediately to my rooms, sat at the desk, shoved on my reading specs. I unfolded the second ransom note carefully and examined it. It appeared to be printed in the same font as the first and the missives sent to Lydia Gillsworth. The right-hand margin was justified. The ink and paper stock seemed identical in all the letters.

The message itself was as Harry Willigan had stated. I was amused by the casual mention of Peaches being in good health but crying a lot. That was clearly intended to pierce the heart of the cat's owner who might have the personality of a Komodo dragon but was obviously sappy with love for his obnoxious pet.

I added the second ransom note to my photocopy of the first, slid both into a manila envelope, and started out again. This time I left my new beret at home but took along my reading glasses tucked into a handsome *petit point* case that mother had made and given to me on my thirty-sixth birthday.

Before leaving, I phoned Mrs. Trelawney, my father's private secretary. I asked if she could persuade the boss to grant me at least fifteen minutes from his rigidly structured daily schedule. I was put on hold while she went to inquire. She came back on the line to tell me His Majesty had graciously acceded to my request if I arrived promptly at eleven-thirty.

"On my way," I promised.

The McNally Building on Royal Palm Way is a stark edifice of glass and stainless steel – so modern it makes my teeth ache. But it's undeniably impressive – which was why my father had approved the architect's design even though I knew he would have preferred a *faux* Georgian mansion.

But the esquire had drawn a line at his private office. *That* was oak paneled and furnished in a style that would have earned the approbation of Oliver Wendell Holmes. The main attraction was an enormous rolltop desk – an original, not a reproduction – that had, by actual count, thirty-six cubbyholes and four concealed compartments that I knew about.

Father was standing in front of this handsome antique when I entered, looking like a handsome antique himself. He glowered at me, and I was happy I had left the linen beret at home.

"This couldn't have waited?" he demanded.

"No, sir," I said. "In my judgment it is a matter that brooks no delay."

Don't ask why, but in his presence I sometimes began to speak like a character from his beloved Dickens. I knew it but couldn't help myself. We sounded like a couple of barristers discussing *Jarndyce vs. Jarndyce*.

"Harry Willigan received a second ransom letter from the catnappers," I told him.

"I am aware of that," he said testily. "Willigan phoned me this morning. In a vile temper, as usual."

"Yes, sir," I said, "but I don't believe you've seen the two letters. I've brought them along. The first is a photocopy, the second is the original. Please take a look, father."

129

I spread them on his desk. Still standing, he bent over to examine them. It didn't take him long to catch it. I heard his sharp intake of breath, and he straightened to stare at me.

"They appear to resemble the poison-pen letters received by the late Lydia Gillsworth," he said stonily.

"More than resemble," I said. "Same type font. Justified right-hand margins. Apparently the same ink and the same paper."

He drew a deep breath and thrust his hands into his trouser pockets. "Where are the Gillsworth letters now?"

"Sergeant Rogoff has them. He's sending them to the FBI lab for analysis."

"Does he know about these letters?"

"Not to my knowledge. I've told him nothing about the disappearance of Peaches."

Hands still in pockets, he began to pace slowly about the office. "I see the problem," he said. "The client has specifically forbidden us to bring the catnapping to the attention of the police."

"And we are obligated to respect our client's wishes and follow his instructions," I added. "But by so doing, are we not impeding an official homicide investigation? That's assuming all the letters were produced on the same word processor or electronic typewriter, as I believe they were."

He stopped his pacing to face me. "And do you also believe they were all composed by the same person?"

"I think it quite possible."

He was silent a moment. Then: "I don't like this, Archy; I don't like it at all. As an officer of the court I don't relish being put in a position where I might fairly be accused of withholding evidence."

"Possibly vital evidence," I said. "In the investigation of a particularly heinous crime."

He took one hand from his pocket and began to tug at his thick mustache, a sure sign of his perturbation. When he's in a mellow mood, he strokes it.

"May I make a suggestion, father?"

"You may."

"I think civic and moral duty outweigh ethical considerations in this case. I believe the police *must* be told of the Willigan letters. Perhaps they have nothing to do with the Gillsworth murder, but we can't take that chance. Let me show them to Sergeant Rogoff, for his eyes only. I'll impress upon him the need for absolute discretion on his part. Al is certainly no blabbermouth. I think we can safely gamble that Willigan will never learn we have told the police about the catnapping."

"It's not so much Willigan I'm concerned about, it's the catnappers. If they learn the police have been informed, it's quite possible they will carry out their threat to kill Peaches. And then McNally & Son may be the target of a malpractice suit brought by our contentious client. It would be difficult to defend our conduct: a clear breach of confidentiality."

We were both silent then, pondering all the ramifications of the problem. The decision was not mine to make, of course. It was my father who might have to take the flak, and it would be presumptuous of me to urge him to any particular course of conduct.

"Very well," he said at last. "Show the Willigan letters to Sergeant Rogoff, explain the circumstances of the catnapping, and try to convince him that the future of Peaches depends on his circumspection." He paused to smile wryly. "To say nothing of the future of McNally & Son."

"I'll convince him," I said, gathering up the letters. "I think you've made the right decision, father."

"Thank you, Archy," he said gravely. "I am happy

131

you approve."

I think he meant it. Irony is not the Governor's strong suit.

I was exiting through the outer office when Mrs. Trelawney beckoned me to her desk. My father's secretary is one of my favorite people, a charming beldame with an ill-fitting gray wig and a penchant for naughty jokes. She was the first to tell me the one about the American, the Englishman, and the Frenchman who visit a – but I digress.

"What have you been up to, young McNally?" she said accusingly. "Romancing married women, are you? And if you are, why wasn't I the first on your list?"

"I am not," I assured her, "but if I were, you would certainly be first, last, and always. Also, my dear, just what, exactly, are you talking about?"

She looked down at a note she had jotted on a telephone message form. "While you were with your father, you received a call from a Mrs. Irma Gloriana, who demanded to speak to you personally. From her voice I would judge her to be of what is termed a 'certain age.' She insists you phone her immediately. What's going on, Archy?"

"A professional relationship," I said haughtily. "The lady happens to be my acupuncturist."

Mrs. Trelawney laughed and handed me the message. "I'm glad someone's giving you the needle," she said.

I had intended to phone Sgt. Rogoff the moment I was in my office, but this call from Mrs. Irma Gloriana seemed more important and more intriguing. I sat at my desk and punched out the phone number. It was not, I noted, the number of the Glorianas' office on Clematis Street.

My call was answered on the second ring.

"The Glorianas' residence," a woman said sharply. A

132

deep voice, very strong, with a rough timbre. Almost a longshoreman's voice.

"This is Archibald McNally," I said. "Am I speaking to Mrs. Irma Gloriana?"

"You are, Mr. McNally," she said, the tone now softened a bit. "Thank you for returning my call so promptly. Hertha has informed me that you wish to arrange a private séance."

"That's correct," I said, "My understanding is that it would be attended by Hertha, her husband, you, myself, and a friend who accompanies me. Will that be satisfactory?"

"Mr. McNally," she said, and I marveled at that voice so deep it was almost a rumble, "I prefer to meet personally with new clients before making plans. You must understand that many people who apply to us simply cannot be helped by Hertha's unique talents. It saves us a great deal of time – and would-be clients a great deal of money, of course – if we might have an interview during which I describe exactly what happens at our séances, what we hope to achieve, and what we cannot do. I must know what you hope to accomplish. I trust this preliminary screening doesn't offend you, Mr. McNally."

"Not at all," I said. "I can understand why – "

"You see," she interrupted, "we are sometimes approached by people who seek the impossible or who are motivated by idle curiosity and have no real interest in sharing the truth of spiritualism."

"That seems to be a – "

"And there are those who come just to mock," she said darkly. "My daughter-in-law is much too sensitive and vulnerable to be forced to cope with stupid and arrogant disbelief."

"I assure you that – "

"When may I expect you, Mr. McNally?" she

133

demanded.

"I can come over now, Mrs. Gloriana," I said. "I could be there in a half-hour."

"That will be satisfactory," she said crisply. "Please make a note of this address. You should also be aware that smoking is not permitted in our home."

So I made a note of her address, hung up, and immediately lighted a cigarette. I smoked it down before venturing out to meet this termagant with the foghorn voice.

On the drive across the bridge to West Palm Beach I tried to make sense of what Mrs. Irma Gloriana had told me. Her insistence on a preliminary screening of would-be clients seemed suspect. Why should the medium and her entourage question the motives of potential customers? Their ability to pay the tariff demanded would seem to be the only necessary requirement.

But then I realized there might indeed be method to this madness. Mrs. Gloriana wanted to know what I hoped to accomplish at the séance. Suppose I told her I wished to contact the spirit of Sir Thomas Crapper. Thus forewarned, Irma, Frank, and Hertha could easily discover that the gentleman in question was the inventor of the water closet, and they could call up a ghost familiar to the workings of that justly famed device.

Similarly, these preliminary interviews could reveal names, dates, even intimate personal details that would be of value in convincing a séance attendee that the medium possessed extraordinary psychic gifts.

This was, I admit, a very jaundiced view of extrasensory powers. But at that stage of the investigation I believed a healthy dollop of cynicism was justified. "Innocent until proven guilty" is the cornerstone of our law. But most detectives, myself included prefer the dictum "Guilty until proven innocent." That's

134

how crimes are solved.

The building in which the Glorianas' condo was located was not as "ratty" as Al Rogoff had described, but it was surely no Trump Plaza either. It had an air of faded elegance, with cooking odors in the hallways and frazzled carpeting.

The matron who opened the door of Apt. 1102 was as I had imagined her: tall, heavy through the hips, but more muscular than plump. There was a solid massiveness about her: a large head held erect on a strong neck. Definitely a dominant woman.

But what I had not been prepared for was her sensuousness, so overt it was almost a scent. It was conveyed, I thought, by her full red lips, glossy black hair as tangled as a basket of snakes, ample bosom, and a certain looseness about the way she moved. It was easy to fantasize that she might be naked beneath her shift, a voluminous gown of flowered nylon.

She shook my hand firmly, got me seated in an armchair covered in a worn brocade. She asked if I would care for an iced tea. I said that would be welcome, and while she was gone I had an opportunity to inspect the apartment – or at least the living room in which I was seated.

It was a dreary place, colors drab, furniture lumpy. It was difficult to believe this was the home of the forthright Irma, the dapper Frank, the delicate Hertha. There was nothing that bespoke luxury, or even comfort. They were ambitious people; this dingy apartment had to be a temporary residence to be endured until something better came along.

Mrs. Gloriana returned with my iced tea – nothing for her – and sat in the middle of a raddled couch, facing me. She wasted no time on preliminaries.

"You believe in spiritualism, Mr. McNally?" she asked.

I took a sip of my tea. It had a hint of mint and was

135

quite good. "Really more of a student," I confessed. "I'm reading as much about it as I can."

"Oh? And what are you reading?"

I mentioned the titles of two of the books Mrs. Gillsworth had lent me.

"Very good," Irma Gloriana said approvingly. "But you must realize they are only instructional. True belief must come from the heart and the soul."

"I understand that," I said, fearing I was about to be proselytized and dreading the prospect. But she dropped the subject of my conversion.

"Hertha tells me you have asked her assistance in finding your missing cat."

"A friend's cat."

"She may be able to help. My daughter-in-law has amazing psychic powers. And did you wish to ask about the cat during the séance?"

"No," I said, "something else. I hope to receive a message from Lydia Gillsworth. I'm sure you knew her and have heard what happened to her."

Her expression didn't change. "Of course I knew Lydia. A sensitive soul. She attended a session here the evening she was killed. A brutal, senseless death."

"Yes," I said, "it was. Do you think there's a possibility that Hertha may be able to contact the spirit of Lydia Gillsworth?"

"There is always a possibility," she said, then added firmly, "But naturally we can offer no guarantees. You wish to ask Lydia the identity of her murderer?"

"Yes, that is what I intended."

"It is worth trying," she said thoughtfully. "Hertha has assisted in many police investigations in the past. With some success, I might add, Our standard fee for a séance is five hundred dollars, Mr. McNally. But that is usually divided amongst several participants. Since only you and

136

your friend will attend, I believe a fee of two hundred dollars will be more equitable. Is that satisfactory?"

"Completely," I said. "And you do accept credit cards?"

"Oh yes. This friend who will accompany you – a man or a woman?"

"A woman."

"Could you tell me her name, please? Numerology is a particular interest of mine, and I enjoy converting names to numerical equivalents and developing psychic profiles."

"Her name is Margaret Trumble."

"A resident in this area?"

Then I was certain she was prying – no doubt about it.

"She is a new resident," I said.

"So many refugees from the north, aren't there?"

If she expected me to divulge Meg Trumble's hometown, she was disappointed; I merely nodded.

"My son tells me you work for a law firm, Mr. McNally."

"Yes, McNally & Son. My father is the attorney."

"But you are not?"

"Regretfully, no," I said, unable to cease staring at her bare neck, the skin seemingly so flawless and tender that it might be bruised by a kiss.

"And what is it you do at McNally & Son?"

It wasn't exactly a third degree. Call it a second degree.

"Research, mostly," I told her. "Usually very dull stuff."

I finished my iced tea, but she didn't offer a refill.

"Did you know Lydia Gillsworth a long time?" she asked.

"Several years. She and her husband were clients. And neighbors as well."

"I have met Roderick Gillsworth. He attended a few of

137

our sessions with his wife. His late wife, I should say. I found him a very intelligent, creative man. A poet, you know."

"Yes, I know."

"He was kind enough to give me autographed volumes of his poems. Have you read his work, Mr. McNally?"

"Some," I said cautiously.

"What is your opinion of his poetry?"

"Ah," I said. Then: "Very cerebral."

"It is that," she said, her deep voice resonating. "But I believe he is more than an intellectual. In his poems I sense a wild, primitive spirit struggling to be free."

"You may be right," I said diplomatically, thinking I had never heard such twaddle. Roderick Gillsworth a wild, primitive spirit? Sure. And I am Vlad the Impaler.

She rose to her feet, a boneless uncoiling. "I'll try to arrange your séance for later this week, Mr. McNally. I'll give you at least a day's notice. Will that be sufficient?"

"Of course," I said. "I may be speaking to your daughter-in-law before that if she is able to receive additional information about Peaches."

"Peaches?"

"The missing cat."

Unexpectedly she smiled, a mischievous smile that made her seem younger. And more attractive, I might add.

I hesitate to use the adjective "seductive" to describe any woman, but I can think of none more fitting for Irma Gloriana. I don't wish to imply her manner was deliberately designed to entice, but I could not believe she was totally unconscious of her physical allure. But perhaps she was. In any event, she projected a strong and smouldering sexuality impossible to ignore.

"Peaches," she repeated. "A charming name. Is the cat charming?"

138

"The cat is a horror," I said, and this time she laughed aloud, a booming laugh. "But my friend loves her," I added.

"Love," she said, suddenly serious. "Such an inexplicable emotion, is it not, Mr. McNally?"

"It is indeed," I said, and her final handclasp was soft and warm, quite different from the hard, cool handshake with which she had greeted me.

I drove back to the office trying to sort out my impressions of Mrs. Irma Gloriana. Al Rogoff had initially dubbed her a "tough broad," and I could understand his reaction. But I thought her more than that: a very deep lady whose contradictions I could not immediately ken. I had a sense that she was playing a role, but what the script might be I had no idea.

The first thing I did on my return to the McNally Building was to phone Sgt. Rogoff. He wasn't in, so I left my name and number, requesting he call me as soon as possible.

I then clattered down the back stairs to our real estate department on the second floor. This section of our legal supermarket advises clients on the purchase and sale of commercial properties and raw land. It also assists on negotiations for private homes, helps arrange mortgages, and represents clients at closings.

The chief of the department was Mrs. Evelyn Sharif, a jovial lady married to a Lebanese who sold Oriental rugs on Worth Avenue. But Evelyn was absent on maternity leave (twins expected!), so I spoke to her assistant, Timothy Hogan, an Irishman who wore Italian suits, English shirts, French cravats, and Spanish shoes. The man was a walking United Nations.

I explained to Tim what I needed: all the skinny he could dig up on the Glorianas' Clematis Street office and their condo near Currie Park. That would include rent,

139

length of lease, maintenance, purchase price of the apartment if they indeed owned it rather than renting, and the references they had furnished.

"Are you sure you don't want the name of their dentist?" Hogan asked.

"I know it's a lot of work, Tim," I said, "but see what you can do, will you?"

"What's in it for me?" he asked.

"I won't tell the old man you're peddling Irish Sweepstakes tickets on company time."

"That's called extortion," he said.

"It is?" I said. "I could have sworn it was blackmail. Whatever, do your best, Tim."

Back in my private closet, I got busy on the phone calling a number of contacts at banks, brokerage houses, and credit rating agencies. Most of the people I buzzed were fellow members of the Pelican Club, and the only price I had to pay for the financial lowdown I sought on the Glorianas was the promise of a dinner at the Pelican.

It was late in the afternoon before I finished my calls, and a subdued growl from the brisket reminded me that other than breakfast the only nourishment I had had all day was a glass of iced tea and a cigarette. I was heading out the door for a pit stop at the nearest watering hole when a jangling phone brought me back to my desk. It was Sgt. Rogoff.

"I'm phoning from the airport," he said. "I just checked with the station and they told me you called."

"What are you doing at the airport?" I asked. "Leaving for Pago Pago?"

"Don't I wish," he said. "Actually I wanted to make sure Roderick Gillsworth made his flight. He's taking the casket up north."

"And he did?"

"Yeah, he's gone. I'm a little antsy about letting him

140

go, but he swears he'll be back in a couple of days. He better be or I'll look like a first-class schmuck for letting him go."

"Al, don't tell me you still suspect him?"

"No, but he's a material witness, isn't he?"

"What kind of condition was he in?"

"It's my guess he was nursing a hangover."

"Shrewd guess," I said. "When I left him last night he was sopping up the sauce like Prohibition was just around the corner. Listen, Al, I've got to talk to you."

"That's what we're doing."

I sighed. "You want me to be precise? Very well, I shall be precise. It is extremely urgent that I meet personally with you, Sergeant Rogoff, since there are certain letters I wish to show you that may prove to be of some importance in your current homicide investigation. There, how's that?"

"What letters?" he demanded.

"Al," I said, "you're going to kill me."

"Cheerfully," he said.

9

Al told me he wanted to drive back to the Gillsworth home to make certain the poet had locked up when he left. I said I'd meet him in an hour.

"Take your time," he said. "I'll be there awhile."

I thought that an odd thing to say but made no comment. I grabbed the envelope with the Willigan letters and rode the elevator down to our underground garage. I waved to the security guard and mounted the Miata for the canter home.

No one was about in the McNally castle so I hustled into the kitchen and slapped together a fat sandwich of salami on sour rye, slathered with a mustard hairy enough to bring tears to your baby blues. I cooled the fire with a chilled can of Buckler non-alcoholic beer, then ran upstairs to get Gillsworth's house keys in case I arrived before Rogoff.

But when I got there, a police car was parked in the driveway and the front door of the house was open. I walked in and called, "Al?"

"In here," he yelled, and I found him sprawled in a flowered armchair in the sitting room where Lydia had been murdered. He hadn't taken off his cap, and he was smoking one of his big cigars.

"Make yourself at home," I said.

"I already have," he said. "Let's see those cockamamy letters you were talking about."

I tossed him the envelope. "Photocopy of the first received by Harry Willigan. The second is the original. Handle it with care; it might have prints."

He read both letters slowly while I lounged on a wicker couch and lighted an English Oval. Then he looked up at me.

"Same paper," he said. "Looks like the same ink, same typeface, same even right-hand margins."

"That's right," I said. "The reason I haven't shown them to you before is that the client forbade it. You know Willigan?"

"I know him," he said grimly. "A peerless horse's ass."

"I concur," I said. "And if he ever finds out I've told you about the catnapping, he'll be an ex-client and probably sue McNally & Son for malpractice. Al, will you please keep a lid on this? My father knows I'm showing you the letters; it was his decision. All we ask in return is your discretion."

"Sure," he said, "I'm good at that. What have you done so far about finding the damned cat?"

"Not a great deal," I said. "One thing I did do – and this will probably give you a laugh: I went to Hertha Gloriana, the psychic, and asked her help in locating Peaches."

But he didn't laugh. "Not so dumb," he said. "Cops hate to admit it, but psychics and mediums are consulted more often than you think. Mostly in missing person cases. What did she say?"

I repeated Hertha's description of the room where she envisioned Peaches was being held prisoner. "She couldn't give me a definite location but said she'll keep trying. Do you think these ransom notes have anything to do with the Gillsworth homicide?"

143

"Definitely," he said. "Too many similarities in the letters to call it coincidence. I'll get these off to the FBI and ask for a comparison. I'm betting they were all printed on the same machine."

"So what do we do now?"

"Nothing, until we get the FBI report. If Willigan gets instructions on delivering the fifty thousand, let me know and we'll try to set up a snare. I wonder if there's anything to drink in this place."

"Let me take a look," I said. "I'm a neighbor; Gillsworth won't mind if I chisel a drink or two."

I went into the kitchen and found my bottle of Sterling vodka in the freezer. It was still a third full. I brought that and two glasses into the sitting room, then made another trip to bring out a bowl of ice cubes and a pitcher of water.

"Help yourself," I said to Rogoff. "It's McNally booze; I loaned it to Gillsworth last night when he ran dry."

We built drinks for ourselves and settled back. It was really a very attractive, comfortable room – if you didn't look at the bloodstains that had not yet been scrubbed away or painted over.

"That cane that killed her," the sergeant said. "You told me Mrs. Gillsworth showed it to you."

"That's right."

"Did you touch it?"

"No, she held it while she was telling me about it."

"The shank has a lot of prints," Al said. "Hers, Gillsworth's, some other."

"Probably the antique dealer who sold it to her."

"Probably, and any other customers who picked it up in his shop. But it also has some interesting partials. Our print expert says they were made by someone wearing latex gloves."

"The killer?"

"Seems likely, doesn't it? The latex prints were over

144

the old ones, so I've got to figure they were the last to be made."

"Where does that leave you?"

"Out in left field – unless you spot a guy in the Pelican Club wearing latex gloves."

"Surgeons use them."

"And house painters, window washers, people who scrub floors, dentists, and your friendly neighborhood proctologist. How are you doing with the Glorianas?"

"They're setting up a private séance for me this week. Irma is handling it."

"So you met that bimbo. Did she come on to you?"

"I don't think she's a bimbo, Al, and she didn't come on to me."

He looked at me quizzically. "But didn't you get the feeling that if you hit on her she wouldn't be insulted?"

"Maybe," I said warily. "But I think she's a very complex woman."

"You and your complexities," he said disgustedly. "You can't call a spade a spade. To you it's a sharped-edge implement used for digging that can be inserted into the ground with the aid of foot pressure. To me Irma Gloriana is a hard case with a bottom-line mentality."

I let it go. Al thinks like a policeman. I think like an aged preppy.

"I know you've checked the Glorianas through records," I said. "Anything?"

"No outstanding warrants," he reported. "I've got a lot of queries out and I'm waiting to hear. Something may turn up – but don't hold your breath."

I told him about the inquiries I had made to determine the Glorianas' financial status.

"Good going," he said. "I'm betting they're on their uppers – but that's just a guess. Elegant vodka, Archy."

"It's all yours," I said, finishing my drink and rising.

"I've got to get home for the family cocktail hour or mommy and daddy will send out the bloodhounds. Something you should be aware of, Al: you're not Roderick Gillsworth's favorite police officer."

"Tell me something I don't know. And you think I lose sleep over it?"

"He asked if he could phone me from up north and get a report on the investigation. He thinks you're holding out on him."

"I am," Rogoff said with a hard smile. "Do me a favor, will you? If he calls you, tell him I've been acting very mysteriously and you think I've got a hot lead I'm not talking about."

"Do you? Have a hot lead?"

"No."

"Then why should I tell him that?"

"Just to stir him up, keep him off balance."

"Is your middle name Machiavelli or Borgia?"

"It happens to be Irving, but don't tell anyone."

I laughed and started out, then paused. "You're staying?" I asked him.

"For a while. I thought I'd look around the house."

"What for?"

"One never knows, do one?"

"Hey," I protested, "that's my line."

"So it is," Al said, "and you're welcome to it."

He was pouring himself another shot of Sterling when I left.

I started the Miata and drove up Via Del Lago toward the beach. As I did, a car turned off Ocean Boulevard and came toward me. I recognised that clunker, an ancient Chevy that needed an IV. And as it passed I recognised the driver from her carroty hair. It was Marita, the Gillsworths' Haitian housekeeper who, according to Roderick, had been given two weeks off. I pulled to the curb,

146

stopped, and watched in my side mirror.

Marita parked next to the police car, not at all daunted, got out, and went into the house. She was a tubby little woman who walked with a rolling gait. And there was no mistaking that dyed hair.

I started up again and drove homeward. I never doubted for a moment that she had been summoned by Sgt. Rogoff. Their meeting was prearranged, but for what purpose I couldn't even guess. Obviously Al wasn't telling me everything about his investigation. But then I wasn't telling him everything about mine: e.g., the relationship between Laverne Willigan and the Glorianas.

There was something else I hadn't told him, something I hadn't really told myself, for it wasn't a fact or even an idea; it was just a vague notion. And I have no intention of telling you what it was at this juncture. You'd only laugh.

The family cocktail hour and dinner went off with no untoward incidents that evening. After coffee, mother went to her television in the second-floor sitting room, father retired to Dickens in his study, and I trotted upstairs and got to work on my journal.

I was interrupted that night by two phone calls. The first was from Connie Garcia.

"You swine," she started. "Why haven't you called?"

"Busy, busy, busy," I said. "I *do* have a job, you know, and I work hard at it. I'm not just another pretty face."

She giggled. "I'll testify to *that*. Have you been seeing Meg Trumble lately?"

"Haven't seen her in days," I said, feeling virtuous because I could be honest. "She may have gone back up north."

"I hope she stays there," Connie said. "Listen, I have a family thing for tomorrow night – a bridal shower for one of my cousins – but I'm available for lunch. Make

147

me an offer."

"Connie, would you care to have lunch with me tomorrow?"

"What a splendid idea! I'd love to. Pick me up around noon – okay?"

"You betcha. I have a new hat to show you – a puce beret."

"Oh God," she said.

I went back to my journal, scribbling along at a lively clip until I started on an account of my meeting with Irma Gloriana. Then I paused to lean back and stare at the stained ceiling, trying to bring her into sharper focus.

I had thought Frank Gloriana functioned as Hertha's business manager. But Irma's role in setting up the séance and her authoritative manner led me to believe that perhaps she was the CEO of the Gloriana ménage.

If the Glorianas were engaged in hanky-panky, as I was beginning to think they were, then Irma was the Ma Barker of the gang, a very robust and attractive chieftain. That would make son Frank her foppish henchman. But what part was Hertha playing? I could not believe that sweet, limpid innocent could be guilty of any wrongdoing. Her lips were too soft and warm for a criminal. (I know that is a ridiculous non sequitur; you don't have to tell me.)

My musings were interrupted by the second phone call, this one from Roderick Gillsworth in Rhode Island.

"How are you getting along, Rod?" I asked.

"As well as can be expected," he said. "Isn't that what doctors say when the patient is in extremis? The funeral is scheduled for tomorrow after a church service at noon. Then I am expected to attend a buffet dinner at the home of an elderly aunt. I fear she may serve dandelion wine or camomile tea so I shall be well fortified beforehand, I assure you. I'll get through it somehow."

148

"Of course you will. When are you returning?"

"I have a flight on Wednesday morning. Tell me, Archy, is there anything new on the investigation?"

I hesitated, long enough for him to say, "Well?"

"Nothing definite, no," I said. "But I spoke to Sergeant Rogoff today and he was rather mystifying. He seemed quite pleased with himself, as if he had uncovered something important. But when I asked questions, all he'd do was wink."

"Dreadful man," Gillsworth said. "If I can't get any satisfaction from him when I return on Wednesday, I intend to go directly to his superior and demand to be told what's going on."

I made no reply to that. "I stopped by your home early this evening, Rod," I said. "Just to make certain it was locked up. Everything is fine."

"Thank you, Archy," he said. "I may call you again tomorrow to ask if you have learned anything new."

"Of course."

"I appreciate all that you and your father have done for me. You might tell him that I've been thinking about my new will. I'll probably have the terms roughed out by the time I return."

"Good," I said. "He'll be happy to hear that."

I hung up, having lied as requested by Al Rogoff and wondering what the sergeant really wanted to accomplish by giving Gillsworth false hopes that the murder of his wife was nearing solution. Sometimes Al moves in mysterious ways.

It was almost midnight before I finished my journal entries. I decided I didn't want to smoke, drink, or listen to Robert Johnson singing "Kindhearted Woman Blues." So I went to bed and thought happily of Meg Trumble arriving on the morrow. I hoped she would be kindhearted and I would have no cause to sing the blues.

149

I was awoken early Tuesday morning by the growling of what sounded like a brigade of power mowers. I stumbled to the window and looked down to see our landscape gardener's crew hard at work. They showed up periodically to mow the lawn, trim shrubbery, and spray everything in sight.

They were making such a racket that I knew it would be futile to try resuming my dreamless slumber – which explains why I was showered, shaved, and dressed in time to breakfast with my parents in the dining room. It was such a rare occurrence that they looked at me in astonishment and mother asked anxiously, "Are you ill, Archy?"

I proved to her I was in fine fettle by consuming a herculean portion of eggs scrambled with onions and smoked salmon. Over coffee, I told my father about Gillsworth's call the previous evening, and that the poet would be returning on Wednesday ready to draw up a new will.

He looked up from *The Wall Street Journal* long enough to nod. I then informed him I expected a hectic day so I would drive to the office in my own car rather than accompany him in the Lexus. That earned me a second nod before he went back to his paper. The master doesn't like to be interrupted while he's checking the current value of his treasury bonds.

I ran upstairs to collect a fresh box of English Ovals, my reading glasses, and the puce beret, which I rolled up and tucked into a jacket pocket. I wore my madras that day, a nifty number gaudy enough to enrage any passing bull.

I arrived at my miniature office just in time to receive a phone call from Mrs. Irma Gloriana.

"Good morning, Mr. McNally," she said crisply and didn't wait for a return greeting. "I have arranged a private séance for you and your companion tomorrow evening at nine o'clock. Will that be satisfactory?"

"Completely," I said. "Shall we – "

"It will be held here in the apartment," she continued. "We have found that an informal, homey setting is more likely to result in a successful session than a meeting held in a commercial office."

"I can – "

"Please be prompt," she went on, and I despaired of contributing to the conversation. "As you can imagine, these sittings are quite a strain on Hertha, and if they are delayed it only adds to her spiritual tension."

"We'll be on time," I said hurriedly and just did get it out before she hung up.

What a peremptory woman she was! I wondered what had happened to her husband. Had he died of frustration because he couldn't get a word in edgewise? Or had he divorced her for a more docile woman who welcomed small talk and could schmooze for hours about his gastritis and her bunions? My own guess was that Irma's husband went to buy a loaf of bread, vamoosed, and was now employed as a tobacco auctioneer.

I worked fitfully on my expense account that morning, a monthly task that challenged my creativity. My labors were interrupted by three phone calls from informants I had queried about the Glorianas' financial status and credit rating.

By the time I had to leave for my luncheon date with Connie Garcia, I was convinced Al Rogoff had been right: the Glorianas were on their uppers. They weren't candidates for welfare – far from it – but their bank balances were distressingly low, and they had an unenviable reputation for bouncing checks. They always made good, eventually, but rubber checks make bankers break out in a rash, and they usually suggest chronic paperhangers take their business elsewhere.

I drove back to the beach to pick up Connie, reflecting

151

on the Glorianas' impecunious state and dreaming up all kinds of fanciful scenarios to link their dreaded ailment, lackamoola, to the catnapping of Peaches. The connection seemed obvious; proving it was another kettle of flounder entirely.

When Ms. Garcia came bouncing out of her office in Lady Horrowitz's mansion, I was lounging nonchalantly alongside the Miata, my new beret atop my dome and tilted dashingly to one side. Connie took a long, open-mouthed look and then bent almost double in a paroxysm of mirth.

"Please!" she gasped. "Archy, *please* take it off. I can't *stand* it! My ribs ache."

Much affronted, I crammed the cap back in my pocket. *Ut quod ali cibus est allis fuat acre venenum.* Translation: one's puce beret is another's aching ribs.

But your hero's generosity of spirit is sufficient to pardon a lapse of taste, and Connie's insult to my headgear was soon forgiven as we headed for the Pelican Club.

There was a goodly crowd at the bar but surprisingly few members were seated in the dining area. We got our favorite corner table, and Priscilla strutted over to take our order.

"Archy," Connie said, "show Pris your new hat."

Obediently I dug the beret from my jacket pocket and tugged it on at a rakish tilt. Priscilla stared, aghast.

"You know, Connie," she said, "the man really should be committed. It's obvious his elevator doesn't go to the top floor."

"What's obvious," I said, removing the beret, "is that the two of you are fashion's slaves but have no appreciation of style. Believe me, linen berets are the coming thing."

"If they're coming," Priscilla said, "I'm going. You folks want to sit here arguing about goofy hats or do you

152

want to order?"

Connie and I had vodka gimlets to start, and we both went for Leroy's special of the day: a grilled grouper sandwich with spicy french fries, served with a salad of Bibb lettuce, red onions, and a vinaigrette sauce. A winner.

Connie attacked her food with enthusiasm and didn't mention a word about proteins, cholesterol, or fat, for which I was thankful. Nutrition nuts are the world's most boring dining companions. They make every bite a guilt trip, which forces me to gorge to prove my disdain for calories. I mean, if God had wanted us to nibble, He wouldn't have created veal cordon bleu.

"By the way," Connie said, looking up from her salad, "I sent in that application to the Glorianas, asking for a psychic profile."

"Good for you," I said. "Thank you, Connie. I hope you didn't make it too ridiculous."

"Nope. I just invented all the vital statistics, birthplace, names of parents, and so forth. And I bought a little red plastic heart at a gift shop and sent it along as my beloved personal possession. You really think the Glorianas will send me a phony profile?'

"As phony as your letter," I assured her. "Let me know as soon as you receive a reply. Meanwhile I'll get you a check from McNally & Son for services rendered."

"I'm not worried," she said. "But don't leave town."

We both laughed. She really was a jolly woman, and there was no side to her; what you saw was what you got. I think our problem – or rather *my* problem – was that we had become so familiar over the years that mystery was lacking; we knew each other too well. We were really more buddies than lovers, more contented than passionate. But content is never enough, is it? Which is why men and women cheat on each other, I suppose.

153

Thoughts like that saddened me, and I resolved to buy Connie a diamond tennis bracelet. Remorse can be costly – right?

I signed the tab for lunch, and Connie preceded me from the dining room and through the bar area. It was gratifying to see how many male noggins turned in her direction and to note the longing looks. She even drew appreciative glances from several of the females present, for Connie was an enormously attractive lady who radiated a buoyant delight in being alive, young, and full of fire.

I knew well that I was a fool to be unfaithful to her. But that knowledge didn't deter me. I consoled myself with the thought that if we all acted in an intelligent, disciplined manner, what a dull world it would be. I'm sure Napoleon thought the same thing as he staggered home from Moscow.

We returned to the Horowitz estate and sat in the car a few moments before Connie went back to work. She turned sideways to look directly at me, her expression set.

"Archy," she said in a firm voice, "you don't want to break up again, do you?"

"Break up?" I cried. "Of course I don't want to break up. What kind of nonsense is that?"

"You've been acting so strangely lately, so distant."

"I told you how busy I've been. I know you've heard about Lydia Gillsworth being killed. Well, she was our client, and father wants me to assist the police find the murderer. We were both very deeply affected by her death."

"I can understand that, but surely you're not busy twenty-four hours a day. We haven't had a night together for ages."

"That's not all my fault," I pointed out. "We did have a small Bacchanalia planned, but then you had to work late.

154

You do recall that, don't you?"

She nodded. "But that doesn't mean we can't plan another mini-orgy. Archy, remember the time we went skinny-dipping in the ocean at midnight?"

"A memory I shall retain forever," I said. "I got stung by a Portuguese man-of-war."

"A very small sting."

"On a very embarrassing portion of my anatomy. But you're right, Connie; it has been a long time since we two were one."

"Tomorrow night?" she suggested.

"Ah," I said, the old neurons and dendrites working at blinding speed, "regretfully I cannot. I have a meeting with Sergeant Al Rogoff to help prepare a statement to the press on the investigation. How about the weekend? Perhaps Saturday night?"

"Sounds good," she said. "I'll plan on it. Don't disappoint me, Archy."

"Have I ever?"

She gave me a rueful smile. "I better not answer that." She leaned forward to kiss my cheek. "Thanks for the lunch, luv. See you Saturday night. But do try to phone me before that – okay?"

"Of course," I said. "Absolutely."

She scampered into her office, and I drove home terrified that on some future date all the women I had wronged might hold a convention, compare grievances, and decided a prompt lynching of yrs. truly would be justified. I even imagined myself swinging from a palm tree, clad in nothing but my silk briefs imprinted with an image of Pan tootling his syrinx to a bevy of naked dryads.

I had no idea when Meg Trumble might call to announce her arrival, so I decided to stick close to the phone, even forgoing my ocean swim so I wouldn't miss her. I went directly to my quarters and switched the air

155

conditioner to High Cool. It wasn't all that hot, but it was oppressively muggy, and I stripped to my skivvies before setting to work.

I remembered I had promised Meg a list of friends and acquaintances who might be interested in employing a personal trainer. Consulting my address book, I compiled a choice selection of men and women, concentrating on the suety and notorious couch potatoes. At the end, just for a giggle, I added the name of Al Rogoff.

It came time to dress for the family cocktail hour, and I still hadn't heard from Meg. It was quite possible she was delayed on the road for one reason or another, so I thought it best to dine at home with my parents. If she called after I had eaten, I could still take her to dinner but limit my own intake to fresh fruit, like a wedge of lime in a frozen daiquiri.

Actually, she didn't phone until a little after nine o'clock. She was all apologies; heavy traffic and road construction had thrown her schedule out of kilter.

"I hope you went ahead and had dinner, Archy," she said. "I'd hate to think you were starving because of me."

"As a matter of fact I have eaten," I confessed. "But that doesn't mean we can't keep our dinner date."

"You don't have to do that," she protested. "I'll just run out for a snack and we can make it another time. Perhaps tomorrow night, if you're free."

"That's what I want to talk to you about," I said. "Listen, suppose we do this: I'll pick up a pizza and something to drink and hustle it over to your place while the pie is still warm. Or you can heat it up in your oven. How does that sound?"

"Marvelous – if you're sure you want to do it."

"I do," I said. "Be there within the hour."

Recently a new pizzeria had opened on Federal Highway south of the Port of Palm Beach. If offered "designer pizzas" to be consumed on the premises or taken out in insulated boxes. I had tried it a few times and found the fare rather exotic. But then I'm strictly a pepperoni addict.

I drove to the pizza boutique to purchase a pie for Meg. I selected one consisting of eggplant, sun-dried tomatoes, and Gorgonzola on a thin crust. I was reminded of the time Peaches had barfed on my lavender loafers, but I was certain the vegetarian Ms. Trumble would love it. I also bought a six-pack of Diet Pepsi, my dream of a frozen daiquiri vanishing.

Meg opened the door for me with a broad smile and a cheek kiss, on the same spot favored by Connie Garcia not too many hours previously. As Willy Loman pointed out, it's important to be well-liked.

Meg looked smashing. She had obviously just showered; her spiky hair was still damp and her face was shiny. She was wearing white duck short-shorts and a skimpy knitted top that left her midriff bare. I swear that rib cage was designed by Brancusi.

Also, she smelled good.

Her apartment was crowded with unpacked suitcases, cartons, and bulging shopping bags. She cleared a space on a clunky cocktail table for the pizza box and brought us both iced Pepsis. She didn't bother heating up the pie but immediately began wolfing it down, occasionally rolling her eyes and uttering, "Yum!"

"Good lord," I said, "didn't you have anything to eat today?"

"A country breakfast at seven this morning," she said. "I'm really famished."

"I should think so. Meg, did you call me from your phone here?"

She shook her head. "From a gas station. But my phone will be connected in the morning. They promised."

"Fine," I said. "I may need to call. About tomorrow night, Meg – how would you like to go to a séance with me?"

I was afraid she might refuse or think the whole idea so hysterically off-the-wall that I wouldn't be able to introduce her to the Glorianas as a serious student of spiritualism. But she surprised me.

"Love to," she said promptly. "Laverne and I used to go to them all the time. I didn't know you were interested in New Age things."

"Oh yes," I lied brazenly. "I'm deep into crystals, ESP, telepathy, and all that. I've arranged a private séance with a local medium, her husband, and mother-in-law for tomorrow evening. The psychic is supposed to be very gifted. I've never attended a séance before, so I'm looking forward to it. You'll go with me then?"

"Of course. What time?"

"Nine o'clock. I thought we'd have dinner first. Suppose I pick you up at seven."

"I'll be ready," she said. She licked her fingers, crossed her sleek legs, settled back with her drink. She had demolished the entire pizza. But of course it was only the eight-inch size.

"That was delicious," she proclaimed. "Thank you, Archy; you saved my life. I wish I had something stronger than Pepsi to offer you. I'm going to load up the fridge tomorrow, get this place organized, and then start looking for clients."

"I'm glad you mentioned that," I said and handed her the list of potential customers I had prepared.

"Wonderful," she said, scanning the names. "I'm so glad you didn't forget. How can I ever thank you?"

I gave her my Groucho Marx leer. "I'll think of something," I said.

She laughed. "Oh, Archy," she said, "what a clown

158

you are. Would you mind awfully if we skipped tonight? Right now I want to get unpacked and catch a million Z's."

"Of course," I said, upper lip stiffening. "You must be exhausted after all that driving." I stood up to leave. "I'll see you at seven tomorrow night, Meg."

She came close and hugged me tightly. I was breathlessly aware of her muscled arms. "Tomorrow will be different," she whispered. "I promise."

"Sleep well," I said as lightly as I could. I drove home thinking there really should be an over-the-counter remedy that cures habitual hoping.

Roderick Gillsworth didn't call that night – for which I was grateful.

10

Why do men's jackets and shirts button left over right while women's button right over left? I have asked this question of people at cocktail parties, and they invariably give me a frozen smile and move away.

But I'm sure there is an explanation for this buttoning conundrum that is at once profound and simple. I felt the same way about the disappearance of Peaches and the murder of Lydia Gillsworth. Those twin mysteries had a logical and satisfying solution if I could but find it.

I spent Wednesday morning slowly going over my

journal, reading every entry twice. I found nothing that even hinted at some devilish plot that would account for a missing *Felis domestica* and the death of a poet's wife. All my diary contained was a jumble of facts and impressions. I could only pray that the séance that evening would yield a spectral suggestion that might inspire me.

I drove to the office and found on my desk, sealed in an envelope, a memo from Tim Hogan, temporary chief of our real estate section. It concerned the Glorianas' office and condo.

The commercial suite on Clematis Street had been leased for a year. The Glorianas had put up two months' rent as security but were currently a month behind in their payments. Similarly, their apartment had not been purchased but was rented on a month-to-month basis. At the moment, the Glorianas were current on their rent.

In both cases the references given were a bank and individuals in Atlanta. Hogan had thoughtfully provided names and addresses, but mentioned he could find no record of the references ever having been checked. That was unusual but not unheard of in the freewheeling world of South Florida real estate.

I called Sgt. Rogoff and told him what I had.

"Why don't you check them out, Al?" I suggested. "Just for the fun of it."

"Yeah," he said, "I will. But first I think I'll contact the Atlanta cops. Just in case."

"Do that," I urged. "It's the first real lead we've had on where the Glorianas operated before they arrived here."

I gave him the names and addresses of the Glorianas' references, and he promised to get back to me as soon as he had something. At that point I had no idea of where I might turn next in my discreet inquiries, so I decided to drive over to Worth Avenue and see if I could buy a tennis bracelet for Connie at a price that wouldn't land me in debtors' prison.

Then fate took a beneficent hand in the investigation – which proves that if you are pure of heart and eat your Wheaties, good things can happen to you.

I went down to the garage to board the Miata for the short drive over to Worth. Herb, our lumbering security guard, had come out of his glass cubicle and was leaning down to stroke the head of a cat rubbing against his shins. I strolled over.

"Got a new friend, Herb?" I asked.

He looked up at me. "A stray, Mr. McNally," he said. "He just came wandering down the ramp."

That had to be the longest, skinniest cat I had ever seen. It was a dusty black with a dirty-white blaze on its chest. One ear was hanging limply and looked bloodied. And the poor animal obviously hadn't had a decent table d'hôte in weeks; its ribs and pelvic bones were poking.

But despite its miserable condition, it seemed to be in a lighthearted mood. It purred loudly under Herb's caresses, then came over to sniff at my shoes. I leaned to scratch under the chin. It liked that.

"Looks hungry, Herb," I said.

"Sure does," he said. "Maybe I'll run up to the cafeteria and get it something to eat."

"*Our* cafeteria?" I said. "You're liable to be arrested for cruelty to animals. Are you going to adopt it?"

"Mebbe," he said. "But if I take it home with me, it's liable to get into my tropical fish tanks. You think it would be all right if I kept it around here? I'll bet it's a great mouser."

"It's okay with me," I said, "if you're willing to take care of it."

"I think I should take it to the vet first," he said worriedly. "I'll have that ear fixed up and get it a bath."

I stared down at the stray, and I swear it grinned at me.

161

That was one devil-may-care cat. It looked a little like Errol Flynn in *The Charge of the Light Brigade*.

"You're going to be okay," the guard said, addressing his new pal. "The vet'll fix you up like new."

That's when it hit me. I clapped Herb on the shoulder. "God bless you," I said hoarsely, and he probably thought I was approving his kindness to a wounded and homeless beast.

I immediately returned to my office and dug out the Yellow Pages for what Southern Bell called Greater West Palm Beach. I turned to the listings for Veterinarians.

This was my reasoning: suppose Peaches got sick while she was in the custody of the catnappers. That was possible, wasn't it? In fact, it was likely when the irascible animal found herself being held prisoner by strangers in unfamiliar surroundings. The thieves wouldn't want to risk the health of their fifty-grand hostage, so they'd hustle her to a vet. All I had to do was contact local veterinarians and ask if they had recently treated a fat, silver-gray Persian with a mean disposition.

It was a long shot, I admitted, but at the moment I didn't have any short shots.

But my brainstorm fizzled when I took a look at the Veterinarian listings in the Yellow Pages. There were pages and pages of them, seemingly hundreds of DVMs. It would take S. Holmes and a regiment of the Baker Street Irregulars a month of Sundays to check out all those names and addresses. Good idea, I decided, but damned impossible to carry out.

But then my roving eye fell on a short section headed Veterinarian Emergency Service and listed animal clinics and hospitals open twenty-four hours a day. The roster contained only fifteen names and addresses, some as far afield as Boynton Beach. It seemed reasonable to guess that if Peaches became ill, her captors would rush her to

162

the nearest emergency facility.

I was back in business again!

I scissored out the vital section and with my gold Mont Blanc I carefully circled the animal emergency wards in the West Palm Beach area. There were seven of them. I estimated I could visit all seven in two days, or perhaps more if I became bored with routine snooping.

Now the only problem that remained was devising a scenario that would insure cooperation at all those infirmaries for ailing faunas. I mean I couldn't just barge in, describe Peaches, and demand to know if they had treated a cat like that lately. The medicos would call the gendarmes for sure and tell them to bring a large butterfly net.

No, what I needed was an imaginary tale that would arouse interest and eager response. In other words, a twenty-four-karat scam. Here is what I came up with:

"Good morning! My name is Archibald McNally and here is my business card. I have a problem I hope you will be able to help me with. I returned from a business trip last night and found on my answering machine a message from a close friend, a lady friend, who apparently had arrived in West Palm Beach during my absence. The message was frantic. Her cat – she always travels with her beloved Peaches – had suddenly become ill and she was rushing it to an emergency animal hospital. But the poor dear was so hysterical that she neglected to inform me where she was staying or to which clinic she was taking her sick pet. I wonder if you could tell me if you have treated such an animal recently and have the address of the owner. It would help me enormously."

I would then describe Peaches.

It seemed to me a plea that would be hard to resist. Naturally I didn't know if the catnapper was male or female, but I planned to put in that bit about a "lady friend" to suggest a romantic attachment that might evoke sympathy. Emerson said all mankind love a lover – but of course he never met Fatty Arbuckle.

Anyway, that's how I spent Wednesday afternoon – driving to four animal hospitals and putting on my act. In all four the receptionist was a young woman, and I would bestow upon her my most winning 100-watt smile and launch into my spiel. The results? Nil.

But I was not discouraged. In fact, as I drove back to the beach for my ocean swim, I was delighted that my monologue had been readily accepted at all four facilities I visited. Although none of them had treated a feline of Peaches' description, all were cooperative in searching their records and sorrowful when they could not provide the assistance requested.

I had my swim and returned to my chambers to prepare for the family cocktail hour, my dinner with Meg Trumble, and the séance with the Glorianas that was to follow. I decided to dress soberly, if not somberly: navy tropical worsted suit, white shirt, maroon tie. But examining myself in the full-length mirror, I realized I looked a bit too much like a mortician, so I exchanged the maroon cravat for a silk jacquard number with a hand-painted design of oriental lilies. Much better.

Over martinis that evening, mother remarked that I looked "very smart." Father took one glance at the lilies, and a single eyebrow shot up in a conditioned reflex. But all he said was, "Gillsworth has returned. He phoned me late this afternoon."

"Is he ready to execute a new will?" I asked.

The patriarch frowned. "He said he would call me next week and set up an appointment. I would have preferred an earlier date – tomorrow, if possible – and told him so. But he said he hadn't yet decided on specific bequests and needed more time. I do believe the man was stalling, but

164

for what purpose I cannot conceive."

"Prescott," mother said softly, "some people find it very difficult to make out a will. It can be a wrenching emotional experience."

"Nonsense," he said. "We're all going to die and it's only prudent to prepare for it. I wrote out my first holographic will at the age of nine."

I laughed. "What possessions did you have to leave at that age, father?"

"All my marbles," he declared.

A derisive comment on that admission was obvious, but I didn't have the courage to utter it.

Later, as I drove northward to Riviera Beach, the problem of Roderick Gillsworth's last will and testament was eclipsed by a more immediate quandary; to wit, where was I going to take Meg Trumble for dinner?

It had to be close enough so that we could arrive at the séance at the time dictated by Mrs. Irma Gloriana. And yet it had to be distant enough and relatively secluded so I had a fighting chance of not being seen in Meg's company by Connie Garcia or any of her corps de snitches.

I finally decided on a Middle Eastern restaurant on 45th Street not far from an area known as Mangonia Park. It was a very small bistro, only six booths, but I had been there once before and thought the food superb, if you liked grape leaves. However, it did have one drawback: it had no bar; only beer and wine were served. But, paraphrasing the Good Book, I consoled myself with the thought that man doth not live by vodka alone.

Meg was ready when I arrived, which was a pleasant surprise. Another was her appearance. She wore a short-sleeved dress of silk crepe divided into two panels of solid color, fuchsia and orange. Sounds awful, I know, but it looked great. It had a jewel neckline, but her only accessories were gold seahorse earrings. Meg still had most of her Florida tan, and she looked so slender, vibrant, and healthy that I immediately resolved to lose weight, grow muscles, and drink nothing but seltzer on the rocks.

I whisked her to the Café Istanbul, assuring her that although it might appear funky, it had become the *in* place for discriminating gourmets. That wasn't a *big* lie, just a slight exaggeration to increase her enjoyment of dining in a joint that had nothing but belly dance music on the jukebox.

It turned out that Meg was fascinated by the place and relaxed her vegetarian discipline sufficiently to order moussaka. I had rotisseried lamb on curried rice. We shared a big salad that was mostly black olives that really were the pits and pickled cauliflower buds. I also ordered a half-bottle of chilled retsina. Meg tried one small sip, then opted for a Coke, so I was forced, *forced*, to drink the entire bottle myself.

It was over the honey-drenched baklava that I finally got around to the séance we were about to attend.

"I didn't know you and your sister were interested in spiritualism," I said as casually as I could.

"Laverne more than me," Meg said. "She's into all that stuff. I think she's had her horoscope done by a dozen astrologers, and she always sleeps with a crystal under her pillow."

"I wonder if she knows Hertha Gloriana, the medium we're going to visit tonight."

"I've never heard her mention the name, but that's understandable. Harry goes into orbit if anyone brings up the subject of parapsychology. He thinks it's all a great big swindle. Do you, Archy?"

The direct question troubled me. "I just don't know," I confessed. "That's one of the reasons I'm looking forward to the session tonight. Meg, do you believe it's possible to communicate with ghosts?"

166

"Of course," she said promptly. "I went to a séance once and talked to my grandmother. I never knew her; she's been dead for fifty years. But her spirit knew things about our family that were true and that the medium couldn't possibly have known."

"Did your grandmother's spirit tell you where she was?"

"In Heaven," Meg said simply, and I finished the retsina.

We arrived at the Glorianas' residence ten minutes before the appointed hour. The family was assembled in that rather shoddy living room, and I introduced Meg. The greetings of Irma and Frank were courteous enough, although not heavy on the cordiality. But Hertha welcomed Meg warmly, held her hand a moment while gazing deeply into her eyes.

"An Aries," she said. "Aren't you?"

"Why, yes," Meg said. "How did you know?"

Hertha only smiled and turned to me. "And how are you tonight, Pisces?" she asked.

She was right again. But of course she could easily have researched my birthday. In all modesty, I must admit my vital statistics are listed in a thin booklet titled: *Palm Beach's Most Eligible Bachelors.* And I could guess how she knew Meg's natal date.

Hertha was wearing a long, flowing gown of lavender georgette which I thought more suitable for a garden party than a séance. Irma Gloriana wore a black, wide-shouldered pant-suit with a mannish shirt and paisley ascot. Son Frank, that fop, flaunted a double-breasted Burberry blazer in white wool with gold buttons. He made me look like an IRS auditor, damn him.

No refreshments were offered, and no preparatory instructions or explanations given. We all moved into a dimly lighted dining room. There, leaves had been

167

removed from an oval oak table, converting it to a round that accommodated the five of us comfortably. The chairs were straightbacked, the seats thinly padded.

I was placed between Irma and Frank. He held Hertha's left hand while Meg grasped her right. From the top of the table, moving clockwise, we were Hertha, Frank, Archy, Irma, Meg. An odd seating arrangement, I thought: the two men side-by-side, and the three women. But perhaps there was a reason for it.

Hertha looked around the circle slowly with that intent, unblinking gaze of hers. And she spoke slowly, too, in her low, breathy voice.

"Please, everyone," she said, "clasp hands tightly. Close your eyes and turn your thoughts to Xatyl, the Mayan shaman who is my channel to the hereafter. With all your spiritual strength try to *will* Xatyl to appear to me."

At first, eyes firmly shut, all I was conscious of was Frank's muscular handclasp and the softer, warmer, moister hand of his mother. But then I tried to think of Xatyl. I had no idea of what a Mayan shaman looked like – certainly not like any member of the Pelican Club – so I concentrated on the name, silently repeating Xatyl, Xatyl, Xatyl, like a mantra.

I thought five soundless minutes must have passed before I heard Hertha speak again in a voice that had become a flat drone.

"Xatyl appears," she reported. "Dimly. From the mists. Greetings, Xatyl, from your supplicants."

The next words I heard were a shock. Not their meaning as much as the tone in which they were uttered. It was the frail, cracked voice of an old man, a worn voice that quavered and sometimes paused weakly.

"Greetings from the beyond," Xatyl said. "I bring you love from a high priest of the Mayan people."

I opened my eyes to stare at Hertha. The words were issuing from her mouth, no doubt of it, but I could scarcely believe that ancient, tremulous voice was hers. I shut my eyes again, grateful for the handholds of Irma and Frank to anchor me to reality.

"Who wishes to contact one of the departed?" Hertha asked in her normal voice.

"I do," Meg Trumble said at once. "I would like to speak to my father, John Trumble, who passed on eight years ago."

"I have heard," the Xatyl voice said. "Be patient, my child."

We waited in silence several long moments. I must tell you honestly that I didn't know what to make of all this. But I confess I was moved by what was going on and had absolutely no inclination to laugh.

"Meg," a man said, "is it you?"

Now the voice was virile, almost booming, and I opened my eyes just wide enough to see the words were being spoken by Hertha.

I heard Meg's sudden, sharp intake of breath. "Yes, dad," she said. "I am here. Are you all right?"

"I am contented since mother joined me last year. Now we are together again as we had prayed. Meg, are you still doing your exercises?"

"Oh yes, dad," she said with a sobbing laugh. "I'm still at it. How is your arthritis?"

"There is no pain here, daughter," John Trumble said. "We are free of your world's suffering. Have you married, Meg?"

"No, father, not yet."

"You must marry," he said gently. "Your mother and I want you to be as happy as we were and are. I must go now, Meg. If you need me, I am here, I am here."

The voice trailed away, and I could hear Meg's

quiet weeping.

"Please," Hertha whispered, "do not let our psychic power weaken. Clasp hands firmly and think only of the other world."

There was silence a few moments, then I heard again the trembling voice of Xatyl.

"There is one among you who is deeply troubled," he said. "Let him speak out now."

"Yes," I said impulsively, hiding behind my closed eyes. "My name is Archibald McNally. I wish to contact Lydia Gillsworth, a friend. She passed over a few days ago."

"I will summon her," Xatyl said. "Be patient, my son."

Once again we waited several minutes. I found myself gripping the hands of Irma and Frank so tightly that my fingers ached, and I was conscious of hyperventilating.

"Archy?" a woman's voice asked. "Is that you?"

After I heard my name I opened my eyes to verify that it was Hertha speaking, but I swear, I *swear* it was Lydia Gillsworth's sweet, peaceful voice. So dulcet.

"It is I, Lydia," I found myself saying, almost choking on the words. "Are you well?"

"Oh yes, Archy," she said, a hint of laughter in her voice. "It is as I told you it would be. Have you read the books I loaned you?"

"Some. Not all."

"You must read *all* of them, dear. The truth is there, Archy."

"Lydia," I said, eager to ask *the* question, "you must tell me another truth: who killed you?"

There was no answer. Just silence. I tried again.

"Please tell me," I implored. "I can never rest until I know. Who murdered you, Lydia?"

What happened next shocked and galvanized us.

"Caprice!" Lydia Gillsworth's voice shrieked.

170

"Caprice!"

Handclasps were loosened, four of us rose, stared at Hertha. She was still seated, head thrown back, bare throat straining. And she continued to scream, "Caprice! Caprice! Caprice!" But now it was her voice, not Lydia's.

Meg Trumble got to her first, held her arms, spoke soothing words. We all clustered around, and gradually those piercing screams diminished. Hertha opened her eyes, looked about wildly. She was ashen, shivering uncontrollably.

Frank left hastily and came back in a moment with a shot glass of what appeared to be brandy. Meg took it from him and held it gently to the medium's lips. Hertha took a small sip, coughed, stared at us and her surroundings as if finally realizing where she was. She took the glass from Meg's fingers and gulped greedily.

We stayed in the dining room until Hertha's color had returned and she was able to stand, somewhat shakily. She gave us a small, apologetic smile, and then we all moved back to the living room.

Frank had the decency to bring us ponies of brandy, and since Meg wouldn't touch hers, I had a double – and needed it. I sat in one corner with Irma and Frank. Across the room, on the couch, Meg Trumble comforted the medium, her muscled arm around the other woman's shoulders. She spoke to her and stroked her hair.

"What on earth happened?" I asked Irma.

She shrugged. "Hertha heard or saw something that terrified her. And she became hysterical. It's happened a few times before. I told you she is a very sensitive and vulnerable spirit."

"Caprice," Frank said, looking at me. "That's what she was screaming. Does that mean anything to you, Mr. McNally?"

I shook my head. "A caprice is a whim, an unplanned

action. Perhaps Lydia Gillsworth was trying to tell us that the killer acted on a sudden impulse, and her murder was totally unpremeditated."

"Yes," Irma said, "I'm sure that was it."

"I'm sorry now that I asked the question," I said. "I didn't mean to frighten Hertha. But I did inform you that I intended to ask."

"No one blames you," Irma said. "There are many things in this world and the next that are beyond our understanding."

Hamlet said it better, but I didn't remind her of that. "You're so right, Mrs. Gloriana," I said.

She nodded. "Did you bring your credit card, Mr. McNally?"

I handed it over; she and Frank left the room to prepare my bill. I remained seated, finishing Meg's brandy and watching the two women on the couch. Hertha seemed fully recovered now. She and Meg were close together, holding hands and giggling like schoolgirls. I found it a bit off-putting.

Irma returned with my bill. I signed it, reclaimed my plastic; and took my receipt.

"I'm sorry the séance ended the way it did," she said. "But I would not call it a total failure, would you?"

"Far from it," I said. "Meg was able to speak to her father and I made contact with Mrs. Gillsworth. I'm perfectly satisfied."

"Good," she said. "Then perhaps you'd like to arrange another private session."

"Of course I would. Let me check my schedule and speak to Meg about a date that will be suitable for her. You'll be here all summer?"

"Oh yes. We have many activities to keep us busy."

"Then you'll be hearing from me."

"When?" she asked.

172

A demon saleswoman, this one.

"Soon," I said, stood up, and motioned to Meg.

I shook hands with all the Glorianas before we left. Meg did the same, but then Hertha embraced her, kissed her on the lips, clung to her a moment. In gratitude for Meg's sympathetic ministrations. No doubt.

On the drive back to Riviera Beach Meg was so voluble that I could scarcely believe this was the same woman who had been so reticent on our first ride together.

"What a *wonderful* medium she is, Archy," she burbled. "So *gifted*. She knew so *many* things about me. And it was so *great* to talk to dad. Wasn't it *incredible* to hear all those voices coming from *her*? And guess what: I told her I hope to become a personal trainer, and she *insisted* on being my first client. Isn't that *marvelous*?"

"Yes."

"And she's going to do my horoscope – for *free*! It must be *scary* having the talent to see into the beyond. She said she usually refuses to predict the future, but after she does my horoscope she'll tell me what she sees ahead for me. Isn't that *fantastic*?"

I didn't want to rain on her parade, so I neither voiced my doubts nor cautioned her against relying on the predictions of a seer. It seemed unnecessarily cruel to tell her my own reactions to what we had just experienced. Being essentially without faith myself, I think it rather infra dig to mock the faith of others.

We arrived outside Meg's apartment, and now her initial ebullience had faded and she was speaking calmly and seriously of spirituality and how she had neglected that side of her nature and really should start seeking answers to what she termed the "big questions." I presumed they included Life, Death, and why only one sock got lost in the laundry.

Somehow it didn't seem the right moment to remind

her of her carnal promise of the previous evening. So, rather than risk rejection, I said:

"Meg, would you mind awfully if I didn't come in? I feel totally shattered by what happened tonight – hearing Lydia Gillsworth's voice and all that. I think I better go home and try to figure things out."

She promptly agreed – so promptly that she severely bruised the ego of A. McNally, who may or may not be suffering from a Don Juan complex.

"I think that would be best, dear," she said in the kindliest way imaginable, patting my hand. "I'm as emotionally wired as you. We'll make it another time, Archy."

So I drove home alone, howling curses at a full moon and wondering why Hertha Gloriana had granted Meg a farewell kiss and not the laughing cavalier who had picked up the tab. Did the medium bestow her osculations freely without regard for sex, age, race, color, or national origin? Was she, in fact, an Equal Opportunity kisser?

I went directly to my rooms when I arrived home. I stripped off the dull costume I was wearing and donned my favorite kimono, a jaunty silk number printed with an overall pattern of leaping gazelles. Then I put on reading glasses, sat at my desk, and went to work.

I was determined to play the devils advocate, to view the evening's events as a cynic who completely disbelieved in alleged manifestations of the occult and had a perfectly rational explanation for what others might consider evidence of the supernatural.

I scribbled furiously, and this is what I came up with:
Hertha's knowledge of Meg Trumble:

Meg's sister, Laverne, was a client of the Glorianas and quite likely had her horoscope prepared by the medium. Hertha could easily be aware of Meg's birthdate, the death of her parents, Meg's interest in physical exercise.

174

The voices:

Of course no one was familiar with the voice of Xatyl, the Mayan shaman, and it would be relatively simple for an actress with a gift of mimicry to imitate the speech of an old man. The voice of John Trumble might offer a problem, but the man had been dead for eight years, and it was doubtful if Meg remembered the exact sound of his voice. More importantly, she *wanted* to believe and was eager to accept any masculine voice as that of her departed father.

Lydia Gillsworth's voice would be easy for Hertha to reproduce since Lydia had been present at several séances and was well known to the medium.

Hertha's knowledge of Archy McNally:

I have already speculated on how my date of birth might have been learned by the Glorianas. And I had mentioned to Irma at our first meeting that I had been reading books on spiritualism. I hadn't revealed that they had been loaned to me by Mrs. Gillsworth, but Lydia had attended her final séance *after* lending me the books and could have casually mentioned that she was assisting me.

I read over what I had written. I didn't claim that all my explanations and suppositions were one hundred percent accurate. But they *could* be. And they certainly had as much or more claim to the truth than ascribing all the revelations made by the medium to paranormal powers. If you had to bet, where would you put *your* money?

But acting the disbeliever and applying cold logic to the occurrences at the séance failed in one vital and bewildering instance. That was the medium's screams "Caprice! Caprice!" in answer to my query as to the identity of the murderer of Lydia Gillsworth. Those shocking screams had been uttered in the voices of both Lydia and Hertha.

I had told Irma and Frank Gloriana that the outburst probably meant that the killer had acted on a whim, a

175

sudden impulse, and the murder was unpremeditated. That was pure malarkey, of course. I thought I knew what that shrieked "Caprice! Caprice!" really signified.

It was the car in which Lydia Gillsworth had driven home to her death.

11

I set out detecting on Thursday morning sans beret – which was certainly more socially acceptable than setting out sans-culotte. It was my intention to visit the remaining three animal hospitals on my list, and I feared outre headgear might tarnish the image I wished to project: a worried swain seeking his lost love and her ailing cat.

But first I had a small chore to perform and phoned Roderick Gillsworth.

"Good morning, Rod," I said. "Archy McNally. Welcome home."

"Thank you, Archy," he said. "You have no idea how wonderful it is to be home."

"Rough time?" I inquired.

"Rough enough," he said. "I meant to call you Tuesday night after the funeral, but I had a duel with a bottle of California brandy. The bottle won."

"That's all right," I said. "There was nothing new to report anyway. Rod, I'd like to return your house keys. Will you be home this morning?"

Short pause. Then: "Only for another half-hour. I have some errands to run – supermarket shopping and all that. Including a liquor store so I can return your vodka."

"Don't worry about that. Could I pop over now? It'll just take a minute; I won't linger."

"Sure," he said, "come ahead."

When I arrived at the Gillsworth home, his gray Bentley was parked on the bricked driveway. I admired that vehicle. Subdued elegance. A bit staid for my taste but undeniably handsome.

I rang the bell, Rod opened the door, and I blinked. He usually wore solid blues, whites, and blacks, nothing flashy. But that morning he was clad in lime-green slacks with yellow patent leather loafers, complete with fringed tongues. And over a pink polo shirt was a Lilly Pulitzer sport jacket.

I don't know if you're familiar with that garment, but about twenty years ago it was de rigueur for the young bloods of Palm Beach. Ms. Pulitzer doted on flower prints, and a jacket of her fabric made every dude a walking hothouse. Rod's was a bouquet of daisies, mini carnations, and Dolores roses.

He saw my surprise and gave me an embarrassed smile. "A transformation," he said. "What?"

"Quite," I said.

"Lydia found the jacket in a thrift shop," he said. "A perfect fit, but I never had the courage to wear it. I'm wearing it now for her. You understand?"

I nodded, thinking that chintzy jacket had to be the world's strangest memorial.

"Come on in, Archy," he said. "Too early in the morning to offer you an eye-opener, I suppose."

"By about two hours," I said. "But thanks for the thought."

I moved inside and we stood talking in the hallway.

177

"Here are the keys, Rod," I said handing them over. "Everything all right in the house when you returned?"

"Shipshape. Thank you for your trouble. And you've learned nothing new about the investigation from Sergeant Rogoff?"

"Not a word. The poison-pen letters Lydia received have been sent to the FBI lab for analysis. Rogoff should be getting a report soon."

"Do you think he'll tell you what the report says?"

"Probably."

"Then I wish you'd tell me," he said, and added testily, "That man simply refuses to let me know what's going on."

I had no desire to listen again to his complaints against Al, so I changed the subject. "By the way, Rod," I remarked, "I had an unusual experience last night. I attended a séance at the Glorianas'."

His face twisted into a tight smile. "Did you now? Good lord, I haven't been to one of those things in ages. I didn't know you were interested in spiritualism."

"Curiosity mostly," I said. "And the Glorianas are fascinating people."

He considered a moment. "Yes," he said finally, "I suppose you could call them fascinating. Lydia always said that the medium had a genuine psychic gift. Did Hertha tell you anything?"

"Nothing I didn't already know," I said. Then a question occurred to me. "Incidentally, Rod, do you happen to know if Irma, the mother-in-law, is widowed, divorced – or what? I was wondering and of course I didn't want to ask her directly. It would have sounded too much like prying."

Again he paused a moment before answering. Then: "I believe Lydia mentioned that Irma is a widow. Yes, now I recall; her husband was an army officer, killed in the Korean War."

"A strong woman," I opined. "Domineering."

"Do you really think so?" he said. "That's a bit extreme, isn't it? Dominant perhaps, but not domineering."

"You poets," I said, smiling. "You make a nice distinction between adjectives."

"I hate adjectives," he said. "And adverbs. They're so weak and floppy. Don't you agree?"

"Indubitably," I said, and we both laughed.

Your hero drove away wondering and happy. Wondering why the bird had suddenly transmogrified from crow to peacock, and happy that I had picked up another item to add to my journal: Mrs. Irma Gloriana was a widow.

I tooled over to West Palm Beach and started my search. It would add immeasurably to the dramatic impact of this narrative if I could detail fruitless visits to two emergency animal clinics and then conclude triumphantly by telling you I struck paydirt at the last on my list. But I have resolved to make this account as honest as is humanly possible, so I must confess that I succeeded at the first hospital I canvassed.

I performed my song and dance for the receptionist, a comely young miss. She seemed sympathetic and spoke into an intercom. In a moment a veterinarian exited from an inner office and accosted me. He was wearing a long white doctors' jacket with five – count 'em, five! – ballpoint pens clipped to a plastic shield in his breast pocket. He was a short, twitchy character who appeared to be of nerdish extraction.

I repeated my fictional plea, and he blinked furiously at me from behind smudged spectacles. I returned his flickering stare with a look I tried to make as honest and sincere as possible.

Apparently it worked, for he said in a reedy voice, "I have recently treated a female cat such as you describe,

179

but a man brought her in, not a lady."

"A man?" I said thoughtfully. "That was undoubtedly her uncle. He frequently travels with her to prevent her being propositioned by uncouth strangers. She is an extremely attractive young woman. Could you describe the man, please, doctor?"

"Tall," he said. "Reddish hair. Broad-shouldered. Very well-dressed in a conservative way. About sixty-five or so, I'd guess."

"Her uncle to a T," I cried. "I'm enormously relieved. And was Peaches seriously ill?"

"I cannot divulge that information," he said sternly. "Medical ethics."

"Of course," I said hastily. "Completely understandable. Would you be willing to give me their address, sir? I'm eager to offer them what assistance I can."

He went back into his office and returned a few minutes later to hand me a scribbled Post-It note.

"The man's name is Charles Girard," he said. "On Federal Highway. A strange address for someone as prosperous as he seemed to be."

"A temporary residence, I'm sure," I said. "I believe Mr. Girard and his niece are on their way to the Lesser Antilles. Thank you so much for your cooperation, doctor."

I had noticed a glass jar on the receptionist's desk. It bore a label requesting contributions for the feeding and rehabilitation of stray felines. The jar was half-filled with coins. I extracted a twenty-dollar bill from my wallet and stuffed it into the jar.

"For the hungry kitties," I said piously.

The vet blinked even more rapidly. "You are very generous," he commented.

"My pleasure," I said, and meant it.

I boogied out to the Miata. I was very, *very* pleased

with the triumph of my charade. Surely you recall Danton's prescription for victory: "Audacity, more audacity, always audacity." How true, how true!

The veterinarian had been correct about the address given him by Charles Girard: it *was* a strange neighborhood. The buildings on that stretch of Federal Highway appeared to have been erected fifty years ago and never painted since. They were mostly one- and two-story commercial structures housing a boggling variety of businesses: taverns, used car lots, fast-food joints, and a depressing plethora of stores selling sickroom equipment and supplies.

But there were many vacant shops with FOR RENT signs in their dusty windows. There was something inexpressibly forlorn and defeated about the entire area, as if the Florida of shining malls and gleaming plazas had passed it by, leaving it to crumble away in the hot sun and salt wind.

I found the address the vet had provided. It proved to be a motel, and when I tell you it consisted of a dozen individual cabins, you can estimate when it was built. I guessed the late 1940s. I drove past and left the Miata in a small parking area beside a seemingly deserted enterprise that sold plastic lawn and patio furniture.

I walked slowly back to the Jo-Jean Motel and entered the office. It was not air conditioned, but a wood-bladed ceiling fan revolved lazily. A large, florid lady was perched on a stool behind the counter, bending over one of those supermarket newspapers that everyone denies reading and which sells about five million copies a week. She didn't look up when I came in.

"I beg your pardon," I said loudly, "but I'm looking for Mr. Charles Girard."

"South row, Cabin Four," she said, still perusing her tabloid. I could read the big headline upside down. It

181

said: "Baby Born Whistling 'Dixie'."

I went out into that searing sunlight again, found the south row of cabins. Then I stopped, stared, turned around, and walked hastily back to my Miata.

Parked alongside Cabin Four was Roderick Gillsworth's gray Bentley.

I headed back to the McNally Building, reflecting that I had refused Gillsworth's offer of an eye-opener that morning, but he had certainly provided one now. I was totally flummoxed. I couldn't conjure up even the most fantastic scenario to account for the poet visiting a man who apparently had catnapped Harry Willigan's pride and joy. It made absolutely no sense to me whatsoever.

And that turned out to be a mistake. I was looking for rationality in a plot that might have been devised by the Three Stooges.

I was making a turn off Federal when it suddenly occurred to me that the Pelican Club was only a few minutes' drive away. The sun was inching toward the yardarm, and I decided that refreshment, liquid and solid, in a cool, dim haven was needed to clear my muddle-headedness and get the old ganglia vibrating again.

I lunched alone, waited upon by the saucy Priscilla. Ordinarily we'd have had a bout of chivying, but Pris recognized my mood, and after taking my order left me alone with my problems. I scarfed determinedly through a giant cheeseburger and a bowl of cold potato salad, and by the time I started on my second schooner of Heineken draft, the McNally spirits were bubbling once again. I finished lunch by devouring a wedge of key lime pie while silently reciting those fatuous lines from Henley's "Invictus," although I wasn't positive I was the captain of my soul. More like a Private First Class.

I paid my bill at the bar. Simon Pettibone was wearing a striped shirt with sleeve garters and a small black leather bow tie. With his square spectacles and tight helmet of gray hair, he radiated the wisdom and understanding of an upright publican familiar with all the world's enigmas.

"Mr. Pettibone," I said, "I need your advice."

"No charge, Mr. McNally," he said.

"I have a small puzzle I'm trying to solve. There are two men utterly dissimilar in occupation and probably education and personal wealth. Now what could those two men possibly have in common?"

Mr. Pettibone stared at me a moment. *"Cherchez la femme,"* he said.

I could have hugged him! I was convinced he had it exactly right, and I was determined to follow his counsel. Unfortunately, as events later proved, I cherchezed the wrong femme.

I stopped briefly at the office, hoping Al Rogoff might have left a message to call him. I wanted to learn if the FBI report had been received and what it contained. I also needed to know if he had spoken to the Atlanta PD about the Glorianas. But there was no message from the sergeant, so I phoned him. He was not available and I left my own message.

Then, acting on Mr. Pettibone's advice, I drove over to Ocean Boulevard and headed south for the Willigans' home. I decided it was time to play the heavy with Laverne, to lean on her enough to discover her relationship with Hertha, the kissing medium.

The lady was home, but Leon Medallion informed me she was having her "bawth" and he'd ask the maid when Mrs. Willigan would be receiving. All very upper class and impressive until you remembered the lord of the manor was a lout. So I cooled my heels in the tiled foyer until the butler returned and notified me I had been granted an audience with milady.

I found Laverne in the master suite, which looked like

183

it had been decorated by someone who specialized in Persian bordellos. I've never seen such a profusion of silken draperies, porcelain knick-knacks, and embroidered pillows. Instead of Laverne, it should have been Theda Bara reclining on that pink satin chaise longue, swaddled in a robe of purple brocade so voluminous it seemed to go around her three times.

"Hiya, Archy," the siren sang. "What's up?"

"Why didn't you tell me you knew Hertha Gloriana?" I demanded, figuring it would stun her.

But she wasn't at all discombobulated. "Because I was afraid you'd tell Harry," she said calmly. "I already told you how he hates all that stuff. He calls it 'fortune-telling bullshit.' If he knew I was going to the Glorianas' séances, he'd break my face."

"Did you go to the one Lydia Gillsworth attended on the night she was killed?"

"No," she said, looking at me wide-eyed. "I had to go to a builders' association dinner with Harry that night. If you don't believe me, ask the Glorianas; they'll tell you I wasn't there. But why all the sudden interest in spiritualism?"

"Because I asked Hertha's help in finding Peaches."

I thought she'd be furious because I had ignored her instructions, but she seemed unperturbed.

"Oh?" she said. "And what did Hertha tell you?"

"Not very much. She saw Peaches in a single room, but she didn't know the location."

Laverne examined the chartreuse polish on her fingernails. "Well, Hertha is very gifted but she can't win them all. No medium can."

"Did she ever do your horoscope?"

"Sure she did. So what?"

"Did you tell her details about your personal life, about Meg and your parents?"

184

"Of course. Hertha has to know those things to draw your psychic profile."

"Uh-huh. Laverne, do you know a man named Charles Girard?"

"Nope," she said promptly. "Never heard of him. Who is he?"

"He may be one of the catnappers."

"No kidding?" she said. "How did you get on to him?"

"Any genius could have done it. Did you ever hear your husband mention him?"

"Not that I recall. You better ask Harry."

"I shall. Laverne, how long have you known the Glorianas?"

"Oh, months and months. I guess it must be almost a year now."

"Where are they from – do you know?"

"Chicago, I think."

"Is Mrs. Irma Gloriana widowed or divorced?"

"Divorced. She said her ex lives in California somewhere with their daughter. Frank went with his mother, and the daughter lives with their father."

"How long have Hertha and Frank been married?"

"I think they said four years. Why all these questions about the Glorianas, Archy?"

I shrugged. "I find them interesting people. Mysterious."

"Mysterious?" She laughed. "Not very. They're just trying to grab the brass ring like everyone else."

"You grabbed it," I said boldly.

She wasn't offended. She looked around that scented chamber with satisfaction, then stroked the raised gold and silver design on her robe. "You bet your sweet ass I grabbed it," she said. "But I've paid my dues. By the way, Meg is back in town. She phoned me this morning. You going to see her again?"

185

From which I deduced that Meg hadn't told her sister about the séance she attended with me. Initially I was thankful for that, but then I realized that Laverne would probably learn about it from the Glorianas.

"Yes, I'd like to see her again," I said.

"Good boy," she said approvingly. "She has to learn that not all men are shitheads. Most, but not all."

I had been standing throughout this interview because Laverne hadn't invited me to sit down. I was weary of standing in one position and couldn't think of any additional questions to ask.

"Thank you for your help," I said. "I'll phone Harry and ask him if he knows Charles Girard."

"Where does Girard live?" she said casually. "Do you know?"

She shouldn't have asked that. I had suspected she might be lying when she denied knowing Charles Girard. Her question convinced me she knew very well who he was and now she was trying to discover how much I knew of him.

"Haven't the slightest idea," I said, furrowing the old brow. "But eventually I'll find him. And Peaches."

"Don't strain yourself, Archy," she advised. "What difference does it really make? Harry can easily afford the fifty grand they're asking."

"Laverne!" I protested. "Don't let your husband hear you say that. He wants his pet back without paying and he wants the catnappers strung up by their thumbs – or whatever other bodily appendages are handy."

"My husband," she repeated darkly. "What he wants and what he gets are two different things."

I figured that was a good moment to make my farewell, so I did. I drove home thinking that Laverne Willigan had more than ozone between her ears. She had lied glibly and shrewdly, I was certain of that, but what her motives

186

were I wasn't yet sure.

And in addition to the Charles Girard business, she had given me another puzzle. Roderick Gillsworth had said Irma Gloriana was widowed. Laverne had just told me she was divorced. I couldn't believe Irma would give varying accounts of her background to different people; she was too clever for that.

Which meant that Gillsworth was lying or Laverne was lying.

Or both.

I used the phone in my father's study to call Harry Willigan. He greeted me with screams, and I had to wait until he ran out of breath before I could get in my question about Charles Girard.

"Never heard of the bozo," he bellowed and took up his ranting again.

I hung up softly, hoping he might continue for another five minutes before he realized he was raving into a dead phone.

I went upstairs and scribbled in my journal for more than an hour. The dossier on the Peaches–Gillsworth case was bulking up nicely, but I still could not see any pattern in all those disparate tidbits of information. Where was Xatyl now that I needed him?

I had returned from my ocean swim and was dressing for the evening when Al Rogoff called. He wasted no time on preliminaries.

"I've got some news for you," he said. "Interesting stuff."

"And I have a few choice morsels for you," I said. "When and where can we meet?"

"I'm up to my pipik in paperwork," he said. "I probably won't be able to get away until late. How about you coming over to my wagon around nine-thirty or so."

"Sounds good to me," I said. "Can I bring something to

187

lubricate your tonsils?"

"Nah," he said, "I have a bottle of wine I'll pop. It's a naive domestic burgundy without any breeding, but I think you'll be amused by its presumption."

"Thank you, Mr. Thurber," I said. "See you tonight."

That evening Ursi Olson served a Florida dinner of conch chowder, grilled swordfish and plantains with a mango salsa and hearts of palm salad. My father relented, and instead of a jug chablis he brought out a vintage muscadet, flinty hard.

I returned to my rooms after dinner and added a few more notes to my journal. Then I phoned Information and asked if they had a new listing for Margaret Trumble in Riviera Beach. They gave me the number and I called. I let it ring seven times before I hung up, wondering where she was. I don't know why I felt uneasy, but I did.

Then I grabbed up a golf jacket and went trotting out to the Miata. It was a super evening, clear and cool enough to sleep without air conditioning. But that night I didn't get much chance.

What Al Rogoff called his "wagon" was actually a mobile home set on a sturdy foundation in a park of similar dwellings off Belvedere Road. It was a pleasant place – lots of lawns and palm trees, a small swimming pool and a smaller recreation room.

Most of the residents were retirees, and I always suspected Al got a discount on his maintenance because the owner of the park liked the idea of having a cop on the premises. I mean if any villain got the idea of ripping off one of the mobile homes – and they didn't provide much security – he might think twice if he spotted a guardian of the law strolling around with a howitzer strapped to his hip.

Al's home was trim outside and snug inside. He had a living room, bedroom, kitchen, and bath, all in a row, like a railroad flat. He had decorated the place himself, and though nothing was lavish or even expensive, I thought it a very attractive and comfortable bachelor's pad – the kind of place where you could kick off your shoes and mellow out.

He had a bottle of wine chilled and uncorked when I arrived. But it wasn't a burgundy, it was an '87 Sterling cabernet. If you think it blasphemous to cool a good red like that, I must tell you that Floridians customarily refrigerate even the most costly Bordeaux. We dine alfresco a great deal of the time, and if the wine isn't chilled, you're slurping soup.

We sat in padded captain's chairs at an oak dining table tucked into one corner of the living room. I sampled the wine, and it was just right.

"Who goes first?" Al asked.

"You start," I said. "My amazing revelations can wait."

He got up to fetch his notebook. He was wearing tan jeans and a T-shirt. He was unshod but his meaty feet were stuffed into white athletic socks. I noticed he was getting a belly, not gross but nascent. Most cops don't eat very well. They think a balanced diet is an anchovy pizza and a can of Dr Pepper.

"Okay," the sergeant said, hunching over his notebook, "here's what I got from Atlanta. Those people the Glorianas named as references just don't exist at the addresses given. The Atlanta bank they named was a savings and loan that folded three years ago."

"Beautiful," I said.

"Then I got through to a detective in the Atlanta PD who knew all about the Glorianas. Jerry Weingarter. A nice guy. He's a cigar smoker, like me. He was a big help so maybe I'll send him a box of the best."

"McNally & Son will pick up the tab," I said.

189

Al grinned. "That's what I figured," he said. "Anyway, this Weingarter told me that Irma Gloriana and her husband were – "

"Whoa," I said, holding up a hand. "You mean Irma is married?"

He looked at me. "Sure she's married. What did you think?"

"I didn't know what to think," I said honestly. "Is her husband still living?"

"He was about six months ago when he got out of the clink. His name is Otto. Otto Gloriana. Got a nice sound to it, doesn't it? Drink your wine; there's another bottle cooling. Irma and Otto were running what my dear old granddaddy used to call a house of ill repute. It wasn't a sleazy crib; the Glorianas had a high-class joint. All their girls were young and beautiful. The johns paid anywhere from a hundred to five hundred, depending on what they wanted. Irma was the madam, Otto the business manager. They had been in business four or five years and had a nice thing going with a well-heeled clientele of upper-crust citizens. The law got on to it when one of their girls OD'd on heroin."

I finished my glass of wine and poured myself another. "A pretty picture," I said. "And what part did the son, Frank, play in all this?"

"He was like a bouncer, providing muscle if any of the johns got out of line."

"And Hertha?"

"Apparently she had no connection with the cathouse. Weingarter says she had her own racket, doing what she does now: holding séances and doing horoscopes. He also said she's a crackerjack psychic. Once she helped the Atlanta cops find a lost kid. Weingarter doesn't know how she did it, but the lead she gave them was right on the money."

He paused to refill his glass, and I had a moment to reflect on what he had told me. I think I was more saddened than shocked.

"What happened after the cops closed them down?" I asked.

"Otto cut a deal. He'd take the rap if his wife and son got suspended sentences and promised to leave town."

"Very noble of Otto," I said. "How long did he get?"

"He drew three-to-five, did a year and a half, and was released about six months ago. No probation. Present whereabouts unknown."

I gazed up at the ceiling fans. "Al," I said, almost dreamily, "do you have a physical description of Otto?"

"Yeah," he said, flipping pages of his notebook, "I've got it somewhere. Here it is. He's – "

I interrupted him. "He's tall," I said. "Reddish hair. Broad-shouldered. Very well-dressed in a conservative way. About sixty-five or so."

The sergeant stared at me. "What the hell," he said hoarsely. "You been taking psychic lessons from Hertha or something?"

"Did I get it right?" I asked.

"You got it right," he acknowledged. "Now tell me how."

"He's down here," I said. "Using the name Charles Girard."

Then I gave Rogoff an account of how I figured Peaches might get sick, how the catnappers would seek medical help, how I canvassed emergency animal hospitals with a flapdoodle story, how I finally found a veterinarian who remembered treating Peaches and gave me the name and address of the man who brought her in.

Al looked at me and shook his head in wonderment. "You know," he said, "You have the testicles of a brazen simian. You also have more luck than you deserve.

191

Where is Otto living?"

"In a fleabag motel on Federal Highway. But I haven't told you the punch line, Al. I went out there this morning to pay a visit to Charles Girard, or, if he wasn't present, to see if Peaches was on the premises and could be rescued. But I took one look and departed forthwith. Roderick Gillsworth's gray Bentley was parked outside Otto's cabin."

The sergeant stared and slowly his face changed. I thought I saw vindictiveness there and perhaps malevolence.

"Gillsworth," he repeated, and it was almost a hiss. "I knew that – "

But I wasn't fated to learn what it was the sergeant knew, for the phone rang at that instant, startlingly loud.

Al waited until the third ring, then hauled himself to his feet. "I'll take it on the bedroom extension," he said.

He went inside and closed the door. I wasn't offended. If it was official business, he had every right to his privacy. And if it was that schoolteacher he dated occasionally, he had every right to his privacy.

He seemed to be in there a long time, long enough for me to finish what was left of the cabernet. Finally he came out. He had pulled on a pair of scuffed Reeboks, the laces flapping, and a khaki nylon jacket. He was affixing his badge to the epaulette of the jacket. After he did that, he took his gunbelt with all its accoutrements from a closet shelf and buckled it about his waist with some difficulty.

Then he looked at me. I could read absolutely nothing in his expression, because there wasn't one; his face was stone.

"There was a fire at Roderick Gillsworth's place," he reported tonelessly. "A grease fire in the kitchen. The neighbors spotted it. The firemen had to break down the door to get in. They put out the fire and went looking for

192

Gillsworth. They found him in the bathtub. His wrists were slit."

I gulped. "Dead?" I asked, hearing the quaver in my own voice.

"Very," Al said.

"Can I come with you?"

"No," he said. "You'd just have to wait outside. I'll phone you as soon as I learn more."

"Al, there's something else I've got to tell you," I said desperately.

"It'll have to wait. Go home, Archy. You better tell your father about this."

"Yes," I said. "Thanks for the wine."

"What?" he said. "Oh. Yeah."

We both went outside and paused while Al locked up. Then he got in his pickup and took off. I stayed right there, smoking a cigarette and looking up at the star-spangled sky. Another spirit had passed over. Another ghost. It had never occurred to me before that the living were a minority.

12

The door to my father's study was open. He was seated at his desk working on a stack of correspondence brought home from the office. He looked up when I entered.

"I'm busy, Archy," he said irritably.

"Yes, sir," I said, "but I have news I think you should hear immediately. Not good news."

He sighed and tossed down his pen. "It's been that kind of day," he said. "Very well, what is it?"

I repeated what Al Rogoff had told me and, like the sergeant's, his face became stone.

"Yes," he said in a quiet voice, "I heard the fire engines go by earlier this evening. The man has definitely expired?"

"According to Rogoff. He promised to phone me when he learns more about it."

"Does the sergeant believe it was suicide?"

"He didn't say, father."

"Do *you* think it was?"

"No, sir," I said, and told him of my early morning meeting with the poet. "He seemed very up, as if he was happy Lydia's funeral was over and he could get on with his life. He said he had some errands to do today, shopping and so forth. A man planning suicide doesn't go to a supermarket first, does he?"

"He was sober, I presume."

"As far as I could tell. He did offer me an eye-opener but in a joking way. Yes, I'd say he was completely sober."

My father drew a deep breath. "And now all my fears come true. As things stand, he leaves all his worldly goods, except for his original manuscripts, to a wife who predeceased him. As far as I know, he has no immediate survivors."

"None?" I said, shocked. "Siblings? Cousins? Aunts? Uncles? No one at all?"

"Not to my knowledge. Would you pour us a port, please, Archy. I believe we both could use it."

I did the honors, and the sire gestured me to the armchair alongside his desk. He sipped his wine thoughtfully.

"If an investigation proves I am correct and he had no survivors, then I imagine Lydia's aunt and cousins will have a claim on the bulk of her estate inherited by Roderick."

"A mess," I offered.

"Yes," he said, "it is that." Suddenly he was angered. "Why the devil the idiot didn't make out a new will immediately after his wife's death I'll never know."

"You tried to persuade him, father," I said, hoping to mollify him.

"I should have been more insistent," he said, and I realized his fury was directed as much at himself as at Gillsworth.

"You couldn't have anticipated what happened," I pointed out.

"I should have," he said, refusing to be assuaged. "I learned long ago that in legal matters it's necessary always to prepare for a worst-case scenario. This time I neglected to do that, and the worst happened. You say Sergeant Rogoff will call you when he learns the details of

195

Roderick's death?"

"He said he would."

"Please let me know as soon as you hear from him."

"It may be very late, father. After midnight."

"Then wake me up," he said sharply. "Is that understood?"

"Yes, sir," I said, drained my glass of port, and left him alone with his anger. The old man likes things tidy, and this affair was anything but.

I went upstairs but I didn't undress, figuring it was possible Al might want to meet me somewhere else. I sat in my swivel chair, put my feet up on the desk, and tried to make some sense, *any* sense, out of Gillsworth's death.

Despite the corpse's slit wrists, no one was going to convince me the poet was a suicide. If I tell you why I refused to accept that, you'll think me an ass, but it's how my mind works: I could never believe that a man with the *joie de vivre* to wear a Lilly Pulitzer sport jacket in the morning could kill himself in the evening. Unless, of course, he had suffered a cataclysmic defeat during the day, and so far there was no evidence of that.

Do you recall my mentioning that I had a vaporish notion of what had gone down and was still going down? It was so vague that I couldn't put it into words. But now Gillsworth's death made a difference. I'm not saying all the mists had cleared, but I began to see a dim outline that had shape if not substance.

I obviously dozed off because when the phone rang I discovered my head was down on the desktop, cradled in my forearms. I roused and glanced at my Mickey Mouse watch: almost two-thirty a.m.

"Rogoff," he said. "Why should you be sleeping when I'm not?"

"You still at Gillsworth's house, Al?"

"Still here. If I take a breather and run up to your

196

place, do you think you could buy me a cup of coffee?"

"You bet. How about a sandwich?"

"Nope, but thanks. Just the coffee, hot and black. I won't stay long."

I went down to my parents' bedroom and knocked softly. Father opened the door so quickly that I guessed he hadn't been sleeping, even though he was wearing Irish linen pajamas: long-sleeved jacket and drawstring pants.

"The sergeant called," I said in a low voice, hoping not to disturb mother. "He's coming for a cup of coffee."

"May I join you?" the pater asked.

That was so *like* him. I mean it was his home, he was the boss, he could have said, "I'll join you." But he had to couch it as a polite request to sustain his image of himself as a courtly gentleman. He's something, he is.

"Of course," I said. "Decaf for you?"

He nodded and I went on down to the kitchen. I put the kettle on and set out three cups and saucers, cream and sugar, spoons. In less than ten minutes I heard tires on our graveled turnaround and looked out the window to see Rogoff's pickup.

He came in a moment later, looking weary and defeated. He collapsed onto one of the chairs without saying a word. He put a heaped teaspoon of regular instant into his cup and I poured boiling water over it.

Then my father came in. He had changed to slacks, open-necked shirt, and old cardigan, and older carpet slippers. The sergeant stood up when he entered. I admired him for that. The two men shook hands, wordlessly, and we all sat down. Father and I had instant decaf with cream, no sugar.

"He *is* dead, sergeant?" the senior asked.

"No doubt about that, sir," Rogoff said. "The exact cause will have to wait for the autopsy. I'm no medic, but I'd say it was loss of blood that finished him."

197

"Exsanguination," I remarked.

Al looked at me. "Thank you, Mr. Webster," he said. "Well, there was enough of it in the tub."

"How do you interpret it?" father asked.

"I don't," Rogoff said. "Not yet. There are too many questions and not enough answers. Let me set the scene for you. The people next door were having a barbecue on their patio. One of the guests spotted flames behind the window of Gillsworth's kitchen. The men ran over there but the back door was locked. Meanwhile the women called nine-one-one. When the firemen arrived, they had to break down the back door. It was locked, bolted, and chained. They also broke through the front door of the house. That was closed with a spring lock but not bolted or chained."

He paused to blow on his coffee and then sipped cautiously. It wasn't too hot for him, and he took a deep gulp. Father and I sampled ours.

"That's significant," I said. "Don't you think? The front door on a spring lock but not bolted or chained?"

"Maybe," Rogoff said. "Maybe not. Anyway it wasn't much of a fire. There was a big frying pan on the range. The pan had grease in it – butter or oil, it hasn't been determined yet. But it caught fire and spattered, igniting the curtains and café drapes. The range coil was still on High when the firemen got there."

"Then he was preparing dinner," my father said, a statement not a question.

"It sure looked like it, sir. There was a plate of six big crab cakes on the countertop, ready for frying. And in the fridge was a huge bowl of salad, already mixed."

"Any booze?" I asked.

"Yeah, an open liter of gin on the countertop, about two slugs gone. Also a highball glass still half-full. Looked like a gin and tonic. It had a slice of lime in it. And there was a six-pack of quinine water in the cabinet under the sink. One of the bottles was half-empty."

I shook my head. "That doesn't compute. A man is making dinner. He has a drink, mixes a salad. He gets ready to sauté his crab cakes. Then he decides to slit his wrists instead. Do you buy that, Al?"

"Right now I'm not buying anything. Could I have another cup of coffee? I'm not going to get any sleep tonight anyway."

I fixed him another regular and another decaf for myself after my father put his palm over his cup.

"Please continue, sergeant," he said. "How was Gillsworth found?"

"The firemen figured things didn't look kosher and went searching for him. They found him in the tub of the downstairs bathroom, the one next to his den. He was fully clothed. There was a bloody single-edge razor blade on the bath mat alongside the tub. Both his wrists were slashed."

"Both?" I said. "If you slit one wrist, do you then have enough strength in that hand to grip a razor blade and slit the other wrist?"

"Don't ask me," Rogoff said. "I've never tried it. We're going to need a forensic pathologist on this one."

"Did the body show any other wounds?" father asked.

The sergeant looked at him admiringly. "Yes, sir, it did," he said. "On the back of the head, high up. The hair was matted with blood. But after he slashed his wrists he could have slipped down in the tub and cracked his head on the rim. In fact, there's a bloody mark on the rim that looks like he did exactly that. It's one of the questions the ME will have to answer."

"What's your guess, Al?" I said. "Suicide or homicide? I'm not asking what you're absolutely certain about, but what's your *guess*?"

199

He hesitated for just a brief instant, then he said. "Homicide."

"Of course!" I said triumphantly. "No one is going to slit his wrists in the middle of preparing dinner – unless he finds worms in the crab cakes."

"That's not my main reason for calling it homicide," Rogoff said. "Suicides sometimes do goofy things before they work up their courage to take the final exit. No, it's something else that makes me think someone cut Gillsworth's wrists for him. Archy, do me a favor. Show me how you'd slit your wrists if you were determined to shuffle off to Buffalo."

I stared at him. "You want me to pretend to slash my wrists?"

He nodded. "Use your spoon."

I picked up the spoon from my saucer. I held it in my right hand, gripping it by the bowl, the handle extended. I held out my left forearm and turned it palm upward. I was wearing a short-sleeved polo shirt; my arm was bare.

"I feel like a perfect fool," I said.

"Nobody's perfect," Al said, "but you come close. Go ahead, slit your wrists."

As my father and the sergeant watched intently, I drew the spoon handle swiftly across my left wrist, just hard enough to depress the skin. Then I transferred the spoon to my left hand and made the same slashing motion down across my right wrist. I admit the playacting gave me the heebie-jeebies.

"Uh-huh," Rogoff said. "That's what I figured."

"*What* did you figure?"

"You cut from the outside of your wrist down to the inside. You did it on both wrists."

I looked at my forearms and then tried slashing with the spoon handle from the underside of each wrist up to the top.

"Of course I did," I said. "It wouldn't be impossible to cut in the other direction, but it's awkward and you wouldn't be able to apply as much force. It would be like a backhand tennis stroke versus a forehand."

"For sure," Rogoff said, nodding. "I've seen slit wrists before, on suicides and would-be suicides. The slash is always made from top to bottom. But the cuts on Gillsworth's wrists looked like they had been made from the underside of the wrist to the top. That was my impression anyhow, but I admit I could be wrong. But there's another thing: Gillsworth's wrists showed no hesitation marks. Those are scratches and shallow cuts a suicide sometimes makes before he finally decides to go for broke. Gillsworth's wrists had single deep slashes. Hey, I've got to get back. Thanks for the coffee, it juiced me up."

"Thank *you*, sergeant," father said, "for being so forthcoming. I assure you that Archy and I will keep what you've told us in strictest confidence."

"Yeah," Rogoff said, "I'd appreciate that."

They shook hands, and I accompanied Al out to his pickup.

"Got just a few more minutes?" I asked him.

He looked at me a sec, then grinned. "Something you didn't want your father to hear?"

"That's right," I said. "Or he'd have me committed."

"Sure, I got a few minutes," Al said. "Gillsworth isn't leaving town."

I climbed into the cab of the pickup with him. He pulled out a cigar and I pulled out a cigarette. We got our weeds burning, and I turned to face him.

"Remember before you took off from your place last evening I said I had something important to tell you? Well, I went to a séance at the Glorianas' on Wednesday night."

201

He didn't seem surprised. "So? Did you talk to your old friend Epicurus?"

"No, but I talked to Lydia Gillsworth. The medium contacted her through Xatyl, a Mayan shaman. He's Hertha's channel to the spirit world."

"Uh-huh. Makes sense to me."

"It does? Anyway, Al, I heard Lydia talking. I know the words were being spoken by Hertha, but I could have sworn it was Lydia. But Hertha knew her well, and if the medium has a gift for mimicry, which she obviously has, she could have imitated Lydia's voice."

"That *does* make sense. What did you and Lydia talk about? Did you ask who offed her?"

"Of course."

"And what did she say?"

"She became hysterical. She screamed, 'Caprice! Caprice!' over and over again."

That shook him. He turned his head slowly to look at me, and his expression was a puzzlement.

"You're sure that's what she said?"

"I'm sure. First it was screamed in Lydia's voice, then Hertha kept shrieking 'Caprice!' in her own voice. You know what she meant, don't you?"

"Yeah, I know. Mrs. Gillsworth's car was a Caprice. She drove it from the séance to her home the night she was murdered."

"That's right. How do you figure it?"

Al was silent a long time. He turned away to stare fixedly through the windshield.

"I'll tell you something, Archy: I suspected Roderick Gillsworth might have killed his wife. He says he talked to her from your place, was told she had just arrived, and immediately drove home to find her dead. He called nine-one-one, and I got there about fifteen minutes later. Tops. After I heard his story, I went out to the garage and felt the engine block on her Caprice. I didn't think it was as hot as it should have been if she had just driven home from the séance. But that was a subjective judgment. Also, she was killed on a warm night, and no one in South Florida drives around in late June without turning on the air conditioning. The interior of Lydia's Caprice wasn't as cool as it should have been if she had just arrived home – another personal judgment. It was nothing I could take to the State Attorney, but I began to wonder about Roderick Gillsworth."

"What about the grandfather clock that was toppled and stopped at the time of death?"

"Doesn't mean a thing, Archy. Anyone could have set the clock at any time desired and then pushed it over to stop it ticking. An easy alibi to fake."

"So far, so good," I said. "But he *did* call his wife from my father's study."

"I know he did," Al said almost mournfully. "There's no getting around that. And then, last night, Roderick gets iced – if it *was* homicide, and I think it was. That helps eliminate him as a suspect, wouldn't you say? It looks like someone, for whatever reason, crazy or not, wanted to wipe out the entire Gillsworth family, wife and husband. But now you tell me the psychic, speaking in the murdered woman's voice, yelled, 'Caprice! Caprice!' So I've got to start thinking again if Lydia's car really does provide a clue to her killer. Maybe I was right in the first place about the lack of engine heat and no air condition- ing inside the car. Listen, Archy, I've really got to get back to the Gillsworth place. There's still a lot to do."

"Sure," I said and started to climb from the truck cab. But he reached out a hand to stop me.

"I'm going to be tied up with this thing for the next few days at least. Will you check on Otto Gloriana and the catnapping?"

"I intend to."

"Good. One more thing: that Atlanta detective said Otto is a nasty piece of work."

I was indignant. "And what do you think I am – Little Lord Fauntleroy?"

"Just watch your step," he warned.

I went back into the house, locked up, and climbed the stairs to bed. I tried to sleep but my mind was a kaleidoscope of scary images, and it must have been five a.m. before I finally conked out. I awoke a little before noon, and I was under the shower, all soaped up, when, in accordance with tradition, my phone rang.

I went dashing out uttering a mild oath – something like "Sheesh!" – and grabbed up the phone only to have it drop to the floor from my slippery grasp. I retrieved it after much fumbling and finally cupped it in both hands.

"H'lo?" I said.

"What the hell's going on?" Harry Willigan demanded. "You drunk or something?"

I started to explain, but he had no time or inclination to listen. He said he was about to leave on a flight to Chicago for a business meeting. He would be gone until Tuesday, and if I had any news about Peaches I was to phone Laverne; she knew where he could be reached. He hung up before I could tell him I was hot on the trail of his beloved.

I finished my shower, dressed, and phoned Meg Trumble again. Again there was no answer. Very frustrating. I went downstairs for breakfast-lunch and found Jamie Olson seated at the kitchen table. He was munching on a thick sandwich that seemed to be mostly slices of raw Spanish onion between slabs of sour rye. It looked good to me so I built one for myself, heavy on the mayo. I sluiced it down with a bottle of Buckler beer (non-alcoholic, if you must know).

"Jamie," I said, "remember my asking if Laverne Willigan had a little something on the side? You said there was talk she was putting horns on dear old Harry."

"Yuh."

"Hear any more on the grapevine about who he is?"

"A dude."

"A dude? That's all? Just a dude?"

"Yuh. Dresses sharp."

"But no name?"

"Nope."

"So all you heard is that Laverne's Consenting Adult or Significant Other is a dude – correct?"

"Tall."

"Ah-ha, a tall dude! Now we're making progress. Young? Old?"

"Half-and-half."

"About my age, you think?"

"Mebbe."

"Better and better. Now we've got a tall, half-and-half dude. Slender or fat?"

"Thin."

"Dark or fair?"

"Darkish."

"Handsome?"

"Mebbe, I guess she thinks so."

"Excellent," I said. I now had a tall, half-and-half, thin, darkish, handsome dude. There were many men in the Palm Beach area answering that description, including you-know-who.

I slipped Jamie a tenner for his enthusiastic cooperation. Then I went into my father's study and looked up the number of the Jo-Jean Motel on Federal Highway. I phoned and was greeted by a woman's voice.

"Jo-Jean," she said, and I wondered which one she was.

"May I speak to Mr. Charles Girard?" I asked. "South row, Cabin Four."

"I know where he is," she said crossly.

There was a clicking, the connection went through, and the ringing started. Nine times, I counted, before the phone was picked up."

"Yeh?" A man's voice, deep and thick.

"Mr. Charles Girard?"

"Yeh. Who's this?"

"Mr. Girard, this is the veterinarian who recently provided medical care for your cat. It is my custom to make follow-up calls regarding the animals I have treated to make certain they have recovered satisfactorily. No charge, of course. Let's see, your cat's name is, ah, Gertrude?"

"Peaches," he said.

"Of course," I said. "It slipped my mind. And how is Peaches feeling, Mr. Girard?"

"She's okay."

"Glad to hear it. Well, remember we're here to serve and ready to provide emergency medical care for your pet should it ever be needed. Thank you, Mr. Girard, and have a nice day."

"Yeh," he said and hung up.

I was enormously pleased with the results of my discreet inquiries that morning. I reckoned that if my good luck continued, before nightfall I might find Judge Crater and identify Jack the Ripper.

I boarded the Miata and started my journey to Federal Highway. I drove slowly, for I meant to beard Otto Gloriana in his den at the Jo-Jean Motel and needed to cobble up a believable scenario to justify my appearing on his doorstep. But I could think of no scam that wasn't sheer lunacy. I decided to trust my modest talent for improvisation.

206

I parked in the same area I had used before and walked back to the Jo-Jean office through the midday heat. The same woman I had spoken to previously was perched on the same high stool behind the same counter, bending over a newspaper. But at least the tabloid was different. The headline was "Chef Slays Six With Spatula."

"I beg your pardon," I said, "but is Mr. Girard in?"

"You just missed him," she said, not looking up. "Him and the missus drove out a coupla minutes ago."

"Drat!" I said. "He told me he was staying here. I haven't seen him in ages, and I came all the way from Fort Lauderdale hoping to surprise him. Is he still driving his Lincoln Continental?"

"Chrysler Imperial."

"Ah, he must have traded in the Lincoln. And is his wife still the same tall, striking blonde?"

"Brunette. Chunky. Built like a bulldog."

"Oh my!" I said, laughing merrily. "Then I guess old Charlie traded in his first wife too. Did he say when he'd be back?"

"Nope."

"Perhaps I'll just drive around awhile, see the sights, and return later. Thank you for your help."

I thought I had been devilishly clever, but suddenly, without looking up, she said. "You got a lot of information for free, didn't you?"

I sighed, took a twenty from my billfold, and placed it on the countertop. She plucked it away so swiftly that I swear the visage of Old Hickory seemed shocked.

I went out into the hot sunlight and wandered down to Cabin Four, south row. It was larger than I had imagined, but it was surely a decrepit structure, badly in need of painting – or a hand grenade. A rusty air conditioner wheezed away in one window, and there was a dented deck chair on the sagging porch, the plastic webbing broken and hanging.

I stepped up to the door and knocked softly. No one opened it, but I heard a single plaintive meow. I put my lips close to the jamb and whispered, "Do not despair, Peaches. The cavalry is on the way."

Then I returned home, realizing that events were moving so rapidly that I needed to update my journal to make sure nothing was forgotten or ignored, no matter how trivial. But first I phoned Meg Trumble again, and this time she answered.

"Meg!" I said. "Where on earth have you been? I've been trying to reach you for ages. I was beginning to get concerned."

"Oh, Archy," she said, her voice positively bubbling. "I've been *so* busy. That list of names you gave me was a godsend. I've already visited four of them, and two are really interested in having a personal trainer. Isn't that wonderful!"

"Absolutely," I said. "How about dinner tonight?"

"Love to," she said promptly. "As a matter of fact, I called Laverne just minutes ago to ask if she'd like to eat with me tonight, but she has a meeting of the Current Affairs Society. Now I'm glad she couldn't make it; I'd much rather we have dinner together."

"Ditto," I said. "Pick you up around seven?"

"Super," she said. "Can we go back to that Café Istanbul again? I loved it. Bye!"

I sat there a moment, adding two and two and coming up with five. To wit: Harry Willigan was out of town. His wife had a lover lurking in the wings. And Laverne couldn't join Meg for dinner because she had a meeting of the Current Affairs Society. Hah!

That Society is a Palm Beach association of men and women, mostly elderly, who meet once a month to hear a lecture on current affairs by a congressman, political

208

science professor, repentant Communist, or the deposed dictator of a banana republic. The lecture would be followed by a Q & A period, and the meeting concluded with the serving of coffee and oatmeal cookies. My mother was a faithful member and had once served as sergeant at arms.

I went galloping downstairs and found the mater in the greenhouse, chatting to her begonias.

"I know it's hot," she was saying, "but it's summer, and you must keep your spirits up."

"Hallo, luv," I said, swooping to kiss her velvety cheek. "And how is mommy baby feeling today?"

"Oh my," she said, "you *are* in a chipper mood. Are you in love again, Archy?"

"Quite possibly," I acknowledged. "I do feel strange stirrings about the heart, but of course it could be the onion sandwich I had for lunch. Listen, Mrs. McNally, do you have a meeting of the Current Affairs Society tonight?"

She paused, sprinkling can in hand, to look at me, puzzled. "Why, no," she said. "The next meeting isn't until July fifteenth. Why do you ask?"

"Just confused," I said. "As usual. See you for cocktails, but I have a dinner date tonight."

"Good for you," she said, beaming. "Someone nice, I hope."

"I hope so too," I said.

I went back upstairs convinced that the only current affair Laverne Willigan would attend to that night was her own. There seems to be a lot of adultery going around these days. I suspect it may be contagious.

I worked on my journal for the remainder of the afternoon, jotting down all the information I had learned about Roderick Gillsworth's death. I added the family history of the Glorianas as related by Al Rogoff, and what

209

I had discovered that day of Otto's probable involvement in the catnapping of Peaches, aka Sweetums. I finished with an account of Laverne Willigan's apparent infidelity and her clumsy attempt to conceal it with a feeble falsehood.

Satisfied with my day's labors and the way in which the Gillsworth–Peaches case was slowly revealing its secrets, I closed up shop and went for my daily swim. I returned to shower and dress with particular care. I intended to dazzle Meg Trumble with sartorial splendor, which was why I selected a knitted shirt of plum-colored Sea Island cotton and a linen sports jacket of British racing green. Slacks of fawn silk. Cordovan loafers. No socks.

I displayed this costume at the family cocktail hour.

"Good God!" my father gasped.

I prayed Meg would be more favorably impressed by my imitation of a male bower bird. I was convinced I had been working dreadfully hard and needed a quiet evening to unwind, with no violent deaths, no catnappings, no shocking messages from the beyond. I imagined Meg and I would spend prime time together smiling and murmuring.

And later, surfeited with moussaka and overcome by *gemütlichkeit*, she would grant me a session of catch-as-catch-can intimacy. Just the two of us. Alone in the world.

I rang her bell, quivering with eagerness like a gun dog on point. Meg greeted me with a winning smile. And behind her, seated in the living room, was Hertha Gloriana, who gave me a smile just as winning.

"Hertha is going to join us," Meg said happily. "Isn't that marvelous?"

13

I had dined with two women before, of course – most lads have – and I usually found it a pleasurable experience. To be honest, it gives one a pasha-like feeling: entertaining two from the harem, or perhaps interviewing wannabes. Male self-esteem, always in need of a lift, is given an injection of helium by the presence and flattering attention of not one but two (count 'em!) attractive ladies.

Having said all that, I must tell you from the outset that the evening was a disaster. Never have I felt so extraneous, so *foreign*. I began to wonder if men and women are not merely two different genders but are actually two different species.

It started when we arrived at the Café Istanbul. I selected a booth, Meg and Hertha preferred another, although as far as I could see the booths were identical. I expected to sit alongside Meg, with Hertha, the third wheel, placed across the table from us. But the women insisted on dining side by side, so I sat alone, facing them.

Nothing so far to elevate a chap's dander, you say – and right you are. But it was only the beginning.

Hertha and Meg seemed to vie with each other in casting snide references to the conjunction of colors I was wearing. Even worse, the medium suggested I'd do well to ask her husband for tips on how to coordinate hues and fabrics in order to present a pleasing appearance.

"It's an idea," I said with a glassy smile, hoping the gnashing of my teeth was not audible. "And where is Frank this evening?"

My innocent question resulted in a convulsion of laughter by both, and it continued until our salad was served and the wine uncorked. I never did receive a reply to my query, though it was obvious that both my dinner partners knew the answer. Is there anything more maddening than an inside joke to which one is neither privy nor offered an explanation?

My essays at light-hearted conversation were similarly rejected. Both women remained po-faced in response to the truly hilarious tale of how Binky Watrous and I, somewhat in our cups, stole a garbage truck and drove it to Boca Raton. Nor did they seem interested in my favorite anecdote about Ferdy Attenborough, a member of the Pelican Club, who was debagged by his cronies and thrust into the ballroom during a formal dance at The Breakers.

As a matter of fact, the ladies didn't seem interested in me at all. But they spent a great deal of time whispering to each other – a shocking breach of good manners – and I recalled my uneasy feeling when I saw them sitting close and holding hands after the séance on Wednesday night. I began to get a disconcerting picture of who the third wheel really was.

Eventually that calamitous dinner came to an end, and I definitely did not suggest we go on to a nightclub for a bottle of bubbly and a spot of dancing. At the moment I felt biodegradable and ready for a New Jersey landfill.

We went back to Meg's apartment, with Hertha sitting on Meg's lap as she had before. I had no desire to linger, since it was painfully obvious that my presence was lending nothing to the festivities. And so, pleading an early morning engagement with my periodontist, I made my escape. The protests of the two women at my early departure were perfunctory, their farewells just as mechanical.

I drove away more thoughtful than angry. You may find this difficult to believe, but there are times, many of them, when my duties as chief of discreet inquiries for McNally & Son take precedence over the *Sturm und Drang* of my personal affairs.

So, in the wake of that discomfiting evening, I pondered less on the outrageous behavior of my two dining companions than on the present whereabouts and activities of Frank Gloriana. I didn't have to be Monsieur C. Auguste Dupin to deduce that Frank and Laverne Willigan had what Jamie Olson once referred to as a "rappaport."

To test my theory I decided to make a quick return trip to the Jo-Jean Motel on Federal Highway. This time I pulled into the motel area just long enough to confirm that Laverne's pink Porsche was parked outside Cabin Four.

Then I drove home, deriving some amusement from imagining Harry Willigan's reaction if he was to learn of his wife's involvement in the catnapping of Peaches. I had no intention of snitching on her, of course. It was simply not something a gentleman would do.

I arrived at my burrow to find a scrawled message slipped under the door. It was from Ursi Olson and stated that Sgt. Al Rogoff had phoned early in the evening and requested I call him back.

I tried him at first at police headquarters but was told he had left for the night. I then phoned him at his mobile home, and he picked up after the third ring.

"McNally," I said.

"You're home so early?" he said. "What happened – the girlfriend kick you out of bed?"

"You're close," I said. "What's happening, Al?"

"A lot. I finally got the FBI report on the Gillsworth and Willigan letters."

"Printed on the same machine?"

"Yep. I also have a preliminary report from the Medical Examiner and some stuff from the lab. There are more tests to be made, but things are beginning to get sorted out. We better meet."

"Fine," I said. "I have something to tell you, too. I know who swiped the cat."

"Don't tell me it was Willie Sutton."

"No," I said, laughing. "Even better. When do you want to make it?"

"Tomorrow morning at ten," he said. "At Gillsworth's house."

"Why there?"

"We're going to reenact the murder. You get to play the victim."

"My favorite role," I said. "I rehearsed this evening."

"What?"

"Nothing," I said. "See you tomorrow."

I poured myself a small marc and spent a few hours reviewing my journal, paying particular attention to the entries dealing with Laverne Willigan, her feelings about her husband, her reactions to the snatching of Peaches, and the gossip Jamie had relayed about her alleged lover.

I poured a second marc and lighted a cigarette. Absorbing alcohol and inhaling nicotine with carefree abandon, I mused on Laverne's motive for assisting in the catnapping, for I was certain she was involved up to her toasted buns. I scribbled a few notes:

1. Laverne is a sensual young woman with a jumbo appetite for the pleasures of the good life.

2. She is married to Harry, an ill-natured dolt much older than she but with the gelt to provide the afore-

mentioned delights.

3. She meets a rakishly handsome immoralist, Frank Gloriana. He is married to the psychic, Hertha, but has no scruples about cheating on his wife, especially when the possibility of a payoff exists. (Or perhaps the medium is aware of his infidelity and couldn't care less, being as amoral as he.)

4. Laverne and Frank become intimate, enjoying each other's company with absolutely no intention of leaving their respective spouses.

5. But Frank suffers from a bad case of the shorts. (Bounced checks, etc.)

6. Question: Did Laverne or Frank dream up the idea of swiping Peaches for a good chunk of walking-around money?

7. Answer: My guess is that it was Frank's scam, but Laverne merrily goes along since it causes distress to her boorish husband, he can easily afford the bite, and *not* to aid Frank might result in her losing him.

8. She sneaks the cat out of the Willigan home in its carrier and delivers it to Cabin Four.

9. Frank slides the ransom notes under the Willigans' front door.

10. Laverne returns the carrier when she learns from her sister that I have noted its absence.

11. All that remains to be done is the glomming of the ransom and the return of Peaches to her hearth.

12. Everyone lives happily ever after.

I reread these notes, and everything seemed logical to me – and so banal I wanted to weep. I went to bed reflecting that there are really no new ways to sin.

If you discover any, I wish you'd let me know.

Saturday morning brought brilliant sunshine and a resurgence of the customary McNally confidence. This high lasted all of forty-five minutes until, while lathering my

215

chops preparatory to shaving, I received a phone call from Consuela Garcia.

"Archy," she wailed, "our orgy tonight – it's off!"

The bright new day immediately dimmed. I had consoled myself, in typical masculine fashion, that despite my rejection by Meg Trumble on Friday night, there was always Connie awaiting me on Saturday. I had envisioned a debauch so profligate that it might even include our reciting in unison the limerick beginning, "There was a young man from Rangoon." But apparently it was not to be.

"Connie," I said, voice choked with frustration, "why ever not?"

"Because," she said, "I got a call from my cousin Lola in Miami. She and Max, her husband, are driving up to Disney World and want to stop off and spend the night in my place."

"Ridiculous!"

"I know, but I've *got* to let them, Archy, because I spent a weekend with them at Christmastime."

I sighed. "At least we can all have dinner together, can't we?"

"Archy," she said, "Max wears Bermuda shorts with white ankle socks and laced black shoes."

"No dinner," I said firmly.

"But I want to see you," she cried. "Can't the two of us have lunch even if there's no tiddledywinks later?"

"Of course we can," I said gamely. "Meet you at the Club noonish."

"You are an admirable man," she proclaimed.

"I concur," I said.

A zingy breakfast did wonders for my morale. Being of Scandinavian origin, the Olsons had a thing for herring. Ursi kept a variety on hand, and that was my morning repast: herring in wine, in mustard sauce, in dilled cream, and one lone kipper. I wolfed all this with schwarzbrot and sweet butter. I know iced vodka is the wash of choice with a feast of herring, but it was too early in the morning; I settled for black coffee.

Much refreshed and happy I had been blessed with a robust gut, I tooled the Miata southward to meet Sergeant Al. It was a splendid day, clear and soft. If you're going to reenact a murder, that was the weather for it. The glory of sun, sea, and sky made homicide seem a lark. No one could possibly die on a day like that.

Rogoff was waiting for me in the flowered sitting room of the Gillsworth manse. I thought his meaty face was sagging with weariness, and I made sympathetic noises about his strenuous labors and obvious lack of sufficient sleep.

He shrugged. "Comes with the territory," he growled. "How to be a successful cop: work your ass off, be patient, and pray that you're lucky. You smell of fish. What did you have for breakfast?"

"Herring."

"I shouldn't complain," he said. "I had a hot pastrami sandwich and a kosher dill. Tell me about the crazy cat."

We sat in facing armchairs, and I recited all the evidence leading to my conclusion that Laverne Willigan and Frank Gloriana had conspired in the catnapping.

Al listened intently and grinned when I finished. "Yeah," he said, "I'll buy it: the two of them making nice-nice and cooking up a plot to swipe the old coot's pet for fifty grand. I love it, just love it. You figure the cat is still out at the motel?"

"There's *a* cat in Cabin Four," I said. "I heard it mewing. I can't swear it's Peaches, but I'd make book on it."

He thought a moment. Then: "It might make our job easier when push comes to shove. That Cabin Four

217

sounds like the combat center of everything that's going down. Otto Gloriana is staying there, and that's where you saw Gillsworth's Bentley and Laverne's Porsche."

"And heard the cat," I reminded him. "And also, the lady in the office said Otto drove off with a woman who could be Irma."

"Probably was."

"You want to raid the place, Al?"

"Not yet," he said. "The cat isn't as important as the homicides. I'd hate to tip our hand and send all the cockroaches scurrying back in the woodwork. But I think I'll put an undercover guy in one of the other cabins, just to keep an eye on things."

"All right," I said, "you play it your way. Now tell me about the FBI report."

He took out his notebook and flipped pages until he got to the section he wanted. Then he paused to light a cigar. I waited patiently until he had it drawing to his satisfaction. Then he started reading.

"The machine is a Smith Corona PWP 100C personal word processor with pica type. Paper is Southworth DeLuxe Four Star. Smith Corona ribbon used throughout. All letters written on same machine, probably by same operator."

"Interesting," I said, "but what good is it? What do we do with it?"

He smiled at me. "Archy, you've got to start thinking like a cop. I just had a rookie assigned to me. What I'll do is have the guy go through the Yellow Pages and make a list of all the companies in the area that sell and service office machines. He hits every one of them and makes his own list of those that handle the Smith Corona PWP 100C. Then he gets the names and addresses of customers who have bought that machine or had it serviced. It's a lot of legwork, I admit, but it's got to be done, and I think

218

it'll pay off."

I thought a moment. "That's one way of doing it," I said. "The hard way."

Al looked at me, a little miffed. "Oh?" he said. "And what's the easy way, Sherlock?"

"Give your rookie a twenty-minute crash course on word processors. Tell him to get a business card from a legitimate company. Send him to call on Frank Gloriana at their office on Clematis Street. The rookie is wearing civvies. He tries to sell Frank a Smith Corona PWP 100C. I'm betting Frank will say. "Sorry, we've already got one.""

The sergeant burst out laughing and slapped his thigh. "What a scamster you are!" he said. "Thank God you're on our side or you'd end up owning Florida. Yeah, that's a great swindle, and we'll try it before the rookie starts pounding the pavement. You really think the letters are coming out of the Glorianas' office?"

"A good bet," I said. "There are some doors up there leading to closed-off rooms I didn't see. It's worth a go."

"It sure is," Rogoff said. "Thanks for the suggestion."

"You're quite welcome," I said. "Al, are you serious about reenacting the murder?"

"Sure I'm serious. Look, we picked up some odds and ends of physical evidence. None of them are heavy by themselves, but taken together they add up to a possible homicide planned to look like a suicide. I'll explain as we go along. Now I want you to go back to the kitchen. I'll go outside and pretend I'm the perp. You try to act like you think Gillsworth did in the few minutes before his death."

I went to the kitchen, which still showed blackened scars from the grease fire. In a moment I heard the front doorbell ring. I paused a moment and then returned to the entrance. I peered through the judas window. The sergeant was standing there. I opened the door.

"All right," Rogoff said, "the victim probably does the same thing: glances through the window, sees someone he knows, and lets him in."

"*Him?*" I said. "Not a woman? Or maybe two people?"

"Possible," he said. He stepped inside, closed the door behind him. "Now the perp is inside but doesn't know Gillsworth has left a pan of oil heating on the range. And before the victim can tell him, the killer does this . . . "

He levelled a forefinger at me thumb up, other fingers clenched.

"Why the gun?" I asked him.

"Because the killer wants to get Gillsworth into the bathtub so he can fake a suicide. A polite invitation just isn't going to do it. Now put your hands in the air and turn around."

I followed orders. In a few seconds I felt a light slap on the back of my skull.

"What was that?" I asked.

"The guy – or lady if you insist – slugs Gillsworth on the back of the noggin. The docs found it: a forcible blow caused by the famous blunt instrument. Could have been a gun butt. Heavy enough to render the victim unconscious. Now fall backward. Don't worry; I'll catch you."

Somewhat nervously I toppled. Al caught me under the arms.

"My God," he said, "what do you weigh?"

"One-seventy."

"Bullshit."

"Well, maybe a little more."

"Yeah, twenty pounds more," he said. "Gillsworth weighed about one-fifty."

"That figures," I said. "He was a scrawny bird."

"And a lot easier to drag than you," Al said, moving backward down the corridor toward the bathroom, pulling me along with him.

"We know it was done like this," the sergeant said, "because the victim's heels made furrows in the carpet. Photographed and the fibers analyzed. And guess what we found in the parallel tracks."

"What?"

"Cat hairs."

"Oh-oh. The motel."

"You got it. So we went upstairs and vacuumed Gillsworth's other clothes and shoes. More cat hair. He must have spent a lot of time in Cabin Four. The hair was silver-gray."

"Peaches," I said. "Definitely."

He made no comment, trying not to huff and puff as he dragged me past the poet's den and through the door of the bathroom.

"Okay," he said, "you can stand up now. I'm not going to put you in the tub; it hasn't been washed out yet." He assisted me to my feet and glanced at his watch. "Less than three minutes from front door to bathroom. Then I figure the killer tugged Gillsworth over the edge of the tub and let him fall. That's when the victim cracked his head on the rim. He had two separate and distinct wounds on the back of his skull: one from the gun butt, the other made when he was dumped in the tub and smashed his head. You can still see the mark on the rim."

I stood erect and gazed down into the tub. Blood had dried and caked on the bottom and inner surfaces of the walls.

"Was the drain closed?" I asked.

"No," Rogoff said. "But Gillsworth was wearing a crazy jacket. The tail blocked the drain enough so the blood didn't run out freely. Now the victim is lying in the tub, face up, unconscious. The killer takes a single-edge razor blade and slashes both his wrists."

221

"In the wrong direction?"

"Correct. And drops the blade on the bath mat to make it look like Gillsworth had let it fall there."

"Any prints on the blade?"

"Nothing usable."

"Where did it come from? Did Gillsworth shave with single-edge blades?"

"Ah-ha," Rogoff said. "The beauty part. I wanted to make sure this wasn't a burglary-homicide, so I called Marita to come over and check out the house. She said nothing was missing. She also said they had no single-edge blades; Gillsworth used an electric shaver. We found it in the upstairs bathroom. So the killer brought the blade with him. Which means the fake suicide was planned. It would make a nice headline: 'Heartbroken Poet Takes Own Life After Tragic Death of Beloved Wife'."

"Uh-huh," I said. "And your mention of Marita reminds me of something. The last time you and I met in this house – that was right after Lydia Gillsworth was killed – I saw Marita drive up. What was she doing here?"

Al gave me a look. "You don't miss much, do you? Well, after his wife was murdered, I asked Roderick to check out the house and see if anything was missing. He did and said nothing was gone as far as he could tell. But I called in Marita to double-check, figuring a housekeeper would know better whether or not anything was missing."

"And was it?"

"Yeah," Al said, staring at me. "A pair of latex gloves. Marita kept them under the sink to use when she scoured pots."

"Latex gloves," I repeated. "Lovely. The final prints on the walking stick that killed Lydia were made with latex gloves, weren't they?"

"That's right."

I took a deep breath. "How do you compute it, Al?"

"I don't," he said, almost angrily. "It makes absolutely no sense that a stranger breaks into the house and goes looking for latex gloves before he kills. I've got that mystery on hold. But meanwhile, what do you think of my scenario on Gillsworth's murder and the faked suicide?"

"Plausible," I said. "There's only one thing wrong with it."

"What's that?"

"You've provided a believable exegesis on *how* it happened, but you haven't said a word about *why*."

"Why?" he said disgustedly. "Why does a chicken cross the road?"

"For the same reason a fireman wears red suspenders," I said. "Let's get the hell out of here, Al. A bloody bathtub is not the most fitting dessert for a herring breakfast."

But he said he wanted to stay, and mumbled something about taking additional measurements. I didn't believe that. Al Rogoff, despite his cop's practicality, is something of a romantic. I reckoned that he wanted to wander through that doomed house for a while, reflect on the two sanguinary murders that had happened within its walls, try to absorb the aura of the place, listen for ghosts, and perhaps conceive a reason for the seemingly senseless killings.

All I wanted was blue sky, hot sunshine, and uncontaminated air to breathe. Evil has a scent all its own, not only sickening but frightening.

I drove directly to the Pelican Club. I was a bit early for my date with Connie Garcia, but having spent the morning impersonating a corpse, I was badly in need of a transfusion. I was certain a frozen daiquiri would bring roses back to the McNally cheeks.

The luncheon crowd had not yet assembled, but Simon Pettibone was on duty behind the bar reading *Barron's*

223

through his Ben Franklin glasses. He put the financial pages aside long enough to mix my drink, an ambrosial concoction with just a wee bit of Cointreau added.

Mr. Pettibone went back to his stock indices, and I nursed my plasma, savoring the quiet, cool, dim ambience of my favorite watering hole. A few members wandered in, but it was a pleasant Saturday afternoon and most Pelicanites were in pools or the ocean, on fairways and courts, or perhaps astride a polo pony out at Wellington. Life is undoubtedly unfair and one would be a fool not to enjoy one's good fortune.

Connie showed up a few minutes after noon. She was wearing stone-washed denim overalls atop a tie-dyed T-shirt. Her long black hair was gathered with a yellow ribbon, and there were leather strap sandals on her bare feet. She looked – oh, maybe sixteen years old, and I told her she might have to show her ID to get a drink.

We went back to the empty dining area, and a yawning Priscilla showed us to our favorite corner table. Connie ordered a white zin and I had a repeat of my daiquiri.

"Sorry about tonight, Archy," she said, "but there was just no way I could turn Lola and Max away: they *are* family."

"No problem," I said. "After they've gone, we'll make up for lost time."

She reached across the table to clasp my hand. "Promise?" she said.

"I swear by Zeus," I said. "And a McNally does not take an oath to Zeus lightly."

"Who's Zeus?" she asked.

"A Greek who owns a luncheonette up near Jupiter," I said.

I was spared further explanation when Pris brought our drinks and rattled off the specials of the day. Connie and I both opted for the mixed seafood salad (scallops, shrimp,

224

Florida lobster) with a loaf of garlic toast.

"I've got news for you," Connie said after we ordered, "and you're not going to like it."

"You're pregnant?"

"No, dammit," she said. "I'd love to have kids, wouldn't you?"

"I can't," I said. "Being of the male gender."

"You know what I mean," she said, laughing. "Anyway, the bad news is this: I was turned down by that medium."

"What!?"

She nodded. "I got a letter from Hertha Gloriana, a very cold letter. She said it was obvious to her that the person I described doesn't actually exist, and therefore she could not provide a psychic profile and was returning my check. She also told me not to apply again unless I told her the truth."

"I'll be damned."

"Archy, how did she know my letter was a phony? There was nothing in it that might tip her off it was a scam."

I shook my head. "I can't figure how she knew. But what's even more puzzling is that she returned your money. If the Glorianas have a swindle going, as I thought, Hertha would have cobbled up a fictitious profile and cashed your check."

"Perhaps she really is clairvoyant and knew at once that my letter was a trick."

"Perhaps."

Our lunch was served, and we talked of other things as we devoured our salads. Connie gave me a long account of her trials and tribulations in planning Lady Horowitz's Fourth of July bash, but I hardly listened; I couldn't stop brooding about Hertha's reaction to the fake letter. How *did* she know?

Connie didn't want any dessert and said she had to get back to her houseguests. I told her I was going to loll around the Club awhile and would phone her on Sunday. I escorted her out to her little Subaru.

"Thanks for the lunch, Archy," she said, "and I'm sorry I depressed you with the bad news about the medium's letter."

"You didn't depress me."

"Sure I did. You've hardly said a word since I told you, and when Archy McNally doesn't chatter, he's depressed."

"I think I'm more mystified than anything else. Connie, you don't happen to have that letter you received from the Glorianas, do you?"

"Yep," she said, fishing in the hip pocket of her overalls. "I'm glad you reminded me; I thought you might want it for your files. Don't forget to call me tomorrow, sweet."

She handed me a folded envelope, kissed my cheek, and hopped into her dinky car. I waved as she drove away. Then I unfolded the envelope, took out the letter, and read it in the bright sunlight. It was coldly phrased and stated pretty much what Connie had already told me. There were no surprises.

But what shocked me was that it had an even right-hand margin and had obviously been written on the same word processor as the Gillsworth letters and Peaches' ransom notes.

I went back into the Pelican Club and used the public phone in the rear of the bar area. I called Al Rogoff but he wasn't in his office, and they refused to tell me where he was. On a hunch, I then phoned Roderick Gillsworth's home and got results.

"Sergeant Rogoff," he said.

"McNally," I said. "You're still there? What on earth

226

are you doing?"

"Reading poetry."

"Gillsworth's? Awful dreck, isn't it?"

"Oh, I don't know," Al said. "Erotic stuff."

"You've got to be kidding," I said. "Gillsworth's poetry is about as erotic as the Corn Laws of England. Which book of his are you reading?"

"I'm not reading a book. I'm going through unpublished poems I found in a locked drawer in his desk. I picked the lock. A piece of cheese. Inside was a file of finished poems. They're dated and all appear to have been written in the past six months or so. And I'm telling you they're hot stuff."

I was flabbergasted. "I don't dig that at all," I told Al. "I've dipped into some of his published things, and believe me they're dull, dull, dull."

"Well, the stuff I've been reading is steamy enough to add a new chapter to *Psycopathia Sexualis*. Maybe he decided to change his style."

"Maybe," I said. "We can talk about that later. Right now I've got something more important."

I told him how the Glorianas were selling psychic profiles by mail, how I tried to prove it a scam by having Consuela Garcia send in a trumped-up letter from a nonexistent woman, how Hertha rejected the fake application, and how her missive was identical in format to the Gillsworth–Willigan letters.

"That does it," Rogoff said decisively. "I'll send the rookie to the Glorianas' office to see if he can confirm that they own a Smith Corona word processor. And instead of one under-cover cop, I'll plant a couple, man and woman, out at the Jo-Jean Motel and put round-the-clock surveillance on Cabin Four. And if the brass will give me the warm bodies, I'll stake out the Glorianas' apartment."

"That should do it," I said. "Al, Frank Gloriana carries a gun. Lydia Gillsworth told me."

"Thanks for the tip. Tell me, Archy, how do you figure the medium knew the letter you sent her was a phony?"

"I don't know," I said. "I just don't know."

I went back to the bar to sign the tab for lunch.

"Mr. Pettibone," I said abruptly, "do you believe in ghosts?"

He stared at me a moment through his square specs. "Why, yes, Mr. McNally," he said finally. "As a matter of fact, I do."

"Surely not the Halloween variety," I said. "The kind who wear white sheets and go 'Whooo! Whooo!'"

"Well, perhaps not those," he admitted. "But I do believe some of the departed return as spirits and are able to communicate with the living."

I had always considered the Pelican Club's majordomo to be the most practical and realistic of men, so it was startling to learn he accepted the existence of disembodied beings. "Have you ever spoken to the spirit of a deceased person?" I asked him.

"I have indeed, Mr. McNally," he said readily. "As you know, I am an active investor in the stock market. On several occasions the spirit of Mr. Bernard Baruch, the successful financier, has appeared to me. We meet on a park bench and he gives me advice on which stocks to buy and what to sell."

"And do you follow the ghost's advice?"

"Frequently."

"Do you win or lose?"

"Invariably I profit. But Mr. Baruch's spirit has a tendency to sell too soon."

"Thank you for the information, Mr. Pettibone," I said gravely and left him a handsome tip.

I drove home, garaged the Miata, and entered the

house through the kitchen. Ursi and Jamie Olson were both working on a rack of lamb dinner we were to have that evening. They looked up as I came in.

"Ursi," I said without preamble, "do you believe in ghosts?"

"I do, Mr. Archy," she said at once. "I frequently speak to my dear departed mother. She's very happy."

"Uh-huh," I said and turned to Jamie. "And how about you?" I asked. "Do you believe in ghosts?"

"Some," he said.

That evening during the family cocktail hour I asked my mother the same question.

"Oh my, yes," she said airily. "I have never seen them myself, but I have been told by people whose opinion I respect that spirits do exist. Mercedes Blair's husband died last year, you know, and she says that ever since he passed, their house has been haunted by his ghost. She knows because she always finds the toilet seat up. No matter how many times she puts the cover down, she always finds the seat up when she returns. She says it must be her dead husband's spirit."

I looked to my father. His hirsute eyebrows were jiggling up and down, a sure sign that he was stifling his mirth. But when he spoke, his voice was gentle and measured.

"Mother," he said, "I would not accept the testimony of Mrs. Blair as proof positive of the existence of disembodied spirits. It's similar to saying, 'I saw a ghost last night. It ran down the alley and jumped over a fence. And if you don't believe me, there's the fence.'"

I asked: "Then you don't believe the spirits of the departed return to earth and communicate with the living?"

He answered carefully. "I think when people report seeing a ghost or talking to a spirit, they sincerely believe they are telling the truth. But I suggest what they are actually reporting is a dream, a fantasy, and the spirit they allegedly see is a memory, a very intense memory, of a loved one who is deceased."

"But what if the spirit they claim to see is a historical character, someone they couldn't possibly have known?"

"Then they are talking rubbish," my father said forthrightly. "Utter and complete rubbish."

I retired to my lair after dinner to add entries to my journal, which was beginning to rival the girth of *War and Peace*, and to sort out the day's confused impressions.

I consider myself a fairly lucid chap. Oh, I admit I might exhibit a few moments of pure lunacy now and then, but generally the McNally hooves are solidly planted on terra firma. But now I was faced with a mystery that baffled me. How *did* Hertha Gloriana know Connie's letter was a hoax? And how was the medium, speaking in the voice of Lydia Gillsworth, able to shriek "Caprice!" and identify a clue that had already intrigued Sgt. Al Rogoff?

It was possible that Hertha had a genuine psychic gift. But if you admitted the existence of such a specialized talent, then you had to allow that the actuality of spirits was also conceivable, communication with the dead tenable, and all the other phenomena of the psi factor similarly capable of realization, including ESP, psychokinesis, telepathy, precognition, and perhaps, eventually, discussing the International Monetary Fund with dolphins.

That afternoon I had discovered that several perfectly normal citizens believed in ghosts and by extension, I supposed, in other manifestations of the supernatural. Could they be right and my father's cogent disbelief wrong?

I went to bed that night and with my eyes firmly shut I

willed with all my strength for the appearance of Carole Lombard's ghost.

She never showed up.

14

Like most people I consider Monday the first day of the week. It is actually the second, of course, but Sunday is usually observed as a day of rest, a *faux* holiday, a twenty-four-hour vacation to be devoted to worship, a big midday meal, and just lollygagging about and recharging one's batteries.

But that particular Sunday turned out to be something entirely different. It deepened my confusion and increased my suspicion that events were moving so swiftly it was impossible to cope. Men who have been in battle have described it to me as disorder in the nth degree. Before that Sunday concluded, I felt I deserved a combat ribbon.

It began when I overslept and went downstairs to find that my parents had already departed for church. And the Olsons had left for *their* church. So I fixed my own matutinal meal, succeeding in dropping a buttered English muffin onto the floor. Butter-side down, inevitably – another puzzle I've never solved. I also knocked over a full cup of coffee. That brunch did not augur a successful Sabbath.

The phone rang as I was mopping up the spilt coffee and I really didn't want to answer, thinking it was sure to be calamitous news. But I girded my loins (how on earth does one gird a loin?) and picked up after the sixth ring.

"The McNally residence," I said.

"Archy?" Meg Trumble said. "Good morning!"

You could have knocked me over with a palm frond. "Good morning, Meg," I said. "What a pleasant surprise."

"What are you doing?" she asked.

"If you must know, I'm wiping up spilled coffee."

She laughed. "That doesn't sound like much fun. Archy, Hertha Gloriana is with me, and she'd like to speak to you."

"Sure," I said. "Put her on."

"No, no. Not on the telephone. Can you come over to my place?"

"Now?"

"Please. We're going to do some aerobics, and then we plan to go to the beach. Could you make it soon, Archy? It's important."

"All right," I said. "Half an hour or so."

The day was muddling up nicely, and as I spun the Miata toward Riviera Beach I didn't even want to imagine what lay ahead. I knew only that it would add to my flummoxization – and if there isn't such a word, there should be.

I walked into quite a scene for an early Sunday afternoon. The two women were wearing exercise costumes of skin-tight gleaming spandex; Meg in a cat-suit of silver and Hertha in a purple leotard and pink biking shorts. Apparently they had finished their workout, for both were sheened with sweat and still panting slightly. And they were sipping glasses of orange sludge.

"Carrot juice, Archy?" Meg asked.

232

I fought nausea valiantly. "Thank you, no," I replied. "I have no desire to see in the dark."

"A cold beer?"

"Thank you, yes."

Hertha patted the couch cushion beside her, and I sat there, a bit gingerly I admit. I had an uneasy feeling of having intruded into a ladies' locker room. I had been invited but couldn't rid myself of feeling an interloper.

Meg brought me a popped can of Bud Light, which I accepted gratefully.

"Hertha," she said commandingly, "tell him."

The medium turned to me. She seemed uncommonly attractive at that moment, her fair skin flushed from exercise and something in her eyes I had never seen before. It was more than happiness, I thought; it was triumph.

"It's about Peaches," she said to me. "I had another vision. Remember I told you I saw her in a plain room? It's in a small building, like a cabin. I think it may be at an old-fashioned motel."

I took a gulp of my beer. "That's interesting," I said. "Did you see where the motel is located?"

"I'm sure it's in the West Palm Beach area."

"Tell him what else you saw, Hertha," Meg ordered.

The medium hesitated a second. "Perhaps I shouldn't be revealing this," she said, "but it troubles me and you did ask for my help. I hope you will keep it confidential."

"Of course."

"I saw my husband, Frank, in the room with the cat."

The two women looked at me expectantly. That they were attempting to manipulate me I had no doubt. There was no alternative but to play along. I'm good at acting the simp; it just seems to come naturally.

"That *is* a shocker," I said. "What on earth do you suppose he was doing there?"

"I don't know," she wide-eyed me. "Do you suppose

233

he had anything to do with the catnapping?"

The greatest actress since Duse.

"Why don't you ask him?" I suggested.

"I've got to be completely honest with you, Archy," she started – and my antennae stiffened. When people say that to you it's time to button your hip pocket to make certain your wallet is secure. "Frank has an awful temper," she went on. "I'm afraid of angering him. He can become quite physical."

"The brute beats her," Meg said wrathfully.

"Not exactly," Hertha said. "But he has struck me on occasion."

I was terribly tempted to remark that if she was truly a seeress she would foreknow the blows in time to duck. I said nothing of the sort of course. I said, "Dreadful."

"So you see I can't ask Frank about it," the medium said sorrowfully. "But I hope it may help you recover the cat."

"I'm sure it will," I said. "And I thank you for being so cooperative."

I finished my beer (sadly, only an 8-oz. can) and bid the ladies adieu. They were both looking at me thoughtfully when I left the apartment.

I drove home slowly, reflecting on what I had just been told. It was obvious the two women had compared notes and Hertha now knew the original reason I had given her for wanting to find Peaches was false. She was aware the cat had been snatched and I had been employed to find it. That much was clear.

What wasn't quite so apparent was how she knew the missing feline was presently incarcerated in a motel cabin. Either she was telling the truth and had seen the cat and Frank in a psychic vision or she had overheard conversation at home revealing the cat's whereabouts and Frank's guilt.

But then I realized *how* she knew was unimportant. What was vital was that she was intent on implicating her husband. The story of the physical abuse she suffered at his hands might or might not be true. But I felt Hertha had a deeper motive for wanting her spouse apprehended and perhaps tucked away for an appreciable period in the clink.

I was still pondering the medium's motive for snitching when I arrived home, saw the Lexus in the garage, and knew my parents had returned from church. When I entered the house, my father was standing in the open doorway of his study.

"Are you acquainted with a woman named Mrs. Irma Gloriana?" he demanded. It was almost an accusation.

"Yes, sir, I am," I replied.

He nodded, beckoned, led the way into his study, and closed the door. He sat behind his desk and motioned me to an armchair.

"I think you better tell me about her," he said.

"It's a long story, father."

"Dinner will not be served for another hour," he said dryly. "Surely that will be sufficient time."

Usually mein papa does not question me about details of my discreet inquiries. I think he suspects I cut ethical corners – which I do – and he'd rather not have knowledge of my *modus operandi*. Successful results are really all that concern him.

But since he wanted to know about Mrs. Irma Gloriana, I told him. And not only Irma, but husband Otto, son Frank, and daughter-in-law Hertha. I also gave him an account of the séance I had attended and related how I had managed to locate Peaches in Cabin Four of the Jo-Jean Motel. I concluded with a brief report on my most recent meeting with Hertha Gloriana and Meg Trumble. In fact, I told him everything you already know.

235

He listened closely and never once interrupted. When I had finished, he rose and walked slowly to the sideboard where he carefully packed one of his silver-mounted Upshall pipes. I took that as permission to light up an English Oval. He regained his swivel chair and held his loaded pipe a moment before flaming it.

"Then I gather you and Sergeant Rogoff believe the Glorianas are guilty of criminal behavior," he pronounced.

"I cannot speak for the sergeant," I said, "but I am convinced that Frank Gloriana connived with Laverne Willigan to steal the cat and hold it for ransom. I also think Otto Gloriana, probably Irma, and possibly Frank were involved in the murders of Lydia and Roderick Gillsworth. But I have no idea as to their motive."

He finally lighted his pipe. When he had it drawing freely without a gurgle, he blew a plume of smoke at the coffered ceiling. "Perhaps we'll learn tomorrow," he remarked.

I was astonished. "Tomorrow, father?" I said.

He nodded. "Shortly after returning from church, I received a phone call from Mrs. Irma Gloriana. A very forceful woman."

"Yes, sir, she is that."

"She wishes to see me tomorrow. She said it was an important matter concerning Roderick Gillsworth. I thought it best to listen to what she has to say. We're meeting in my office at ten o'clock. I'd like you to be present, Archy."

"Of course," I said, grinning. "Absolutely. Looking forward to it, sir. May I tell Sergeant Rogoff about the meeting?"

He considered that request a long, long time. I had learned to wait patiently, knowing that eventually his mulling would end and he'd come to a decision.

236

"Yes," he said at last, "you may tell the sergeant. And he will be informed as to the results of the meeting if circumstances and ethics allow. It may possibly aid his investigation. You say this woman was formerly the madam of a brothel?"

"Yes, sir. According to the Atlanta Police."

"A coarse woman?"

"No, sir, I would not say that – although Al Rogoff might possibly disagree. As you said, she is a forceful woman. I find her almost domineering. Very sure of herself, very heavy in the willpower department. I see her as the Chief Executive Officer of the Gloriana family, the dynamo, with perhaps a tendency to tyrannize." I hesitated a second. Then: "There is something else. In my opinion she is a disturbing woman. Physically, that is. She exudes a certain sensuality. I believe she is aware of it and uses it. I put her age at close to sixty, but there has certainly been no diminution of her sexual attractiveness."

One of my father's hairy eyebrows slowly ascended. But all he said was, "Interesting."

But then, as I rose to leave, he added, "I usually find your reaction to people very perceptive, Archy."

Praise! How sweet it was.

That evening I called Al Rogoff, reported on my meeting with Hertha Gloriana, and informed him of my father's Monday morning appointment with Mrs. Irma Gloriana.

"Oh boy," Al said. "I have a feeling the lady is about to drop a bomb. Keep me up to speed on what happens, Archy."

"Did you get your spies into the Jo-Jean Motel?"

"Yep. Man and woman in Cabin Five, right next to Otto's pad. They've already reported by radio. He's had two visitors so far. I make them as Frank and Irma. Be

237

sure to call me tomorrow after your father's meeting."

"Wait a minute," I cried. "Don't hang up. Those erotic poems Gillsworth wrote – did he mention any names?"

"No one you know," Rogoff said.

"Come on, Al," I said, "don't play games. What names did he mention?"

"Just one. Astarte. I looked it up. Goddess of fertility and sexual love."

"I know her well," I said. "She lives in Miami Beach."

Then he did hang up.

But that long, aggravating day had not yet ended. Later that evening I was in my sanctum, working on my journal, when Laverne Willigan phoned.

"Another ransom note, Archy," she told me. "It was slipped under the front door sometime tonight."

"Uh-huh," I said. "Will you read it to me, please?"

She did. The letter commanded Harry Willigan to assemble fifty thousand dollars in fifty-dollar bills, unmarked with no numbers in sequence. Then he or his representative would deliver the money to a messenger. That was the term used: "Messenger." He would be waiting in the parking area of a twenty-four-hour convenience store on Federal Highway at midnight on Monday. The address given, I judged, was about a mile from the Jo-Jean Motel.

After the ransom had been handed over, the messenger would leave, but Willigan or his representative was ordered to remain in the parking area. When the fifty thousand had been counted and the bills examined and approved, Peaches would be delivered, hale and hearty.

Laverne continued: "It also says if the messenger sees or suspects the presence of the police, Harry will never see his pet alive again."

"I don't like the setup," I said immediately. "What if the fifty thousand is handed over to the messenger, he

238

disappears, and Peaches is never produced? It seems to me they're asking Harry to take a horrendous risk."

"He doesn't have much choice, does he?" Laverne said. "Not if he wants to rub noses with Sweetums again. I called Harry in Chicago and told him what the letter said. He cursed a blue streak but finally said he'll play ball. He's going to phone his Palm Beach bank in the morning and tell them to get the cash together. The bank will call me when it's ready. Then I'll phone you. Harry wants you to deliver the money and get Peaches back. Will you do it, Archy?"

"Of course," I said. "It's the least I can do after failing to locate the catnappers. Let me know when the bank has the cash ready. I'll pick it up from them. And sometime tomorrow I'll stop by your place and get the letter. If you're going out, leave it with Leon."

"Thank you, Archy," she said briskly. "I'm sure everything will work out just fine."

"I think so, too," I said. "Harry will be back on Tuesday?"

"Yes. Early in the morning. By that time you should have Peaches."

After she hung up I phoned Al Rogoff again to alert him to this new development. But I was unable to locate him and decided it could wait until the morning. Then we'd devise a plan to thwart the villains.

Monday was shaping up as a hellacious day. I only hoped I'd live to see Tuesday.

15

I awoke Monday morning with a dread feeling of having forgotten to do something I should have done. I recognized my lapse while scraping my jowls, and if it hadn't been a safety razor I might have nicked the old jug, I was that mortified. What I had disremembered was to phone Connie Garcia on Sunday as I had promised. Not for the first time did I wonder why I treated that dear woman with such thoughtless neglect. I suppose it was because I knew she was *there*.

I had roused in time to breakfast with my parents in the dining room. While scarfing my way through a stack of buck-wheat pancakes, I informed the governor of Laverne Willigan's phone call the previous night.

He glanced up from *The Wall Street Journal* long enough to gaze at me speculatively. "You actually intend to deliver the money to the catnappers yourself, Archy?"

"Yes, sir. I expect Sergeant Rogoff will come up with a plan for a trap."

He nodded. "When you receive the fifty thousand at the bank," he advised, "count it before you sign a receipt."

I sighed. "Yes, father," I said. Sometimes he treated me as if I were the village idiot. I do have a brain, you know, even though occasionally I choose not to use it.

Before leaving for the Willigan hacienda, I phoned Al Rogoff at his office and found him in a surprisingly lively mood.

"What are you so chirpy about?" I asked him.

"It's all coming together, old buddy. I'll fill you in later. What's up?"

I repeated what Laverne Willigan had told me of the catnappers' letter and the instructions as to how the ransom was to be paid.

"I don't like it," Al said at once. "Too much risk of a double X."

"I told Laverne that but she said Harry has no choice and is willing to shell out the fifty grand."

"Which makes her and the boyfriend happy – right? Okay, Archy, I'll start working on a snare for midnight tonight."

"After I collect the money from the bank, do you want to mark the bills?"

"Haven't got time," he said. "And too dangerous if they've got a lamp to read the markings. We'll make a list of the serial numbers; that'll hold up in court. Stay in touch; it's going to be a rackety day."

"Tell me about it. Al, do you think you'll be able to keep Laverne Willigan out of it?'

He was silent a moment. Then he said, "It depends," and I had to be satisfied with that.

Then I buzzed down to the Willigan manse. Leon told me the lady of the house was busy with her pedicurist, but he handed me the latest ransom note in its white envelope.

"I guess Peaches is coming home," he said.

"Looks like it," I agreed.

"And I start sneezing again," he said mournfully.

"If you don't like cats," I said, "why don't you buy yourself a koala or a wallaby? Just to remind you of down under."

"I've been down *and* under since I got here," he complained. "Florida is the outback with oranges."

Have you ever noticed that some people aren't happy unless they're unhappy?

Then I scooted for the McNally Building somewhat in excess of the legal speed limit. I arrived in time to smoke a cigarette before joining my father. I noted my hands weren't exactly shaking, but I would not have selected that moment to thread a needle. It was amazing how the prospect of a meeting with Mrs. Irma Gloriana rasped my nerves.

I went up to my father's office a few minutes before ten o'clock.

"I think it best, Archy," he said, "if you serve as a witness, a silent witness. Please let me ask the questions. If you are addressed directly, of course, you may respond. But I would prefer the conversation be limited to Mrs. Gloriana and myself."

"I'll be a fly on the wall," I assured him.

"Exactly," he said with his wintry smile.

His phone rang, and he glanced at the antique railroad clock on the wall over his rolltop desk. "The lady is prompt," he said. He picked up the phone. "Yes, show her in, please."

Mrs. Trelawney opened the door and stood aside to allow Mrs. Irma Gloriana to enter. Then the secretary closed the door softly.

Father was standing at his desk and I was across the room next to the bottle-green leather chesterfield. Irma took two steps into the office, her eyes on my father. Then she became aware of my presence, stared at me for a beat or two, and turned back to father.

"What is he doing here?" she demanded.

"I am Prescott McNally," he said in a plummy voice,

"and I presume you are Mrs. Irma Gloriana. Since you are already acquainted with my son, I have asked him to attend this meeting as witness and adviser. You may be assured of his discretion."

Irma shook her head angrily. "It won't do," she said. "I don't need a witness and I don't need an adviser. I insist on a private, confidential conversation between you and me."

"In that case," my father said, "I suggest this meeting be terminated forthwith. Good day, madam." (He accented the "madam" ever so slightly.)

How I admired his tactics! Not only was he establishing his command of the situation but he was determining her anxiety level. If she marched out, then she felt she held a winning hand. If she remained, then her role was that of a supplicant, anxious to cut a deal.

She stood a moment in silence, and I reflected it was the first time I had seen her irresolute.

She was wearing a tailored suit of pale pink linen with a high-necked blouse. It was certainly a conservative costume; but not even a chador could conceal that woman's sexual radiance, and I wondered if my father was aware of it. I suspected he was. He might be stodgy but he was not torpid.

We waited.

"Very well," Mrs. Gloriana said finally. "If you wish . . ."

Father gestured toward an armchair upholstered in the same leather as the chesterfield. He sat in his swivel chair, turned to face his visitor. I remained standing in a position where I could observe them both without making like a fan at a tennis match.

"Mr. McNally," she said crisply, "I understand you were the attorney for the late Roderick Gillsworth."

"That is correct."

"Then I suppose you're handling his estate?"

He inclined his head, and she took that for assent. In addition to a black calfskin handbag she was carrying a zippered envelope of beige suede, large enough to hold legal documents. She opened the three-sided zipper with one swift motion and withdrew two sheets of white paper stapled together.

"I have here," she began (and I marveled at how assertive her voice was), "a photocopy of a handwritten last will and testament executed by Roderick Gillsworth approximately a month ago. It has been properly prepared, dated, and witnessed. Attached is a photocopy of an affidavit signed by the testator and both witnesses in the presence of a notary public and so certified. I believe the affidavit makes Mr. Gillsworth's will self-proving, and it may be admitted to probate without further testimony by the witnesses."

She leaned forward to proffer the documents. My father bent forward to accept them. He remained in that position a moment, staring at her expressionlessly. Then he leaned back and began to read. He perused the two sheets slowly, then read them again. He turned his swivel chair a bit to face me.

"Archy," he said, his voice dry, "this purportedly holographic will, allegedly signed by Roderick Gillsworth and witnessed by Irma Gloriana and Frank Gloriana, states that the original manuscripts of the testator's poems shall be given to the Library of Congress. Other than that, the total assets of Roderick Gillsworth at the time of his death are bequeathed to Irma Gloriana."

Al Rogoff had been right; the bomb had been dropped.

My father's aplomb was something to see. He showed absolutely no sign of the turmoil I knew must be racking him. The face he turned to Mrs. Gloriana was peaceable, and when he spoke, his voice and

244

manner were pleasantness personified.

"You were a friend of the late Mr. Gillsworth?" he inquired.

"A close personal friend," she said defiantly, lifting her chin. "Especially after his dear wife passed over. I believe my family and I provided him with spiritual comfort."

"My son tells me your daughter-in-law is a medium."

"She is. And very gifted, I might add."

"Did Mr. Gillsworth attend the séances I understand are held at your home?"

"Occasionally. He attended with his wife."

Father nodded and seemed to relax. He looked down at the papers he was holding, rolled them in a loose tube, tapped them gently on his knee. He didn't speak, and his silence obviously perturbed Mrs Gloriana.

"Is there any reason why this will cannot be filed for probate immediately?" she said. "It is absolutely authentic."

"Well, naturally that must be determined," he said smoothly. "The testator's signature must be verified, as well as that of the certifying notary public. A search must be conducted to locate immediate survivors – family members – if such exist. In addition, I wish to review the statutes of the State of Florida dealing with holographic wills."

That last, of course, was complete nonsense. My father knew Florida law as well or better than any attorney practicing in the State. He knew the music, knew the lyrics, and could sing you verse and refrain. He was simply stalling this would-be client.

"How long will you need?" Irma asked. "I know that probating a will takes months, so I want to get it started as soon as possible."

"Very understandable," he said. "And I shall attempt to expedite the process as much as possible. Where are

245

the originals of these documents now?"

"In my safe deposit box."

He nodded. "And do you have any evidence, Mrs. Gloriana – personal letters from Mr. Gillsworth, for instance – that might attest to your friendship with the testator?"

"Why should that be necessary?" she asked indignantly. "Take my word for it, we were close friends."

"Oh, I do take your word," he said. "But sometimes probate judges make inquiries to establish to their own satisfaction the relationship between testator and beneficiary."

"Well, yes," she admitted, "I do have some letters from Rod. And a few unpublished poems he sent to me. And autographed copies of two of his books."

"Excellent. And where is this material at present?"

"Also in my safe deposit box."

"I suggest you have photocopies made of anything that relates to your friendship with Mr. Gillsworth and have the copies delivered to my office."

"Must I do all that?"

"I strongly urge it. It is my duty to anticipate any questions the presiding judge might have and be prepared to answer them. Do you have any notion of the size of Mr. Gillsworth's estate, madam?"

That last was asked suddenly in a sharp voice, and I could see it flustered her for a brief moment.

"Why, no," she said. "Not exactly. At the time Rod wrote out his will, he said he didn't have much."

That at least, I acknowledged, was the truth.

"And did he give you any reason why he was making a holographic will rather than coming to me, his attorney of record, to have his last testament revised?"

She was obviously ready for that query; her answer was immediate and glib: "He said that because you also rep-

246

resented his wife, he didn't want to run the risk of Lydia learning he had changed his will."

That implied Prescott McNally might be guilty of unethical conduct, but father voiced no objection. He stood and waited until she had gathered up handbag and suede envelope.

"Thank you for coming in, Mrs. Gloriana," he said cordially. "If you will supply me with copies of the personal correspondence in your safe deposit box, I will start preparing an application for probate as well as initiating those other inquiries I mentioned. Please feel free to phone me if you have any further questions or desire a progress report."

She nodded coolly. I wondered if they would shake hands on parting. They didn't. He opened the office door for her and she swept through, head high, indomitable.

Father returned to his swivel chair, and I collapsed onto the couch, weary from standing erect for so long.

"As you said, Archy," the sire remarked with a wry smile, "a disturbing woman."

"Sir," I said, "is a handwritten will legal in Florida?"

"Oh yes," he said, "if it is properly prepared, as this one apparently is. In addition, the attached affidavit serves as self-proof of the authenticity of the will."

"And is a witness allowed to inherit?"

"Yes, a witness to a last will and testament may also be a beneficiary, under Florida law. Archy, methinks the lady and Gillsworth had the assistance of an attorney in preparing this will and the accompanying affidavit. Some of the language she used was legalese, borrowed from the lawyer I'm certain she consulted. The question then arises: why did she come to me? The will I prepared for Gillsworth has been superseded by this holographic will. And, in effect, I have been superseded. Mrs. Gloriana could just as easily have retained the attorney who as-

247

sisted her and ask him to file for probate. But she came to me. Why?"

"Father, I think she figured that by retaining you she would eliminate the possibility of your asking embarrassing questions, causing trouble, delaying her receiving what she considers her rightful due. And if you raise too many objections, she'll offer to cut you in on her inheritance."

He looked at me thoughtfully. "Yes," he said, "I do believe you may be correct. The lady is using me, and I don't relish it."

We sat in a moody silence awhile, chewing our mental cud, and then my father drew a deep breath.

"Archy," he said, "yesterday you told me you thought the Glorianas were involved in the murders of Lydia and Roderick Gillsworth but you had no idea as to their motive." He held up the copy of the holographic will. "Now you have a motive."

I rose to my feet. "I better call Sergeant Rogoff," I said. "Interesting morning, sir."

"Wasn't it," he agreed.

On my way through the outer office Mrs. Trelawney took one look at my expression and evidently decided not to crack any jokes or make any reference to our recent visitor. Instead she silently handed me a message: Mrs. Laverne Willigan had phoned and I was to call her as soon as possible.

I returned to my closet, phoned the Willigan house, spoke to Leon, and eventually Laverne came on the line. She told me she had heard from the bank, the fifty thousand was ready, and I could pick it up anytime. I thanked her and hung up at once, fearing she might ask questions about plans for delivery of the ransom.

Then I phoned Sgt. Rogoff.

"Al," I said, "I'm in my office, Irma Gloriana just left,

and you were right. But that bomb she dropped was a blockbuster. Can you come over?"

"On my way," he said. "Fifteen minutes."

He was as good as his word. He came barging in and plumped down in the uncomfortable steel chair alongside my desk. He lighted a cigar and took out his notebook. "All right," he said, "let's have it."

I gave him a complete account of what had transpired in my father's office. When I started, he tried to keep up by scribbling notes, but then he became so entranced by my report that he left off writing, let his cigar go out, and just listened, bending forward intently.

I finished, and he leaned back, relighted the cold cigar and stared at me. I lighted a cigarette, and within minutes my tiny office was fuggy.

"A handwritten will is legal?" he asked finally.

"My father says so. And a witness can be a beneficiary."

"And Irma gets everything?"

"Everything but the original manuscripts."

He made a grimace of disgust. "Why did the idiot do it?"

"That's obvious," I said. "Sexual obsession."

"I love the way you talk," he said. "You mean he had the hots for her."

"That's exactly what I mean," I said.

Then, when we both grasped the implications of the poet's folly, I think we became excited – hunters on a fresh spoor. We couldn't talk fast enough.

"Look, Al," I said. "Lydia was a lovely woman but something of a bluestocking. The gossip in Palm Beach was that the Gillsworths had a marriage in name only."

"Then Roderick goes to one of those cockamamy séances with his wife and meets Mrs. Irma Gloriana. Snap, crackle, and pop!"

"Irma was everything Lydia wasn't: voluptuous, dominant, and a wanton when it suited her purpose."

"And as rapacious as a shrike."

"So they have an affair. Rod learns there's more to life than iambic pentameters, and Irma calculates this besotted fool might be the answer to her family's money problems. Do you buy all that?"

"Every word of it," Rogoff said. "That's why he began writing those erotic poems; the poor devil couldn't control his glands. It happens to all of us sooner or later."

"But not many of us end up dead because of it."

"Thank God."

"You think Gillsworth knew Otto was Irma's husband?"

"I doubt that. I think she passed him off as her brother or a friend."

"You're probably right," I said. "How's this scenario: Irma learns that Rod is practically penniless but his wife is loaded."

"And if she dies, her husband inherits the bulk of her estate."

"Who do you think made the first fatal suggestion?"

"The husband," Al said promptly. "If that was the price he had to pay to keep enjoying Irma, he was willing."

"Maybe Irma promised to marry him once Lydia was out of the picture. That's assuming he didn't know she was already married."

"And I'm betting Irma told him he wouldn't have to do the dirty deed himself; her so-called brother or friend would take care of Lydia – for a price, of course."

"Maybe the price was Gillsworth writing out that holographic will, leaving everything to Irma. A lovely quid pro quo. But why the poison-pen letters, Al?"

"Just to send the cops galloping off in all directions

250

looking for a psycho who didn't exist. By the way, I sent that rookie up to the Glorianas' office to try to sell Frank a Smith Corona word processor. You were right; Frank already owns a model PWP 100C."

"You think he was in on the plot to murder the Gillsworths?"

Rogoff pondered a moment. "I doubt it," he said finally. "He obviously knew about it – he witnessed the will, didn't he? – but I don't think he was a partner. Frankie boy had his own plot in the works: the catnapping of Peaches with the loving assistance of Laverne Willigan."

"Who he probably met at a séance. Those séances are beginning to resemble the bawdyhouse the Glorianas operated in Atlanta."

"Archy, you figure the medium knew what was going down?"

"Hertha? I don't think she knew about the murder plan. She knew her husband was nuzzling Laverne Willigan, but she just didn't care. Hertha isn't guilty of any crimes, Al."

He looked at me, amused. "How about conduct that violates the ethical code of psychics?"

"Well, yes, she may possibly be guilty of that."

He laughed. "Listen, let's go through the whole megillah one more time from the top and see if we can spot any holes."

So we reviewed out entire scenario, starting with Roderick Gillsworth meeting Irma Gloriana and falling in love – or whatever he fell into. It seemed a reasonable script with only a few minor questions to be answered, such as the date Otto Gloriana arrived in Greater West Palm Beach, where Irma and Rod consummated their illicit union, and why Lydia Gillsworth had opened her locked door to allow her murderer to enter.

251

"We'll clear those things up," the sergeant said confidently. "Now that we've got a logical hypothesis, we'll know what evidence to look for and what's just garbage."

"Whoa!" I said. "I hope you're not going to discard facts simply because they don't fit our theory. That's ridiculous – and dangerous."

"It's not a question of discarding facts," he argued. "It's a matter of interpretation. Let me give you a for-instance. When Gillsworth's body was found, there was a big meal he had been preparing in the kitchen: six huge crab cakes and an enormous salad. Now there were three interpretations of that humongous meal. One: he was famished and was going to eat the whole thing himself. Two: he was making enough food so he could have a leftover dinner the next day. And three: he was expecting a guest and was preparing dinner for two people. According to our theory, the third supposition is the most likely. He was expecting Irma Gloriana to join him for dinner. The doorbell rings, he looks through the judas window, sees her, and unlocks the door. Otto is standing to one side, out of sight, and the moment the door is open, he comes barreling in with his single-edge razor blade. Doesn't that sound right to you? It's what I mean by interpreting facts. They don't become evidence until you can establish their significance. If you don't have a reasonable supposition, you can drown in facts."

"Thank you, professor," I said. "I've enjoyed your lecture enormously. Of course it's based on the belief that our scenario is accurate."

"You believe that, don't you?"

"I do," I said. "It seems to me the only plausible explanation of what happened."

But that wasn't the whole truth. Do you recall my mentioning a vague notion I had early on, something so tenuous that I couldn't put it into words? Then, as more

252

was learned about the homicides, I began to see an outline. Now, with the most recent revelations, the outline was filling in and taking on substance. If it proved valid, it would radically alter the script Sgt. Rogoff had adopted so enthusiastically. But I didn't tell him that.

"Al," I said, "the bank has the ransom money ready. Will you go with me to pick it up? You're the man with the gun."

"Sure," he agreed readily. "Then I want you to come back to headquarters with me. We've got to go over the program for tonight's payoff."

"I hope you've devised an effective plan."

"It should work," he said.

I sighed. "Can't you be more positive than that? After all, it's my neck that's at risk."

"Well . . . " he said doubtfully, "maybe you better not buy any green bananas."

Then he laughed. I didn't.

16

I spent that entire afternoon with Sgt. Rogoff and an ad hoc squad of uniformed officers assigned to him. As the night's action was outlined to me, and my own role described, I realized Al had done a remarkable job of organizing a complex operation in a short time.

Of course, in accordance with Murphy's Law, some

253

things were bound to go wrong, and we spent much of our time brainstorming possible contingencies and planning how they might best be handled. I was satisfied that the overall plan was workable and, with a little bit o' luck, would achieve its objectives.

I wanted to leave the ransom money with Rogoff, but he was loath to accept the responsibility. He did keep a copy of the list of serial numbers the bank had thoughtfully provided. But when I left the Palm Beach police headquarters, which looks like a Mediterranean villa, I was lugging fifty thousand dollars in fifty-dollar bills. The bank had supplied a K-Mart shopping bag as a carrier. Why do all the great dramas of my life contain the elements of farce?

Naturally my mother had not been informed that her dear little boy was engaged in a perilous enterprise that might involve violence. Father and I tried to make our family cocktail hour and dinner that night no different from the umpteen that had gone before. We talked, we laughed, we each devoured a half-dozen delightful quail, and I don't believe mother had an inkling that I was – well, I won't say I was scared out of my wits, but I admit my trepidation level was high.

After dinner, she left us to go upstairs to her television program, and I resisted the temptation to kiss her farewell. I mean I wasn't going off to the Battle of Blenheim, was I? It was really just a small piece of law enforcement business from which I was certain to emerge with all my limited faculties intact. I told myself that. Several times.

My self-induced euphoria was rather diminished when father invited me into his study for a cognac. I knew he meant well, but I considered offering me a brandy was somewhat akin to being supplied with a blindfold and final cigarette. But at least he didn't say, "Be careful." He did say, "Call me as soon as it's over."

Then I went upstairs to change. Al Rogoff had suggested I dress in black, and when I had asked why, he replied, "You'll make a harder target." The other cops on his special squad thought that uproariously funny, but I considered their levity in poor taste.

About nine o'clock I came downstairs, dressed completely in black and carrying my shopping bag of cash. I went out to the Miata and paused to look about. It was a warm night, the dark sky swirled with horsetail clouds. Stars were there, a pale moon and, as I stared heavenward, an airliner droned overhead, going north. I wished I was on it.

I drove directly to police headquarters. Sgt. Rogoff and his cohorts were donning bulletproof vests and inspecting their weapons which, I noted, included shotguns and tear gas and smoke grenades and launchers. There was also a variety of electronic gizmos being tested. I wasn't certain of their function and intended use.

I stripped to the waist and a technician "wired" me, an unpleasant experience involving what seemed to be yards of adhesive tape. When he finished, I was equipped with microphone, battery pack, and transmitter. I put on shirt and jacket again, and we moved outside to test my efficacy as a mobile radio station.

The sergeant instructed me to move a hundred feet away, turn on the power switch, and say something. I did as ordered, activated myself and recited the "Tomorrow, and tomorrow . . . " speech from *Macbeth*. Rogoff waved me to return. "Loud and clear," he said. "Let's get this show on the road."

It was a veritable parade. This was a joint operation, and we had cars and personnel from the police departments of the Town of Palm Beach, the City of West Palm Beach, and the Sheriff's Office of Palm Beach County. All for Peaches! The three jurisdictions were cooperating under a long-standing system Sgt. Rogoff described as "Share the glory and spread the blame."

And in the middle of this procession was a flag-red open convertible sports car inhabited by yr. humble servant, Archibald McNally.

I soon cut out and let the armada proceed without me. The script called for my arrival at the parking area of the convenience store on Federal Highway at 11.45 p.m. I was right on schedule and pulled into a parking slot that provided a good view of the storefront. I switched on my transmitter.

"McNally on station," I reported in a normal voice.

I watched, and in a moment the policewoman in civvies, planted in the store by Rogoff, came to the front window and began to fuss with a display of junk foods: the signal that she was receiving my transmission and would relay it to the task force via her more powerful radio.

I settled down, lighted an English Oval, and wondered why I hadn't relieved myself before setting out on this adventure. All my anxiety and discomfort, I realized, resulted from my trying to assist that fatheaded Willigan, and I was trying to recall lines from *Henry V*: "Unto the breach, lads, for Harry and . . . " when an old Chrysler Imperial pulled slowly into the lighted parking area and stopped in a space about twenty feet away from me.

"I think he's here," I said aloud. "Black Chrysler Imperial. Man getting out and walking toward me."

Rogoff and I had agreed that the messenger was not likely to be Frank Gloriana; he would have no desire to be identified by me as the catnapper. The logical choice for collector would be Otto Gloriana, Frank's daddy.

And as he came closer, I had no doubt whatsoever that this tall, reddish-haired, broad-shouldered man of about sixty-five was indeed Otto Gloriana, aka Charles Girard, former bordello owner and the ex-con described by

Atlanta police as "a nasty piece of work." What surprised me was how handsome he was.

He was wearing a rumpled seersucker suit, and his hands were thrust deep into the jacket pockets. He came near, almost pressing against my door. That was fine with me; it brought him closer to my concealed microphone.

"You from Harry Willigan?" he asked in a resonant baritone.

"That's correct," I said.

"You have the fifty thousand?"

"Right here," I said and started to lift the shopping bag from the passenger seat to hand it to him. But he moved back one step.

"Get out of the car," he said. "Carry the money."

I was astonished. "Why should I do that?" I said.

"Because if you don't," he said pleasantly, "I'll kill you."

He withdrew his right hand from his jacket pocket far enough to reveal that he was gripping a short-barreled revolver that appeared to be a .38 Special. His back was to the window of the convenience store, and there was no one nearby. I was certain his action was unobserved.

"You have a gun?" I said in a tone of disbelief, praying this conversation was being received "loud and clear" by the officer inside the store. "That's not necessary. Just take the money and bring the cat back."

He sighed. "You're not very swift, are you? I'll say it just once more, and if you don't do what I say, you'll have three eyes. Now get out of this baby carriage slowly. Carry the money. Walk to my car. I'll be right behind you."

I did as ordered, thinking sadly that we had prepared for every possible contingency except my being taken hostage. At least that's what I hoped was happening. I had no wish to meet my Maker in the parking lot of a store that sold Twinkies and diet root beer.

We came up to the Chrysler and the rear door was opened from within by the man sitting behind the wheel.

"Get in," Otto commanded.

I did, swinging the bag of cash onto the floor. I sat back in one corner and got a look at the driver.

"Why, Frank Gloriana," I said in a loud voice. "What a surprise!"

"Shut your face," the older Gloriana said to me. And to his son, "Drive."

We pulled out and headed south on Federal Highway. I reckoned we were out of range of the receiver in the store, but just in case, I said, "Going to the Jo-Jean Motel, are we?"

Otto took the revolver from his pocket and rapped the side of my skull with the steel barrel. What can I tell you? It hurt.

"I told you to keep your yap shut," my captor said. "I'll do all the talking."

So I remained silent and tried to calculate the odds against my ever playing the harpsichord again. Rather heavy, I concluded. The fact that I had been allowed to witness Frank's involvement in this caper boded ill for my future. It seemed highly unlikely that I would be allowed to live, even if I vowed to keep my yap permanently sealed.

We turned into the driveway of the Jo-Jean Motel. I knew there were two police officers in Cabin Five and two more in the back room of the motel office. They had been stationed there with the enthusiastic cooperation of the owner who probably hoped the Jo-Jean would rival the O.K. Corral, and she'd be featured on the front page of her favorite tabloid.

But I saw no police cars and no signs that snipers had been deployed to hold Cabin Four in their sights. I could only have faith that Sgt. Rogoff was aware of my plight and was feverishly revising his plans to give my safety precedence over that of Peaches.

We pulled up alongside Cabin Four and Otto nudged my ribs with his weapon. "Out," he said. "Take the money. Walk around to the front door. Frank, you go first and unlock."

Within moments we were all inside, the door closed, a floor lamp lighted. I looked about. It was a simple room, exactly like the one Hertha had claimed to see in her vision. There was also a pan of cat litter, a bowl of water, and a plate of cat food.

"Where is Peaches?" I inquired.

"At the movies," Frank sniggered, the first words he had spoken. He needn't have bothered.

"Count the money," his father ordered.

Frank dumped the contents of the bag onto the bed, stacked the bundles of banded bills. Otto and I remained standing. Nothing was said until Frank finished.

"All here," he said. "The bills look legit."

"They got the numbers," Otto growled, "but so what? Where we'll pass them no one looks at numbers."

"May I take the cat now?" I asked, figuring I had nothing to lose.

Otto looked at me somberly. "I finally figured how you found Charles Girard," he said. "It was the vet, wasn't it? At the animal hospital. That was cute."

For a minute or two I couldn't comprehend how he knew I had identified him. Then I remembered I had mentioned the name Charles Girard to Laverne. She had undoubtedly told Frank and he, in turn, had reported to his father that Archy McNally, a blabbermouthed gumshoe, was on his trail.

"So now you know about me," Otto said. "And you know about Frank. We don't have much choice, do we?"

His meaning was clear and more chilling than a brutal threat.

"It's no big deal," I pointed out. "Catnapping is hardly a capital crime. How heavy a sentence can you possibly get?"

"When you've been inside," he said darkly, "one more day is too much."

He stared at me, and I knew it wasn't only a charge of catnapping that concerned him. He wouldn't kill for that. But he was calculating how much I might know or guess about his other activities, including the vicious murders of the Gillsworths. Finally I could see that he had made up his mind, and his fatal decision seemed to relax him.

"Put the money back in the bag," he told his son. "Shove the bag under the bed. Then get the cat. We'll do them both at the same time. I spotted a good place. A deserted canal."

It was all I could do to keep from crying, "But I can't swim!" and laughing hysterically. Somehow I restrained myself.

Frank hid the money, went into the bathroom, and came out carrying a large cardboard carton that had once held bottles of Jim Beam. It was tied shut with heavy twine, and air holes had been cut in the sides. I heard a few faint meows and the box rocked a bit as Peaches moved.

"Let's go," Otto said.

Up to that point the motel cabin had been illuminated by a single floor lamp with a low-wattage bulb. But now, suddenly, the interior was flooded with a hard white glare. Beams of bright spotlights came stabbing through the front and side windows of the cabin.

"What the hell!" Frank yelped.

Otto moved swiftly. He stood behind the wooden door and leaned to peer cautiously out the corner of the front window.

"Police cars," he reported tonelessly. "Four or five at least. And an army of cops."

"Oh God," Frank said despairingly.

Then I heard Sgt. Rogoff. The bullhorn made him sound harsh and metallic, but there was no mistaking his voice.

"Cabin Four," he boomed. "Everyone come out of the front door with your hands raised. Now!"

Frank appealed to his father. "What should we do?" he asked nervously.

Otto went into the bathroom, stood on the closed toilet lid, and glanced out the small window. He returned to the main room. "No good," he said. "The back is covered."

"Please," I said. "Give yourselves up. It's only a charge of catnapping. It's not worth a shoot-out."

"He's right," Frank said. "Let's do what they want."

His father looked at him with disgust. "You do what you like," he said. "I'm getting out. I'm not taking a fall for you again."

He reached under the bed, jerked out the bag of cash. He removed several bundles and stuffed them into his pockets. Then he leveled his revolver at me.

"Turn around," he said. "You and I are going out of here together. You first."

"Cabin Four!" Rogoff's voice came crashing. "Come out the front door, hands raised. You have exactly one minute."

Otto Gloriana stepped up close behind me. He put a heavy hand on my left shoulder. He pressed the muzzle of his weapon behind my right ear.

"Nothing cute," he warned. "Or you're dead. You understand?"

"Yes," I said.

"Now open the door. Slowly. Step out slowly. Move to

261

the Chrysler. Everything nice and slow."

I did as he ordered. We moved out onto the porch almost in lockstep.

"Hold your fire!" Al screamed. "Hold your fire!"

The spotlights half-blinded me. I could see nothing but the dark bulk of the cars. I walked as slowly as I could toward the Chrysler.

We were alongside the car when the bullhorn barked: "Otto! Otto!" But Rogoff didn't pronounce it "Oddo." He split the name into two distinct syllables: "Ot-to! Ot-to!"

Gloriana was so shocked that the police knew his real name that his grip loosened, his left hand slid from my shoulder. The pressure of the gun behind my ear lessened. I was vaguely aware that he had turned slightly toward the source of that raucous shout.

Then I did something that anyone with an IQ greater than their waistline would have done: I fell down.

Sounds simple, does it? Well, it isn't. I am not a tumbler or circus clown trained to fall without risk or injury. I just let myself go and crumpled, bruising shoulders, elbows, rump.

I hoped Al Rogoff and his troops would have the wit to take advantage of my sudden collapse. They did. I was on the ground and Otto Gloriana was still standing, stunned, when there was an ear-cracking fusillade. I cowered.

I heard Otto grunt, and he was driven back. His body went slack and he flopped to his knees. Then, as the firing continued, his head bowed and he seemed to stretch out prone onto the earth.

"Cease firing!" the sergeant bawled. "Cease firing!"

The silence was deafening. I lay where I had fallen, knowing I was alive but fearing to move my limbs lest broken bones came poking through the skin. I was still shaken by the gunfire and trying to determine what bullets flying overhead sounded like. They did not whine, hum, or whistle. I finally decided the sound was like a sheet of good rag paper being ripped.

I raised my head cautiously. Sgt. Rogoff and two officers were standing next to Gloriana. One of them plucked away the revolver. The other knelt and turned Otto's head to peer at his face.

"He's gone, sarge," he said.

"Yeah," Al said. "A clear case of lead poisoning. Call for the meat wagon." He turned and gently assisted me to my feet. I stood shakily. "You okay?" he asked anxiously.

"I've got to get to a john," I said.

He laughed, and we started for the cabin door. Two officers came out gripping Frank Gloriana by the arms. He was limp and his feet were dragging. As they hauled him away he raised his head and glanced at me.

"Glad you're alive," he mumbled. "Really."

"Thank you," I said.

He didn't look at the corpse of his father.

We went into the cabin. Al started to pack the spilled money back into the shopping bag. I headed directly for the bathroom. When I came out, Rogoff had gone. The cardboard carton was still sitting in the middle of the floor.

I leaned down and untied the twine. I lifted the flaps warily. I feared that Peaches, thinking I was one of the miscreants, might leap at my throat and try to wrench out my Adam's apple with her teeth. But she hopped out of the box and began rubbing against my shins, purring like a maniac.

"Why, Peaches," I said, "you know a hero when you smell one, don't you?"

When Rogoff returned, I was seated on the bed and the cat was lying on her back next to me, all four paws raised

263

in the air. I was scratching her stomach, and her eyes were closed in ecstasy.

Al said, "That's the most sickening sight I've ever witnessed in my life."

"You're just jealous," I said, "because no one does it for you."

"What makes you so sure?" he said.

"Al, can I return Peaches to Harry Willigan?"

"Yep. Tell him we'll have to hang on to his fifty grand for a while. Evidence. He'll get it back eventually. Come on, I'll give you a lift back to your car."

"I have to call the old man first. I promised."

I used the phone in the motel office. Father answered so promptly that I knew he hadn't been sleeping. It was then about two a.m.

"Archy, sir," I said. "I'm fine, and the cat has been rescued."

"Glad to hear it," he said. "Tell me about it tomorrow." Then he added precisely, "Or I should say later today."

Rogoff drove me back to the convenience store in a squad car. I had left the cardboard carton in Cabin Four and held Peaches on my lap. She was content.

"What about Irma?" I asked.

"We picked her up at midnight. She's acting the haughty, insulted grande dame and won't say a word until she sees a lawyer."

"And Hertha?"

"She wasn't in the apartment. Neighbors say they haven't seen her around for two or three days. They don't know where she is."

I could guess, but said nothing to the sergeant.

When I got out to transfer to the Miata, he said casually, "Nice work tonight, Archy."

"Thank you," I said. "You behaved admirably yourself. I'll call you after I get some sleep. Al, I don't believe Frank Gloriana is a strong character. Sweat him."

"I intend to," he said grimly.

I drove with Peaches curled up in the passenger bucket. When we arrived home I thought she might be hungry and offered her a slice of pastrami from the fridge. She ate it with obvious enjoyment. Smart cat.

She slept at the foot of my bed for the rest of the night. When I awoke around eight o'clock I discovered she had upchucked the pastrami onto the cover of my journal.

You can't win 'em all.

17

I breakfasted with my parents on Tuesday morning. Peaches sat patiently alongside the dining room table, and when I gave her a hunk of brioche, she nibbled it daintily, a perfect lady. Mother was delighted with her. We had had no animal in the family since Max, our golden retriever, died, and I wondered aloud if we might invite a pup, perhaps a Dandie Dinmont, to join our ménage. Father promised to consider the suggestion.

After breakfast I drew him aside and gave him an abbreviated account of the police action the previous night.

"Then Otto is dead?" he asked when I had finished.

"Definitely."

"And the son is in custody?"

"That's correct, sir. And also Mrs. Irma Gloriana. I expect Al Rogoff will be questioning them today."

He nodded. "I'd like to speak to the sergeant," he said. "Do you think he could come over this evening?"

"I'm sure he's awfully busy, father, but he might be ready for a break by tonight."

"Ask him," he said. "Tell him it concerns Roderick Gillsworth's holographic will and may possibly affect his investigation."

I knew it would be useless to ask questions, so I told him I'd try to reach Rogoff. Then he departed for the office in his Lexus, and I lifted Peaches into my Miata and headed for the Willigan home. The cat sat upright in her bucket seat, sniffed the morning air, and looked about rather grandly.

I carried her up the Willigans' stoop, but before I had a chance to ring, the door was flung open and Harry rushed out, arms outflung. "Peaches!" he screamed. "Peaches is home!" I swear there were tears in the poor goof's eyes.

He reached for his pet, but the cat had other ideas. She leaped from my arms, darted through the opened door, and went scampering down the long corridor. Willigan lumbered after her, shouting. "Sweetums! Sweetums baby! Papa is here! Come to papa, darling!"

Gruesome.

They disappeared, and I entered the house, closing the door behind me. I wandered down the hallway and out onto the back lawn. Laverne was lying supine on a chaise, wearing a hot-pink French-cut bikini. She also had a plastic shield over her eyes.

"Good morning, Laverne," I called as I approached.

She lifted the shield long enough to glance at me, then replaced it. "Hi, Archy," she said in a flat voice.

"I just returned Peaches," I said. "She was recovered

last night."

"I know," she said tonelessly. "We heard it on the radio this morning."

"Will you please tell Harry the police have his fifty thousand? They're holding it temporarily as evidence. He'll get it back eventually."

"I'll tell him," she said.

I don't know why I felt sorry for her. One has to pay for one's stupidity in this world – ask me; I know! – and Laverne had certainly behaved stupidly. But I supposed she had her reasons and obviously they were sufficient for her.

"I'll try to keep you out of it," I said, "but I'm not sure it can be done."

"Out of what?" she said.

"Laverne, please," I said. "The police are holding Frank Gloriana. I don't know how much he'll tell them."

"What are you talking about?" she said listlessly.

I sighed and started away. I was almost at the screen door when she called, "Archy," and I turned back. Now she was sitting on the chaise, hunched over, head bowed. She was twirling the eye shield in nervous fingers.

"You really think you can keep my name out of it?" she asked, looking up at me.

"Laverne," I said, "let me be frank . . . " Then I caught myself. "Oh lordy," I said, "don't let me be Frank!"

She smiled for the first time.

"Look," I said, "Frank is not a stand-up guy. He's liable to tell the police you talked him into it, that he went along because he was in love with you."

Then she frowned. "That's crazy. How could he say that? The ransom notes were written on his word processor."

"The police already know that. But you did sneak

Peaches out of here in her carrier, didn't you?"

"It was a laugh," she said. "Frank needed money, and Harry has plenty. As for Frank being in love with me, that's bullshit. It was just a game with us."

"It's gone sour, Laverne. If Harry finds out, you know what'll happen to you, don't you?"

"Yeah," she said dolefully. "Out on my can. With no pre-nup."

"You took an awful risk," I marveled.

"A girl gets bored," she said, shrugging. "Listen, Archy, if you can keep me out of it, I'll make it worth your while."

And she put her hands behind her, leaned back, crossed her legs. She looked up at me, smiling again. There was a lot of her.

I laughed. "Laverne," I said, "You're incorrigible."

She licked her glossed lips, still smiling. "Think about it," she said.

I got out of there as hastily as I could. I don't care how macho a man claims to be, when a woman says Yes, his first reaction is not desire, it's fear.

I drove away with the feeling that this was going to be Denouement Day with all current problems solved and complexities unraveled. It didn't turn out *quite* that way, but it came close.

There was a question I wanted to ask Hertha Gloriana, and I thought I knew exactly where to find her. I guided the Miata up to Riviera Beach and within a half-hour I was tapping on the door of Meg Trumble's apartment.

"Why, Archy," she said, "what a pleasant surprise."

The "surprise" I could buy; the "pleasant" was iffy. But she allowed me to enter and, sure enough, Hertha was curled up on the couch. There was a box of Kleenex on the cushion beside her, and she was dabbing at her eyes.

268

Despite the medium's tears and Meg's rather frosty demeanor, both women looked extraordinarily attractive to me. They were wearing identical short-shorts of white twill with men's workshirts, the tails knotted about their waists to reveal a few inches of midriff. And they displayed a quartet of splendidly tanned legs.

"Did you hear the news?" Meg demanded. "About Hertha's husband and her in-laws?"

"I heard," I said, nodding. "Have you been to the police, Hertha?"

She shook her head.

"I really think you should," I said gently. "They may want to question you. Ask to speak to Sergeant Rogoff."

"Hertha knows nothing about that cat," Meg said angrily. "I don't see why she should get involved."

I sighed. "Meg," I said, "she *is* involved. Her husband and mother-in-law have been arrested and her father-in-law shot dead. If she doesn't go to the police, they'll start looking for her. Sooner or later they're sure to find her, and then they'll want to know why she didn't come forward."

"Perhaps I should talk to them," Hertha said timidly. "Meg, will you come with me?"

Meg sat down beside her, put an arm about her shoulders. "Of course I will, darling," she said in a soothing voice. "We'll go together. Who did you say to ask for, Archy?"

"Sergeant Al Rogoff. He's a friend of mine, and I suggest you tell him that you already spoke to me. You'll find him very sympathetic."

"What do you think he'll ask me?" Hertha said.

It was a perfect opportunity to pose my own question. "He'll probably want to know if Roderick Gillsworth came to your office frequently."

The medium looked at me with widened eyes. "What

an odd question."

"Well, did he?" I persisted. "Did Gillsworth come to your office and talk to Frank?"

"Several times," she said, nodding. "But they always went into the room where we did our mailings. I don't know what they talked about."

"Just tell Sergeant Rogoff that," I advised. "I'm sure he'll be interested. Hertha, will you be staying here?"

"Of course she will," Meg said definitely. "As long as she wants. Forever, I hope."

The medium turned and embraced the other woman tightly, kissing her on the lips. "Oh sweetheart," she cried, "what would I ever do without you?"

The two were hugging and whispering to each other when I left. I headed for the Pelican Club, hoping a wee bit of the old nasty might help restore my sanity. As I drove, I reflected on the strange convolutions of human behavior.

I could understand Meg's decision. After all, she had been betrayed by a man in a particularly cruel and humiliating manner. But Hertha's actions puzzled me. The married medium who dispensed her kisses so freely seemed a contradiction: she was a very *physical* spiritualist.

But that, I realized, was occupational stereotyping. Most of us are guilty of it.

For instance, librarians are generally thought to be sexless, dried-up biddies who affect a pince-nez and don rubber gloves before shaking hands with a man. I know from personal experience that this image is totally, *totally* false. (I wonder what Nancy is doing now?)

So it was really not too surprising to learn that being a psychic did not preclude Hertha from having urges of a more corporeal sort. A horny medium? Well, why not? And if she was subject to nymphomaniacal twinges, who

270

was I, a hapless lothario, to condemn her? And if her nature included a predilection for sapphic relationships, so be it.

When I walked into the Pelican Club, the radio behind the bar was on, and Vikki Carr was singing "It Must Be Him." It was just too much, and I burst out laughing.

"You seem in a happy mood today, Mr. McNally," Simon Pettibone said.

"Pondering life's ironies, Mr. Pettibone," I said. "It is indeed a mad, mad world."

"But the only one we have," he reminded me.

"A frozen daiquiri, please," I responded.

I left the bar to use the public phone. Of course I called Rogoff, and of course he was unavailable. I slowly sipped my way through two daiquiries, called the sergeant every ten minutes with no results, and finally got through to him on my fifth call. He was brusque, obviously under pressure, and I hurriedly blurted out an invitation to stop by the McNally home that night at nine. "Okay," he said and hung up abruptly.

I had lunch while seated at the bar. Priscilla brought me a jumbo cheeseburger with side orders of french fries and coleslaw. I wolfed this cholesterol Special with great enjoyment and had an iced Galliano for dessert. I suspected my arteries might soon require the services of a Roto-Rooter man.

I drove back to Worth Avenue to take up a project I had started days ago and never completed: buying a tennis bracelet for Consuela Garcia. The need for a gift seemed more important now than when the idea had first occurred to me, for I had neglected that marvelous woman shamefully. The morning's encounters with Laverne Willigan, Meg Trumble, and Hertha Gloriana made me realize how important Connie was to me. Vital, one might even say, and I do say it.

271

I visited four jewelry shops before I found a bracelet that appealed to me: two-carat, cushion-cut diamonds set in 18K gold. It was horribly expensive, but I handed over my plastic gaily, following McNally's First Law of Shopping: if you can afford it, it's not worth buying.

I went directly home, stripped to the buff, and fell into bed for a nap, for I enjoyed only five hours of shuteye the previous night. Before sleep claimed me, I thought again of my experiences that morning and laughed aloud. I simply could not take them seriously.

It is my conviction that solemnity is the curse of civilization. Think of all the earnest people who had sacrificed themselves for gods now forgotten or wasted their lives on causes no one remembers. Laughter is our only salvation. Pray with a giggle and mourn with a smile. And if you happen to believe, as I do, that women are nature's noblest work, know ye that long face ne'er won fair lady.

Thus endeth the scripture according to St. Archy.

18

It had been a sunny day with a scattering of popcorn clouds, but when I awoke from my nap around six p.m., a dark overhang had moved in from the east and rain had started. There was no wind, so the drizzle fell vertically and soon became a steady downpour that threatened to drive us all to the rooftops.

I wondered if Al Rogoff would show up in that drencher, and by nine o'clock I was waiting in the kitchen, peering out the window and ready to go out with my big golfing umbrella if he arrived. He plowed up in his pickup only fifteen minutes late, parked close to our back door, and came rushing in before I had a chance to unfurl my bumbershoot.

He looked godawful. His features were slack with weariness and there were puddles of shadow under his eyes. Even worse, he seemed harried and uncertain, as if he was faced with momentous decisions and didn't know which way to jump. I took his dripping slicker, hung it away to dry, and led him to the study.

Father was waiting for us, took one look at the sergeant, and immediately broke out his bottle of Rémy Martin XO. He reserved this superb cognac, he said, for "special occasions." To my knowledge there had been two in the past ten years.

Rogoff flopped into a club chair, accepted his glass gratefully, and took a deep pull. Then he sucked in a long breath, exhaled noisily, and said, "Manna."

"Sorry to bring you out on a night like this, sergeant," father said. "It could have waited."

"No, sir," Al said, "I don't think so. Things are moving too quickly. Right now it's all a big mishmash, and I'm hoping you can help make some sense out of what we know and what we guess."

I had poured tots of brandy for father and myself. He was enthroned behind his desk, as usual, and I took an armchair to one side, facing both of them. Rogoff fished a cigar from an inside pocket and looked at the old man questioningly.

"Of course," father said. "Light up. Are you hungry? We can supply combat rations."

"No, thanks, counselor," he said. "I had an anchovy

273

pizza an hour ago. I'm just stressed out. The cognac will do fine."

"How are things going, Al?" I asked. "Making any progress?"

He flipped a palm back and forth. "*Comme ci, comme ça*. Right now I'm working with an Assistant State Attorney, a brainy lady, and we're trying to get a handle on our options and figure out the best deal we can make."

"Is Frank Gloriana talking?"

"Some. We've got him cold on the catnapping. The ransom notes were written on his word processor and he was found with the money. But he claims it was all Laverne Willigan's idea, and she was the one who snatched the cat. He says he played along because he's madly in love with her."

"Oh sure," I said. "I was afraid he'd pull something like that. Any chance at all of keeping Laverne's name out of it?"

"Very thin," Al said. "We're trying to work a deal with his lawyer. If Frank tells us what he knows about his parents' murder plot, charges may be reduced and he could get off with a fine and suspended sentence."

My father spoke up. "As you know, sergeant, I represent Harry Willigan, and I'm just as eager as Archy to keep Mrs. Willigan out of any court proceedings. I presume everything said here tonight is *entre nous*."

"If that means will I keep my mouth shut, the answer is yes."

"Good. Is this Frank Gloriana a man of means?"

"He's stone-broke. His lawyer will probably end up with Frank's office furniture as his fee."

"I see," father said thoughtfully. "Archy, to your knowledge, does Laverne have any liquid assets?"

"I don't know about her bank balance, father, but I do know she's got a heavy collection of jewelry. Gifts from

Harry. Expensive things."

"Better and better. Perhaps, sergeant, you might suggest to Frank Gloriana's attorney that he have a confidential talk with Laverne Willigan. She might be willing to pawn or sell enough of her gems to provide funds for Frank's legal defense. In return, of course, he would avoid mentioning her name. But this arrangement, I strongly urge, should be approved only after Frank tells you what he knows of his parents' involvement in the Gillsworth homicides. Frank might be disinclined to agree to that but if you explain the deal thoroughly to his attorney, I expect he'll recommend that Frank accept it. Especially if the ASA promises to do what she can to have charges reduced."

"Yeah," Al said slowly, "that plot might work. We clear up a catnapping and Frank gives us what he has on the murders. He gets off with a slap on the wrist. His lawyer gets paid. And Laverne keeps her name out of it. Everyone wins. A slick plan, Mr. McNally. I'll bring it up with the ASA."

I saw that his cognac was gone and my glass was getting low. I rose and refilled our snifters without asking permission. My father made no objection although he had barely touched his drink.

"Okay, Al," I said, "so much for the catnapping. Now what's happening with the homicides?"

He sighed deeply. "This is where things get sticky. First of all, you've got to know the whole thing started with Roderick Gillsworth's obsession with Irma Gloriana. We're trying to get a court order to open her safe deposit box, but even without the letters he wrote her, we have the evidence of his holographic will and the erotic poems he started writing after he met her. It's obvious the guy was nuts about her. I'm not saying he was temporarily insane; let's just say that after meeting Irma he became

275

mentally disadvantaged."

"But penniless," I observed.

"Right," Rogoff said. "Which wasn't the way to win Irma's heart. The lady is Queen of the Bottom Line. So Roderick, knowing he was slated to inherit most of his wife's estate, suggested Lydia be knocked off. Irma said she could get it done if Roderick would sign over his inherited wealth to her."

"Wait just a minute, please," my father interrupted. "That doesn't quite compute. Why did Roderick make Irma his beneficiary? The fee for the murder was going to someone else."

"I admit it's fuzzy," the sergeant said. "But I figure Roderick wanted to marry Irma after Lydia was dead. He didn't know Irma was already married. And she agreed to marry him when he was a widower only if he made her the sole beneficiary of his estate. I think Roderick executed that hand-written will and signed it cheerfully because he knew that if Irma reneged, he could cancel out the holographic will at any time by writing a more recent will that superseded it. Am I correct, counselor?"

"Yes," father said slowly, "that's generally true. The most recently executed will at the time of death takes precedence."

But he and I looked at each other. I know we were both troubled by the sergeant's tortuous explanation of why Roderick had made Irma his beneficiary.

"There is something you should know about that holographic will, sergeant," father said. "It was executed about a month ago. At that time Lydia Gillsworth was still alive. Florida statutes provide that the surviving spouse of a decedent has a right to thirty percent of the decedent's estate regardless of the provisions of the decedent's will."

Rogoff was startled. "You mean Gillsworth's holographic will was null and void when it was written?"

276

"Not necessarily," father replied. "But if Roderick had predeceased Lydia and had left a sizable estate, Lydia could either let his will stand or 'elect against the will,' as it's called, and claim her rightful thirty percent. But the whole question is moot because Lydia died before Roderick, and if he had predeceased her, he had no estate to leave."

Al and I exchanged a brief glance. I knew what he was thinking: If the whole matter was moot, why had Prescott McNally mentioned it? I could have told him: If there was a nit to be picked, my father would be the first to volunteer.

"Well," Rogoff said, shaking his head, "all I know is that when Roderick signed that handwritten will he signed his own death warrant. I figure Irma and Otto had it worked out from the start, but Roderick was too pussy-whipped to suspect it. First, they knocked off Lydia. That made Roderick a rich man. Then Roderick was snuffed. And that was supposed to make Irma wealthy according to the terms of his last will and testament."

"You're probably right, sergeant," father said, nodding. "It's a likely scenario. But how much of it can you prove?"

"That Otto bashed in Lydia's skull with a walking stick? Not sufficient evidence to make a case. But things are different with the murder of Roderick, framed to look like a suicide. The most important piece of hard evidence is that we found a package of single-edge razor blades in Cabin Four of the Jo-Jean Motel. Otto Gloriana shaved with them. The same brand was left on the bath mat beside Roderick Gillsworth's corpse.

Father was obviously disappointed. "Hardly conclusive evidence," he said.

"I agree, sir. But we have something much better. Irma Gloriana states she was with her husband when he en-

277

tered Gillsworth's house to kill him. She claims she didn't witness the actual murder but that Otto announced his intention to kill the poet beforehand and bragged about it afterward."

Both my father and I were astounded. "Why on earth would she admit that?" I said. "It makes her an accessory."

"Why?" Rogoff said disgustedly. "Because she thinks it'll get her off the hook. Otto is dead. He can't refute what she says or defend himself in any way, shape, or form. So his widow now says he was the sole killer. His motive, according to Irma, was to kill the man having an affair with his wife. He was aware of it, Irma says, and vowed revenge. He knew she had a dinner date at Gillsworth's home, put a gun to her head, and forced her to ring the doorbell so he could gain entrance to slit Roderick's wrists. She says she was in deathly fear of Otto, a man known to have a violent temper and who had already served time in prison. But she was totally innocent of complicity in Gillsworth's death, she claims. She was coerced, in fear of her life. But since she played no voluntary role in the homicide, she is free to walk and inherit Roderick's estate. A load of kaka – right? The only problem is that she may get away with it. It's the kind of story a jury just might buy if she ever comes to trial. And she's got an awfully smart lawyer who's probably charging her a nice hunk of Gillsworth's estate."

Father and I were silent. Rogoff was correct. Irma Gloriana had concocted a defense that just might work. If she told her story to judge and jury with all the sincere forcefulness of which I knew she was capable, she had a better than fifty-fifty chance of strolling out of the courtroom a free woman with no worries other than how long it might take to probate Roderick's will and collect his millions.

"It stinks," I said wrathfully and stood to refill our glasses.

"Counselor," Rogoff said, "isn't it true that under Florida law a murderer can't inherit anything from the victim?"

Father nodded. "Anyone who unlawfully and intentionally kills or participates in procuring the death of a decedent is not entitled to any benefits from the decedent's estate whatsoever."

"Then somehow," Al said determinedly, "I don't know how, but *somehow* I'm going to nail that lady. She's guilty as hell, and I don't want to see her getting one thin dime."

As I had listened to all the foregoing, my originally dim vision that had gained an outline and then taken on substance now suddenly snapped into sharp focus, and I knew it was time to display the McNally genius. If, in what follows, you feel I acted like a hambone, you must realize it was my Big Dramatic Moment. I could not let it pass without exhibiting my historic gifts, inherited, no doubt, from my grandfather, the famed burlesque comic.

I was still standing and addressed both men. "There is something you should know," I said portentously, "and I believe it may help the cause of justice. Otto didn't kill Lydia Gillsworth. And Irma didn't. Roderick murdered his wife."

Their jaws didn't sag, but Rogoff spluttered brandy and father looked at me sadly as if he finally realized his Number One (and only) son had gone completely bonkers.

"Impossible, Archy," he said hoarsely. "You and I sat in this room and heard Roderick talk to his wife. She was alive when he left here."

I made a great pretense of looking at my watch. "Damn!" I said. "It's getting late, and I promised Binky Watrous I'd call. May I use your phone, father?"

279

He glared at me. "You wish to make a personal call at this moment? Can't it wait?"

"No, sir," I said. "It's important."

"Very well," he said huffily. "Make it short."

I used the phone on his desk, punched out a number, waited half a mo.

"Binky?" I said. "Archy McNally here. How are you feeling? Glad to hear it. Listen, how about dinner tomorrow night at the Pelican Club. Great! About eight-ish? Good-o. See you then, Binky."

I hung up and turned to the others. "Who did I just speak to?" I asked them.

They looked at each other, silent a moment, then Rogoff said, "All right, I'll play your little game. You talked to a guy named Binky."

"Binky Watrous is in Portofino," I said gently. "He's been there for the past two weeks and expects to stay another two. I was talking to a dead phone."

They caught it immediately, of course. The sergeant smote his forehead with a palm, then rose and began to walk in agitated circles. "Snookered," he said, his voice a gargle. My father groaned once, then shook his head in wonderment – at his own credulity, I suspect.

"Father," I said, "you and I didn't hear Roderick speak to his wife; we heard him talking, and that's all we heard. We just assumed his wife was alive and conversing with him."

He sighed heavily. "All my professional life I've sought never to assume *anything*, and yet I allowed myself to be deceived by Gillsworth. The man was a consummate actor."

"He had to be," I pointed out. "His fate depended on it. I reckon he killed his wife about an hour before he showed up here. He deliberately murdered her so he could inherit her wealth and marry Irma, just as the

280

sergeant suggested. He set the grandfather clock an hour ahead and pushed it over to stop it. Then he put on fresh clothes and came to our house."

"Wait a minute," Rogoff said, sitting down again. "If you've got it right, then Lydia arrived home an hour before Roderick told you she did. But Irma Gloriana told me that Lydia had stayed late at the séance."

"That's easy," I said. "Irma lied to you. She was setting up an alibi for Roderick. And her price for lying was the holographic will. She made him pay in advance."

"Yes," my father said, "that's credible."

Rogoff swore a horrible oath. "I suspected that guy from the start," he said wrathfully. "The spouse is always the first choice in a homicide case. But I couldn't get around that phone call he made from here. How did you get on to the dead phone trick, Archy?"

"I really don't know," I confessed. "Maybe it's because I'm such a scamster myself – only when the occasion demands it, you understand."

"We were used," my father said angrily. "Roderick Gillsworth *used* us."

"That's right, sir," I agreed. "His attorney and his attorney's son – perfect witnesses to confirm his alibi. We were an important part of his plot."

Rogoff had been reflecting on my reconstruction of the murder. "Hold on," he said suddenly. "You say Roderick killed his wife and then changed his clothes. I'll buy that because his clean duds helped convince me he was innocent. But what did he do with the bloodstained clothes? We searched his entire house the moment we got there. No bloody clothes. He didn't have time to burn them or dump them somewhere. So what did he do with them?"

I didn't know then and if I live a millennium I don't think I'll ever know why I said what I did.

"Caprice!" I almost shouted. "Did you search

281

Lydia's car, Al?"

He stared at me. "I told you I felt the engine block to test the heat, and I stuck my head inside the car to see how long the air conditioning had been off. But I didn't search the trunk." He stood up abruptly. " I think I'll do it right now. I've still got the keys to the house and garage. It's just possible . . . "

"I'll come along," I said.

"May I join you?" my father asked.

Al pulled on his slicker and went out to his pickup. I took my big multicolored umbrella. My father donned his rain jacket. He and I ran out to the Lexus, and we followed Rogoff's truck southward to the Gillsworth home. We went slowly, for the roads were hubcap deep, and the rain showed no sign of lessening.

We pulled into the Gillsworth driveway, got out, and I opened my umbrella. Before it became soaked through, the sergeant had unlocked the garage door and lifted it up. We all crowded in, and Al switched on the light. The gray Bentley nestled close to the white Caprice. There was something ineffably sad about those two silent, empty cars, their owners slain.

Rogoff examined the lock on the trunk of the Caprice. "I can't pick that," he said. "This calls for surgery."

He went out to his pickup and came back with a two-foot crowbar. "Look the other way, gents," he said with heavy jocularity. "Then you can't testify against me." But we watched as, with some difficulty, he jammed the wedge end into the trunk's seal and then leaned all his weight onto the crowbar. The lock popped with a screech of metal. Al lifted the lid and we all pressed close.

It was in plain sight alongside the spare: a blue plastic garbage bag.

"Bingo," Rogoff said softly.

He used the crowbar to pry open the mouth of the bag,

then hooked out the contents. We saw skivvies, T-shirt, khaki slacks. And a wadded pair of latex gloves. Everything was darkly blotched with blood.

"He didn't wear much," I observed.

"Did you expect him to put on soup and fish to snuff his wife?" Al said. "It's plenty." He closed the trunk lid with the bag of clothing inside. "I'll use the phone in the house. I need lab technicians on this stuff. I think it'll make the case."

"Sure it will," I said. "The clothes will be identified as Roderick's from the laundrymarks, and the blood will be identified as Lydia's. The holographic will and those letters he wrote to Irma will establish motive. Hertha Gloriana told me that Roderick came to the office frequently, and he and Frank would go into a back room to confer. Frank will probably testify that Roderick composed and mailed the threatening letters to his wife. You've got a strong case, Al."

"I concur," my father said. "I believe that when presented with the evidence Archy detailed, the court will make a determination that Roderick Gillsworth murdered his wife. Congratulations, sergeant. You get your wish."

Al was puzzled. "What wish?"

"You didn't want Irma Gloriana to get one thin dime. If it's determined that Roderick did indeed kill his wife, then he is not entitled to any benefits from her estate. And so, even if Irma manages to go free, she will inherit nothing from Roderick."

The sergeant walked out of the garage and turned his face up to the streaming heavens.

"Thank you, God," he said.

19

I have frequently heard northerners denigrate South Florida because, they say, we have no seasons, meaning there are no radical weather changes from January through December. Actually, Palm Beach has two: the *in* season and the off-season. Many of our citizens are in residence only from October through May. Then, to escape summer heat and humidity and avoid hurricanes, they scatter to their villas in Antibes, Monte Carlo, St. Tropez, and the Costa del Sol.

But some of us, gainfully employed or not, are content to enjoy the island year-round. I will not claim Palm Beach is a paradise, but it does have its unique charms. Where else in the world would a Rolls-Royce Silver Shadow be dropped in the ocean to provide an artificial reef for fish?

So Lady Cynthia Horowitz's Fourth of July party was attended by more than a hundred distinguished permanent residents, most of whom knew each other and were linked by their off-season loyalty to this spit of sand that could be submerged by a thirty-foot storm surge.

It was a black-tie affair, and the ladies welcomed the opportunity to step out of their old tennis togs and into new evening gowns purchased at designer boutiques on Worth Avenue. I had never seen such a profusion of billowing summer silks, and the rainbow of sequins out-glittered the stars.

It was a stupendous bash that was talked about for weeks afterward. In the pool area behind the Horowitz mansion, three service bars had been set up, a six-piece dance band played, and the buffet tables were so heavily laden with exotic (and sclerotic) viands that they were not groaning boards; they whimpered.

This extravaganza had been planned and was overseen by Consuela Garcia, Lady C.'s social secretary, and shortly after the McNally family arrived, I deserted my parents, grabbed a Bellini from the nearest bar, and went looking for Connie. Tucked into the pocket of my dinner jacket was the tennis bracelet. It was, I had decided, a night to make amends.

I found her reading the riot act to the caterer who apparently had failed to provide Amaretto-flavored gâteau as promised. I waited until Connie's tirade was completed, and the poor fellow had slunk away in dis-grace, his professional competence belittled and his ancestry questioned. Then I approached.

Connie looked absolutely stunning. She was wearing a silver tank dress of metallic knit, and with her long black hair and glorious suntan she presented a vision that made me question my own sanity for giving other women even a glance.

The glance she gave me I can only describe as scathing.

"I do not wish to speak to you," she said coldly.

"Connie, I – "

"Never once did you call."

"Connie, I – "

"You didn't care if I was alive or dead."

"Connie, I – "

"I never want to see you again. Never, never, never!"

"Connie, ai-yi-yi!" I cried. I plucked the gift-wrapped

package from my pocket and held it out to her, speaking earnestly and rapidly to forestall interruption. "Nothing you can say to me is worse than what I've told myself. I have acted in a cruel, heartless fashion, and I am ashamed of it. I want you to have this. I know it won't make up for my atrocious conduct, but it is a small symbol of the way I truly feel about you."

She accepted the gift gingerly, looking at me with a slight softening. Then: "This isn't going to make everything right between us. You know that, don't you?"

"Of course," I said. "It is intended as a plea to let me prove to you, by my future actions, how sincerely I regret my past neglect and my resolve to treat you henceforth with the respect and love you so richly deserve. Open it."

She tore the wrapping away, lifted the lid and tissue paper. I saw her lustrous eyes widen. She was so overwhelmed she lapsed into her mother tongue.

"Por Dios!" she shouted, *"Magnifico!"*

A warm *abrazo* was my reward.

She insisted on wearing the bracelet immediately. It needed adjustment, but she pushed it up almost to her elbow and vowed she would never remove it. Never, never, never!

Then we discussed plans. She would have to remain after the fireworks display, scheduled for midnight. In fact, her presence was required until most of the guests had departed and the debris cleaned up.

"I probably won't be able to get away until two in the morning," she said. "Can you wait for me, Archy?"

"I can," I said. "Gladly. But I fear I won't be able to resist those pitchers of Bellinis. By two a.m. I may be comatose."

"We can't have that," she said. "Tonight I want you alert and loving and in full possession of your powers. Suppose we do this: I'll give you my house keys, and you

286

go to my place whenever you like and wait for me. You can even take a nap if you want to. I'll be along as soon as I can get away."

So that's what we did. I left the party, bright-eyed and bushy-tailed, even before the fireworks started. I drove to Connie's condo in a high-rise facing Lake Worth. The balcony of her apartment, on the fourteenth floor, overlooked the lake and provided a fine view of the Flagler Memorial Bridge and all the yacht clubs and marinas on the far shore.

I made myself at home, for I had been there many times before and knew where she kept the Absolut – in the freezer. I went out onto the balcony with a small vodka and watched fireworks being lofted from West Palm Beach. I knew I had a few hours before Connie arrived, and I vowed to drink moderately and stay sober.

And this solitary wait gave me an opportunity to muse on everything that had happened during the past fortnight.

On that rainy Tuesday, after father and I had driven home from the Gillsworths' garage, we went into his study for a nightcap. We discussed the end of the investigations into the catnapping and the homicides, and we exchanged platitudes on the unpredictability of human behavior.

Then father looked at me with a quirky smile. "Archy," said he, "I suppose you believe Lydia's ghost came back to haunt Roderick."

"Yes, sir," said I. "Something like that."

"Nonsense," said he.

But now, sitting on the balcony, sipping vodka, and watching fireworks, I wondered if there really might be a supernatural world beyond reason and logic. Hertha had known the letter she received from Connie was a fake, and she had accurately visualized the room in which Peaches was being held prisoner. There might be reasonable explanations of both those insights. But there was certainly no logical way to account for Hertha's shriek of "Caprice! Caprice!" in the voice of Lydia Gillsworth during the séance. And was that the reason I so promptly shouted "Caprice!" when Rogoff had asked where the murderer's bloody clothes might be hidden?

I brooded about that a long time, thinking of Hertha's psychic gifts, the existence of ghosts, and all the other mindnumbing manifestations of the paranormal I had recently witnessed.

The display of fireworks ended at the same time I came to the conclusion that I shall never know the truth.

Nor shall you.

But then I realized the whole subject came perilously close to being *serious*, and I resolutely reminded myself that life is just a bowl of kiwis. And so when Connie finally arrived, glowing, I rushed to embrace her, eager for a larky interlude of laughter and delight.